THE RICHMOND EXCHANGE

A novel by

Forest Bowman

In memory of my parents
Forest & Gladys Bowman
whose love, discipline,
generosity & sound advice
made everything possible for me.

SPECIAL THANKS

One of the basic necessities of an author who is self-publishing a novel is editorial support, other eyes who can look at a manuscript and ferret out typos and grammatical errors and point out when something simply doesn't make sense or when a character or scene needs fleshing out. I have been incredibly blessed with the editorial review advice of five very special friends who have had the courage to take on this demanding job: My fellow members of the Mason-Dixon Civil War Round Table of Morgantown, **Linda & John Fredrick** and **Steve Walker**; my fellow Rotarian and sometime columnist for the Morgantown *Dominion-Post*, **Harry Grandon;** and, for the second time, my neighbor and avid supporter, **Christa Elder Kupec**. Finally, as with my two earlier novels, I could not have done without **my wife Myla**, who put her English Literature background into play and read the manuscript at least four times, all the while patiently, and with great tact, making the book a better one.

Chapter 1

Monday, February 13, 1865

The rider, dressed in the black suit of a country parson, stopped at the top of Good Hope Hill and looked out over the city of Washington. It was an impressive sight, even if it was the enemy's capital. Out of low swamp land, with no particularly good harbor or other natural advantages the Yankees had fashioned a bustling center of commerce, a city that promised to become one of the giants of the Eastern seaboard. Of course this site had been picked by President Washington, who was a Southerner. That would explain some of the city's success.

Suddenly there was a commotion coming from the bridge at the foot of the hill and the rider gave it his close attention. A wagon had been stopped by a sentry at the guard shack at the end of the bridge and the driver of the wagon was objecting vehemently to having his wagon searched. One of the sentries had lowered his rifle menacingly as the driver gestured wildly, backing away from the weapon which was tipped with a broad-edged sword-bayonet.

The rider sat at the top of the hill for better than a half hour watching the spectacle below. To those who rode past nothing about his dress or behavior directed attention to him. He was merely a weary preacher, his face shaded and partially concealed by the black hat of a parson. As he rested his horse before entering the city, he tried to hide his intense interest in the Navy Yard Bridge and the sentries' patterns of behavior.

However, the sentries were a real concern. After the row with the wagon driver they were searching everyone who wanted to enter the city, carefully scrutinizing their papers and going through their personal effects, poking into trunks and emptying saddlebags.

The rider patted his left breast and felt the slight crinkle of the paper he carried there. If those sentries discovered the order sewn into his coat lining he would enter Washington at gunpoint and swing from a Federal scaffold within a matter of weeks. Even without the order he would be in trouble as his cover story could be easily pierced. Any halfway suspicious sentry would arrest him, especially if he came across the Federal chaplain's uniform in his saddlebag and began asking questions. No, the rider could not be searched, that was certain.

He could always go back about a half mile and take the Bowen Road up to Benning's Road and cross the Anacostia River further upstream by way of Benning's Bridge. But that would add another hour and a half to the trip and there was no guarantee Benning's Bridge wouldn't be guarded, too. And, he had an important meeting in the city in just under an hour. He had to cross the Navy Yard Bridge and he had to do it quickly. He looked at the bridge again.

It was narrow and sat low to the river which on that day reflected the grey cloud cover broken up here and there by choppy waves that slapped against the bridge abutments. Some of the horses, frightened by the broad, brooding expanse of water, shied at crossing the bridge after their riders had been waved on by the sentries. One young man had to dismount and place his coat over his mount's eyes before the frightened creature could be led across the bridge.

After a while an idea formed in the rider's mind and he nudged his horse forward, gently stroking its neck and talking softly to the animal as it carried him slowly down the hill.

When he was about ten yards from the sentry he dug his spurs viciously into the horse's sides and yanked harshly on the reins, jamming the bit into the animal's mouth. The horse screamed loudly and reared up on its hind legs, front legs pawing the air.

The rider yelled at the sentries, "My horse is scared of the water. I'm afraid he's going to throw me. Can one of you slap her on the rump with the side of your bayonet and drive her onto the bridge?"

One of the sentries grinned and grabbed his bayonet from the end of his rifle. As the rider drew near, with the horse dancing wildly from the spur jabs it was receiving, the sentry slapped the animal on the rump and sent her scurrying onto the bridge. The other sentry howled with laughter and the rider waved gratefully at the two men.

"Thank you! I couldn't have made it without your help."

The two sentries returned the rider's wave and turned to face the next horseman coming down the hill.

The master spy of the Confederacy rode on across the Navy Yard Bridge and entered Washington with his orders from the Richmond high command safe in his coat lining.

Chapter 2

Monday, February 13

In the beginning it was just a suspicion, a hunch, a vague feeling that something important was afoot. First he'd noticed the sudden increase in activity among the Rebel underground in lower Maryland. Then there were those remarkably similar coded messages that began to show up in the "To the South" *Personals* section of the pro-Confederate New York *Daily News* – all talking about "George's new bride" and the "cousin from Baltimore." And all the while there had been the unusual silence from the National Detective Police's usually "chatty" news sources along the underground route between Washington and Richmond. All this, and not the slightest hint of what it may portend.

But whatever it was, it smelled of trouble for Lieutenant Sam Reid, and it added immeasurably to his foul mood, a mood that was intensified by the bitter cold which gripped Washington, D.C. in February 1865. It mattered not at all that the capital was always this cold and miserable in February. When the thermometer read 6° Fahrenheit and the damp chill penetrated to the bone, a man was entitled to forget past years' experience with the elements and wallow in despair at the present weather. Bad omens from the enemy could only exacerbate an already depressing situation.

In his cramped, dingy office on the second floor of the War Department Annex on 17th Street, Sam edged his chair closer to the fireplace and struggled to make sense out of the jumble of messages before him. Usually he approached this task as if it were a giant puzzle. A bit of gossip here, a piece of solid news there, someone else's observation over here - and it could all add up to something meaningful about Confederate intentions. *If* he were lucky. But today it wasn't coming together. Nothing fit. And Sam wadded yet another sheet of paper into a ball, tossed it angrily into the fire, and looked about the office, staring at nothing in particular.

The room was about ten by fourteen feet with unpainted plaster walls that bore the accumulated grit and grime of two score previous occupants. Two heavy oak tables, both rather large for the room, served as desks and were covered with stacks of newspapers, personal letters, telegrams, and other communications. The papers on Sam's desk were held down by various items: a coffee cup containing the cold remains of this morning's coffee, two flat and heavy cobblestones which had been picked up on Pennsylvania Avenue and carried in for this very purpose, and a battered coffee pot lid which had last seen wartime service in the War of 1812.

The other desk was little neater and differed from Sam's only in that, being closer to the fireplace, its layer of dust and soot was, if anything, deeper. That fact did not bother Lieutenant David Petersen, a fair-haired, sunny-side-up Scandinavian who shared the office with Sam. David sat at his chair as he always did - shoulders erect and uniform buttoned and creased as if on parade, totally oblivious to the mess about him.

Sam had often pondered on the fact that this room, dingy, cluttered and utterly without character, had none of the sterile cleanliness usually associated with the United States Army. But then, when he thought about it at all, he realized that his job, counter-intelligence, was not a task usually associated with the U. S. Army. This war had changed a lot of things.

One of the greatest changes, Sam thought, was in the all-too-frequent suspension of common sense. He bit his lip and recalled the act of chance that had made him a spy.

In 1864, stationed with the Quartermaster Depot along Tiber Creek, not far from the Capitol Building, his job involved planning and organizing wagon trains supplying Federal units within a day or so ride from Washington. These small trains were protected by a company of cavalry, assigned at random from the three cavalry regiments containing a total of over twenty-five hundred cavalrymen, who protected the capital.

In October of that year Sam had sent out eleven wagon trains of basic necessities: beef, salt & fresh pork, bacon, flour, hard bread, cornmeal, coffee, sugar, beans, rice, hominy, molasses, vinegar, soap, and candles. With winter coming on these supplies were vital to the soldiers holed up in isolated units around rural northern Virginia and eastern West Virginia. Five of the wagon trains Sam had sent out into West Virginia had been attacked by a local Rebel guerrilla band known as McNeill's Rangers. The cavalry companies escorting two of the trains had fought valiantly, driving the guerrillas back and saving the trains. But three of the companies had folded quickly, retreating after putting up only token opposition and giving the wagon trains over to the guerrillas. Since attacks on wagon trains were common and occasionally the trains were lost to the Rebels, no one in Sam's command appeared to be particularly concerned about these three lost trains.

But to Sam, something didn't seem right. On his own he began looking at the three failed companies and learned that they had all been led by the same man, a Captain Archibald Miller who, Sam discovered had been born and raised in Louden County, Virginia, in the heart of Mosby's Confederacy. Miller had graduated from Franklin & Marshall College in Lancaster, Pennsylvania and, after graduation stayed in the state, working as a bank teller in Harrisburg. When war came he did not enlist but avoided service, even paying for a substitute for the draft. But by the late summer of 1863 he had enlisted in a Pennsylvania cavalry unit where he stood out because of his college background. By the following year Miller had risen to the rank of captain and commanded a company in one of the regiments charged with defending the capital city and with protecting supply trains sent out from the city. Sam searched and could find no records of a cavalry company protecting a wagon train folding so quickly when under attack.

He brought his discovery to the attention of his superiors who, after interviewing some of the men in Miller's company, secured permission to arrest Miller and interrogate him carefully.

Sam accompanied his commanding officer, Major Tom Swanson, to Miller's office to make the arrest. When they approached Miller and announced he was under arrest, he grabbed the .38 caliber Navy Colt revolver which lay on his desk and swung it against Swanson's head, dropping him to the floor. Sam, who had been nervous about the arrest and already had his revolver in hand, immediately fired point blank at Miller. The round crashed into Miller's abdomen, ripped through his stomach and pancreas, and severed his spinal cord as it exited. Miller was dead before he hit the floor.

Sam tended to Major Swanson, who was dizzy and had a crashing headache but was soon able to be helped back to his office. There Swanson made a report of the incident and much to Sam's relief, praised and assured him that he acted properly when he took the life of Captain Miller.

Major Swanson's report made the rounds of the War Department just as Colonel Lafayette C. Baker, the ruthless head of the National Detective Police, had requested a replacement of a detective who had died in a whorehouse beside the City Canal with a knife shoved between the fifth and sixth ribs. Upon reading the report Baker immediately arranged for Sam's transfer from the Quartermaster Corps to Baker's spy headquarters.

So Sam became a spy, an "agent" in Army nomenclature, and learned to his utter despair that spying was even more tedious and boring than buying and overseeing the shipment of goods to cold and hungry troops. For four months he had done nothing but read intercepted messages - personal letters, coded telegrams, cryptic notes that hinted at a great deal but usually told very little - and interviewed captured Rebels suspected of spying.

He also spent a good deal of time reliving the moment when he had shot Captain Archie Miller. It bothered him greatly that he had taken a human life, even though he knew, on a rational level, that it was a clear case of *I kill you before you kill me.* On a purely emotional level, however, he had *taken a human life!* It was a tough thing to ignore and he had trouble with it. It didn't help much that his work was dull, characterized more by plodding and grinding than by sudden flashes of genius.

Now, however, there was that gnawing sensation that something was going on right before his eyes and he was missing it. It was a sensation Sam did not like.

Wearily he picked up a letter and stared at the spidery hand. "Damn!" he snorted and slammed the letter down on the table.

David looked up from his desk. "What's the matter? Is it getting you down?" His eyebrows were arched, questioning, the way he always did when there was something he clearly didn't understand. And David didn't understand outbursts. They weren't consistent with his cool, methodical style. He stared at Sam, waiting for an answer.

Sam picked up the letter. "Listen to this." He began reading in a high-pitched, sing-song falsetto, mimicking a girl's voice.

"My Dear Nicole,

Carl will pick up the bonnet on his next trip to the city.

Much love, Alice."

"Now, you tell me," Sam shook the letter at David, "is 'bonnet' a code word for 'guns' or 'messages'? Is 'Alice' some Rebel agent's code name? How in the hell are we supposed to make sense out of this damned stuff?"

"Or, listen to this." He picked up another letter. This time he read in a deep baritone, the words measured, precise and masculine.

"Victor-

The line is set. Tomorrow night. The landing.

Red No. 4."

Sam jabbed his forefinger at David. "That, by God, *is* a Rebel secret service message. But it could just as well have been written in Egyptian. But like everything else we've picked up at that Rebel mail drop in lower Maryland, it's a mystery."

Sam shrugged and shook his head slowly. He picked up the latest issue of the New York *Daily News,* turned to the *personal* ads and began scanning the items under "To the South." They all had a crazy double-talk quality that was at the same time both ludicrous and frustrating. One item caught his eye:

> "Sue, in Lynchburg. Your brother Robert, who has been in Harrisonburg, is ill again and wishes to see you. Please call at same time and place next Tuesday. Rhoda. Richmond papers please copy."

He glanced at a list of code names he had been compiling. There had been a message to Rhoda in Montreal three weeks ago. Something about business being good and inquiring about the health of the new baby. Sam made a note to dig out the ad and compare it with this latest message. There was little chance that it was the same Rhoda or, if it were, that anything could be made of it, but there was always that possibility.

There were footsteps in the hallway and Sam looked up to see Sergeant Pollack, his mammoth chest heaving from the exertion of climbing the stairs, come puffing through the door carrying a tissue-thin message and a small manila folder tied with a red ribbon.

The sergeant grinned broadly. "Sir, we just got a message that might interest you, a chance to find out what them Rebels is up to. And it sounds mighty big. Here, read this."

Sam took the flimsy piece of paper from the Sergeant and began to read. In a few seconds his brow was furrowed and a look of puzzlement swept over his face.

Chapter 3

Monday, February 13

The message was brief and to the point:

"Headquarters, National Detective Police Washington, D.C. February 11, 1865

Captain Bishop of the Secret Service left Richmond this morning for Washington on what appears to be a mission of some importance. He met at the President's home for over three hours last night with President Davis and Secretaries Breckinridge and Benjamin. Nothing further is known except that the President was heard to say that this mission would win the war for the Confederacy.

STEADFAST."

"'Steadfast.' That's Edna Van Lew, isn't it?"

"Yessir, Elizabeth Van Lew. 'Crazy Bette' the Rebels call her. She goes about Richmond lookin' wild-eyed and mutterin' under her breath and the Rebels think she's a looney. But she's one of our best agents. Very reliable. Knows what's goin' on in Richmond."

Sam pointed at the calendar on the wall by the door. "She doesn't waste any time does she? Captain Bishop met with Jeff Davis and his Secretaries of State and War on Friday night and Crazy Bette wrote us about it on Saturday. What's she have, an operator in the Rebel White House?"

The sergeant shrugged and wiped his brow with a red bandanna stained from several weeks uninterrupted use. "I don't know, but that'd be my guess. Probably one of the darkies that works there.

"What do you make of it, Sergeant?"

"Haven't the slightest idee, Sir. It's maybe nothin'. Jeff Davis shootin' off his mouth or a servant thinkin' he hears somethin' he didn't. But the major wants you to look into it right away. Myself, I think it might lead to somethin'. You never know."

Sam nodded toward the chair by his desk. "Let me see the file on Captain Bishop."

Sergeant Pollack pulled the chair away from the desk and plopped down heavily, betraying a weariness intensified by obesity and advancing years. He opened the file he had brought with him, glanced over it quickly, and handed it to Sam.

There wasn't much there.

George Washington Bishop, known as *G.W.*, was born February 23, 1836, on a farm near Manassas, Virginia. His father's family had farmed the area for three generations. His mother, also the daughter of a farmer, was determined to leave the drab country existence that was a smalltime Virginia farmer's lot and take up residence in the city. In 1845, when their only child was nine, they sold the family farm that Jesse Bishop had inherited and moved to Georgetown, just across Rock Creek from Washington, D.C. In Georgetown Jesse became a butcher, no difficult matter since he had butchered his own livestock for over a quarter century, and Erma Bishop became a minor socialite and middle-aged busybody.

Despite their Virginia background, the Bishops sent their son to school in the North, to Franklin & Marshall College in Lancaster, Pennsylvania, where he graduated with Honors in 1857. After graduation he opened a girls' seminary - the Georgetown Institute - which was closed in 1861 because of what the file called the "treasonable behavior of the principal and the students."

"What's this 'treasonable behavior' that closed Bishop's school in Georgetown?" Sam asked.

"One of the girls was caught up on the roof signalin' to the Rebel batteries at the Lee Place over in Arlington. Bishop was slapped in the Old Capitol and paroled after six weeks on the condition that he not leave the District. He moved in with his parents in Georgetown after he got out of prison. There was some talk that he was involved in a plot to kill General Scott but there's nothin' about that in the file."

Sam read on. There was the parole paper, clearly marked with the words "not to leave the District of Columbia."

But he did. In July, shortly after the Rebel victory at First Bull Run, which was fought across part of the farm on which he had grown up, Bishop fled to Richmond where he secured a chaplaincy in the 3rd Virginia Cavalry, Stuart's Division, with the rank of captain.

Since then he had been reported to be in Washington on several occasions, most recently around the time of the 1864 elections.

Sam looked up at the Sergeant. "What's a Rebel *chaplain* doing in Washington?"

"The chaplaincy's a cover. And a damned good one. The man is a lay reader in the Methodist Church. He can preach one hell of a sermon, if you'll excuse the expression, sir, according to some of his men I've talked to."

"What's he look like? All the file says is 'short, with dark hair'."

"It's hard to say, sir. That's one of the mysteries."

There were no more papers in the file. "Is this all? Isn't there any more information on this man?"

"Nothin' more in the file, sir ..."

Sam smiled. "But you know something more. Right?"

The sergeant grinned and shifted about in his chair, obviously pleased, both at the opportunity to display his knowledge of the Rebel underground, which Sam knew from experience to be substantial, and at the fact that such further knowledge on his part would be expected.

"Yessir, I do. Last summer I was involved in that business of tryin' to find out how the Rebels get their information out of Washington and into Richmond so damned fast. You remember, Crazy Bette was pickin' up our plans in the Rebel War Office forty-eight hours after they were put together in the War Department here. We know they use couriers, in fact Bishop hisself has served as a courier, but even when we stopped ALL traffic south, the mail still got through. We never did figger out how they do it."

Sergeant Pollack nodded vigorously "Yessir. Anyhow, I went down to the lower Potomac and while I was down there I talked to the cook at the tavern in Surrattsville. You know the place I mean?"

"Yes," Sam replied, "a regular den of rebellion."

"Well, this here cook - she was a slave - tole me that Bishop stopped by there ever week or so. Said he looked different just about ever time he came by - you know, changed his hair style and beard and what not. Sometimes, she said, she hardly know'd him. And she said he was hot tempered and cocky, always lookin' for a fight.

"She didn't think much of him but she said Mrs. Surratt made over him like he was somethin' special. The cook said Bishop hadn't stopped there since spring - it was last summer when I talked to her. 'Course Mrs. Surratt moved into the District back in November and leased her place to a feller name of Lloyd. We watched the place for a while and then give up on it. That's all I know about him."

"Not much, is there? I guess Major Swanson realizes that. And I have one or two other matters I want to check out first." Sam handed the file back to the sergeant.

"Yessir, I'm sure the Major will understand. But that won't make no nevermind to Colonel Baker."

Sam sighed at the mention of the Colonel's name. "I'm sure you're right. Leave the file with me."

The Sergeant nodded, rose and left the room without further ceremony. Sam liked Sergeant Pollack and he knew the Sergeant liked and even respected him, though he also knew that the Sergeant felt, as did most of the other officers and men in the National Detective Police headquarters, that he was a naive young man without much knowledge of the ways of the wicked world in which secret service agents must operate. And, in a way, Sam knew they were right.

Barely twenty-three, Sam Reid was a young man blessed (or cursed, depending on how you viewed it) with the face and physique of perpetual youth. He was tall and slender with a thin face set off by deep-set dark eyes that reflected a sadness that was not all-together an illusion.

He had grown up more or less alone, a "late-in-life baby" whose closest sibling was twelve years older. When he was seven his mother died. Five years later his father married again - to a woman who saw Sam only as a reminder of her husband's first wife and who treated him with polite but cool detachment.

Sam's reaction to her presence had been one of complete rebellion. He caught spiders and put them in her dresser drawer, switched the sugar and salt in the canisters in the kitchen so she would appear to be a poor cook, deliberately dragged mud into the parlor and, when punished by his father for his behavior, ran away from home in Steubenville, Ohio. Once he got all the way upriver to Pittsburgh, before the captain of the paddlewheeler *The Indian Queen* became suspicious of why a well-dressed twelve-year-old boy would volunteer as a deck hand and turned him over to the authorities.

Gradually he and Anna Clarke Reid reached a compromise, marked by grudging acceptance of one another's presence and the unspoken agreement to stay out of each other's way.

At fourteen Sam went to work in his father's general store, the largest mercantile establishment in Steubenville. His pleasant ways and his shy, almost self-effacing personality endeared him to the customers, especially to the ladies, who read into his sad face a desperate need to be mothered.

Steubenville, which was situated across the Ohio River from Virginia's Northern Panhandle, was a vital link in the Underground Railroad west of the Alleghenies. So Nathaniel Reid vented his deep-seated abolitionist feelings by offering his house, which stood in a grove of tall poplars at the edge of town, as a station on this slave escape network. Thus Sam came of age in a clandestine world filled with whispered messages at midnight and followed by the arrival of a handful of frightened, shivering negroes, with their few pitiful possessions wrapped in a gunny sack and their eyes set firmly on the North Star. It was a sobering experience, one that matured the boy in a way that nothing else could.

But so youthful was Sam's appearance that the combined experience of losing his mother at the age of seven, aiding hundreds of runaway slaves on the underground railroad, attending college for three years, and losing a brother at Stone's River - plus the uniform of a Lieutenant in the United States Volunteers - did not erase the image of naivete and wide-eyed youth that hung about him.

Suddenly there was a rustle of crinoline at the door and David Petersen stood up abruptly.

"Hello, Miss Ellie," he said. "Sam, you've got a mighty pretty caller here to see you."

Sam looked up just as Ellie Richards swept into the room, her long, thick eyelashes aflutter and her hands encased in a muff of pure white rabbit fur. He jumped up quickly, came around in front of the desk and took the girl's outstretched hands which were cold despite the muff she had laid on Sam's desk. In total contrast to the miserable weather, she was radiant.

"I declare, it's like a smokehouse in here," she said, throwing Sam an exaggerated look of disgust. "I don't know how you men stand it. Please sit down, David."

She smiled at Sam, the smile lines curling around the corners of her mouth, and the two moved closer together. "Darlin', Momma wants to know if you can come to dinner Sunday. Or can you leave your spying long enough?"

Sam stared intently into the girl's large brown eyes. She was of medium height, amply built, with sensuous hips that were evident even beneath all the crinolines and large breasts that strained at the top of her low-cut dress and always drew a second glance from the men. Her skin was clear, with a light olive tint, made all the more striking by her shiny, almost coal black hair.

"Of course. I wouldn't miss it if I had to pass up a chance to read Jeff Davis' mail." He glanced at his watch lying open on the desk. "It's nearly 4:30. Why don't we go to Willard's for supper?"

Ellie laughed. "Momma said I was just asking for an invitation to supper by coming here at this time to invite you to Sunday dinner. So she's not expecting me home 'til after six. You see, I do know you pretty well, don't I?"

She turned to Lieutenant Petersen, who was intently studying a paper on his desk. "Won't you join us, David?"

"No thank you, Miss Ellie. Sam would kill me if he had to share you with me."

"Oh posh. There'll be so many people in Willard's dining room that we'll probably have to share a table with total strangers. I'd much rather have you two handsome lieutenants as companions than to have to make conversation with some beady-eyed old colonel who loses half of his supper in his beard."

"Miss Ellie, I have to stay here and finish some work. I'm going out of town tomorrow and may be gone the rest of the week. If I don't finish this report Colonel Baker will chew my hide off."

Ellie smiled at the young officer. "I'm sorry, David. I do enjoy your company so much. Where are you going? Off to Richmond to spy on Jeff Davis?"

"No, I'm taking the train to Chicago."

"Oh posh, David. I don't see what could possibly interest you or your Colonel Baker in Chicago. It must be a million miles from the war. You just don't want to join us for supper. Come on, Sam dear, let's go."

David jumped up, protesting. "Ask Sam what's happenin' in Chicago with the inauguration coming up. Ask him about the prison there and the Rebel plots we've heard about."

Ellie broke into a grin. "Oh, David, can't you see I'm just joshing you? I understand. We know you'd join us if you could, don't we, Sam? You have a nice trip."

Ellie smiled at the young officer. "I'm sorry, David. I do enjoy your company so much." She smiled broadly. "I understand. We know you'd join us if you could, don't we, Sam?"

David smiled weakly and sat back down. "You two have a pleasant evening. I'll see you later, Sam."

As Sam and Ellie walked down the narrow, dingy passageway toward the stairs, Ellie held her muff in her right hand and sought out Sam's hand with her free left hand. They walked down the stairs to the landing and Ellie stopped and faced Sam. When she was satisfied that no one was coming in either direction and that they were quite alone on the landing, she pressed her body tightly against his and pulled his lips to hers. After a few seconds she pulled her head away slightly, leaving her breasts pushed firmly against Sam's chest, and whispered softly, "I love you so much, Darling. I'm not sure I can wait 'til this war's over to marry you."

"Ellie, you know I'll marry you anytime you say," Sam replied.

"I know, but with all the uncertainty Momma says we have to wait. And she's right. Here, wipe off your forehead. You've smudged it tending the fire. It's a wonder that you ever keep clean in that awful dingy office. But you do look so handsome in your uniform. I'll probably lose you to the first pretty girl who comes along."

"She'll have to drag me from you," Sam said.

When the couple emerged from the War Department building onto 17th Street the sky was leaden and overcast. Ellie shivered, took Sam's arm and slid her hands deep into her muff. They turned left and walked toward Lafayette Square chatting merrily, Ellie the very picture of radiant beauty.

After a block they reached the Square and turned right onto Pennsylvania Avenue. As they walked past the White House two men who were standing across the street in Lafayette Square beside the bronze equestrian statue of Andrew Jackson watched them intently. Finally, one of the men, who was dressed in the dark blue uniform of the United States Army, turned to the other and spoke.

"Captain Bishop," he said. "That young man is Lieutenant Reid."

"Well," Bishop said tensely, "it's good to get a look at the man I intend to kill."

Chapter 4

Monday, February 13

The actor known as "the handsomest man in Washington" made his way through the late supper crowd at Gautier's Restaurant, nodding graciously to all who called him by name. And there were many, for at twenty-six John Wilkes Booth was darkly and romantically handsome. His silky jet-black hair and thick, drooping mustache highlighted the splendor of flawless ivory skin. And dark, lustrous heavy-lidded eyes hinted at the sensual nature that lay at his heart.

The diners looked up at Booth from tables laden with a variety of foods - roast venison, thick pan-fried beef steaks, Cornish game hens, wild turkey, platters of chops, steaming tureens of soup, mounds of thick creamy mashed potatoes and dishes piled with vegetables of every description, usually swimming in a rich buttery broth. Here and there a quiet, elegantly-attired waiter moved effortlessly among the tables with more food or a tall, frosty bottle of imported French Champagne, fresh from the ice-packed cellar beneath the restaurant.

In deference to the advancing hour the gas jets had been turned up and the restaurant basked in a warm twilight glow that blended together the subtle colors and tints of the establishment's imported red French wallpaper, the multi-shaded greens of the potted palms and ferns, the crisp golds and blues of the stained glass windows along the avenue, and the shiny elegance of the cut crystal chandeliers.

If the restaurant at Willard's were more famous, Gautier's was nonetheless bidding fair to be *the* place to dine and be seen dining in the capital. With its cosmopolitan crowds it was also an ideal place for one secret service agent to meet another.

Captain G. W. Bishop watched Wilkes Booth thread his way slowly between the tightly-packed tables in the ornate dining room. The man was the picture of nonchalant elegance. An expensive greatcoat, with its flowing cape, collared in fur, was draped carelessly over his left arm. His flawlessly dressed hair curled casually to the velvet collar of his braid-bound jacket. The jacket, which was claret colored, hung open to reveal a soft, fawn-colored waistcoat. A diamond stickpin, large enough to be noticed but not so large as to be gaudy, was thrust through the center of his expensive silk cravat. Even the tailoring of his dove-gray trousers had been so expertly done as to play down the only flaw in the actor's otherwise perfect appearance - his bowed legs.

As he neared Bishop's table Booth stopped and turned at mention of his name in a heavy French accent. Bishop watched as Gautier, the fashionable French restaurateur and caterer, hurried up to Booth and shook his hand warmly, publicly welcoming the famous actor to his establishment and assuring that a portion of the actor's glamour would attach to the elegant restaurant.

After a few polite words with the restaurateur, Booth turned again toward the table. Bishop rose and held out his hand. "Good evening, Mr. Booth," he said. "My name is Wilson."

"Ah, yes. Of the Annapolis Wilsons?" Booth replied.

"No, my family is from Baltimore."

Booth smiled broadly when the recognition code was finished and took the proffered hand. "My pleasure, sir," he replied, and the two men were seated.

The conversation was light and trifling during the meal of roast wild duck with currant sauce, wild rice sauté and alligator pear salad. As they chatted casually each man carefully probed for bits and pieces of the other's background.

Bishop quickly confirmed what he had been told in the Confederate capital, that despite his profession and his dandified appearance, John Wilkes Booth was no soft character. His appearance and his personality were entirely consistent with his reputation as an athletic actor, a reputation that proceeded from his inclination to rely on frenzied physical activity to carry difficult scenes where more subtle theatrics were generally called for. As he watched the actor eat, Bishop recalled the story of the time Booth, playing in the title role of *Richard III*, got carried away with his enthusiastic sword play and drove E. L. Tilton, a powerful six-footer and excellent swordsman, into the orchestra pit. Tilton suffered a painfully dislocated shoulder but Booth had what he wanted, the thunderous applause of the audience and the attention of the press.

Booth, for all his idle chatter and seeming indifference to his surroundings was carefully sizing up his companion, whose identity was, as yet, unknown to him. His quick eyes darted about the spy's Northern garb between snatches of polite conversation and occasional forays to his plate. He ran his eyes across the Southerner's mutton chop and carefully scrutinized his expensively-tailored black broadcloth suit.

The Southerner's face had an innocent quality to it, a wide-eyed, full-mouthed look Booth figured would be quite an advantage to a spy. Yet at moments, particularly when he was answering a question, his eyes would narrow and Booth could sense a hardness that not even the spy's forced congeniality could cover.

But the most significant factor about his physical appearance was the absolute lack of any distinguishing characteristics and the total normality of appearance. The spy played on this, Booth noticed, dressing quietly, wearing his hair at medium length, keeping his whiskers trimmed and blending into the crowd with perfect anonymity. He was short, but not too short, dapper, but not showy, a non-entity in a game where being a nonentity could spell the difference between life and death.

He was a hearty eater, too. Booth noted how he carefully rounded up every bit of wild duck, swished it around in the currant sauce and then methodically went after the remainder of the sauce with thick chunks of Gautier's heavy French bread. He ate neither swiftly nor ravishingly, but with a deliberateness and purpose that spoke of a man who loved his food. In Richmond, where acorns were being boiled as a substitute for coffee and a barrel of flour sold for $1,000 Confederate money, such an appetite must suffer greatly.

Booth kept searching his companion, masking his interest with idle chatter. Finally he stopped abruptly. He leaned forward and lowered his voice slightly. "I must congratulate you. You look very much the Yankee businessman. I pride myself in keen powers of observation and there is nothing about you to suggest," he glanced about quickly and lowered his voice again, "your background and political preference. I could easily have mistaken you for a Pennsylvanian."

The man lay down his fork. "When in Rome," he said quietly, "you MUST do as the Romans do. It's quite simple. I'm an actor, too, only the whole eastern theater of war is my stage. And my audience - the people of the North - will hang me if my performance is not entirely convincing."

Booth laughed. "I've had many an audience ready to hang me, too. But not for my political preferences."

When they were finishing their dessert of pumpkin pie with American cheese and coffee creamed to within an inch of its life, Booth eyed Bishop squarely and said softly, "Well, sir. What is this all about? What do you want of me?"

Bishop reached into his inside coat pocket and pulled a paper from it. He handed it to Booth who unfolded it and read.

> "Confederate States of America
> War Department
> Richmond, Virginia, Feby. 10, 1865.
>
> Lt. Col. Mosby and Lieut. Cawood are hereby directed to aid and facilitate the movements of Capt. Bishop.
>
> John C. Breckinridge
> Secretary of War."

Booth looked up. "So you're . . . ." His voice trailed off. "I don't suppose I should mention your name, even in a whisper. It is, sir, a great honor to make your acquaintance. You have a vast reputation in the circles in which we mutually travel." Then he said in a whisper: "What do you, what does the Secretary of War, want of me?"

Bishop took a sip of rich, cream-laden coffee and belched softly. Then, eyeing the restaurant crowd, he responded. "Is there someplace where we can talk in absolute security?"

"Yes. My room at the National," Booth replied. "Shall we go there now?"

"I'd like another cup of coffee if you don't mind. You can't imagine what a treat real coffee is." Bishop looked around the restaurant. "It probably sounds hedonistic but the opportunity to eat like this is one of the finer compensations for the risks I must take in my line of work."

Booth waved the waiter aside when he was offered a second cup. When the man had left he spoke softly. "Are things as bad there as I hear?"

"I don't know what you hear but, yes, things are bad. Corn meal was selling for $100 a peck Confederate the morning I left. The night before I feasted on a meal of rice, dried peas and stewed apples - and I've no doubt I ate as well as anyone in Richmond. There is a scarcity of soap and the lady with whom I took my meal, a widow of long acquaintance, paid $35.00 a yard for calico that goes for 12 cents a yard in New York City. Coal and scraps of firewood are hoarded as if they are gold."

"We black our shoes with polish made at home of lard mixed with soot. Lard, scented with rose petals, is our hair oil. Our womenfolk arrange their hair with combs carved from wood or cows horn and hairpins improvised from thorns. We haven't enough salt to preserve what little hog meat we produce. We are, Mr. Booth, on the edge of collapse, deprived of simple necessities. But enough of this. I'm finished now. Are we ready to go?"

Booth nodded and after settling for their meal the pair started for the door. Booth's exit was as ceremonious as his entrance, with the actor bowing left and right to those who called out his name. Twice he stopped to shake hands with admirers. Both times Bishop hung back until the actor moved on. Finally they were outside.

As they picked their way across the frozen, snow-covered pavement of Pennsylvania Avenue between the hustling hacks and mounted horsemen, Booth sought to make small talk. "Some 'Grand and Imposing Boulevard' our Pennsylvania Avenue, isn't it? Poor Pierre L'Enfant must be spinning in his grave to see what desolation the Yankees have wrought from the grand design he prepared for this city."

He threw his right arm dramatically about, making a broad sweep of the Avenue with his walking stick. "Look at it, the whores of 'Hooker's Division' on your right, our 'glorious' barely finished Capitol dead ahead, and the drab establishments of Yankee commerce, their cathedrals, if you will, on our left. And, after the thaw, the odor, we call it the perfume of the City Canal. They say it smells like Abe Lincoln's breath."

Bishop smiled quietly but did not respond. He knew that the actor was showing off a bit for him, emphasizing his distaste for the Federal City and its Yankee masters. With some agents this would have raised suspicions rather than quieting them. But Booth was known, even among his most ardent supporters, as a loud, cocky, show-off. Still, he had his contacts and could be useful under the proper circumstances. Listening to a little puffing was all a part of the job.

As they made their way up the Avenue a bleary-eyed, unshaven man, dressed in rags, who had been huddled against the brick storefront of Harper and Mitchell, the dry goods merchants, pushed away from the storefront and started down the brick sidewalk in an unsteady gait. Although his pace was irregular and his attention apparently concentrated on something deeply within himself, he very carefully stayed just within sight of the two men he had been watching since their exit from Gautiers. When Booth and Bishop entered the lobby of the National Hotel the man staggered across the Avenue and leaned up against the disreputable front of the Hotel Murray, pulling his shabby collar up against the numbing cold. There, unobtrusively, he kept watch over the entrance to the National Hotel.

Chapter 5

Monday, February 13

David was getting ready to leave when Sam returned to the office. He looked at Sam and grinned the tight-mouthed, sheepish grin that announced he had something on someone else. "Surprised to see you here. I thought you'd stay at Ellie's all night."

"I would have liked to but I finally got tired of her mother glaring at the two of us and took the hint and left. The damned old bat, she just sits there in that damnable squeaky rocker and knits. Never leaves the room unless there's something on the stove in the kitchen. The only way we can be alone is to go out in the kitchen and make candy or hot chocolate. And then she's always coming in and out to check on us."

"Sam, if I were a mother and had a daughter as statuesque as Ellie, I'd never let her out of my sight."

"Well, she certainly doesn't let Ellie out of her sight now, that's for sure," Sam said as he backed up to the fire and warmed his hands.

David picked a paper off his desk and waved it. "Last week one of our agents, a fellow named Felix Stidger, seemed to be on to something big around the Camp Douglas prisoner of war camp in Chicago, when he was killed by a runaway horse. Looks like an accident but the Colonel doesn't think so. He wants me to go out to Chicago and have a look. I'm to check out the camp and try to learn what I can about the existence of any Rebel underground in Chicago. Mostly I guess I'll just nose about for a few days and come home."

"Sounds rather vague, like this Bishop business of mine."

David stacked some papers on his desk and wiped the dust from his hands. "Yes, I guess so. But since when have we ever had an assignment that made any real sense?"

Sam turned and faced the fire. "I suppose I shouldn't complain too much about this job not making sense. Nothing has made much sense since my mother died. My witch of a step-mother and my bratty half-brother have taken all of my old man's attention. College was such a bore I quit before getting a degree. The Underground Railway was a study in human misery and the Quartermaster Corps was a farce."

"I thought you got along all right with your father."

"Oh, Pa's all right. He just knows it all. Used to be a school teacher and, even after he became a success in the store business, he never quite lost the teacher's itch to tell everyone how to do everything. And he's something of a religious nut, has a strong hatred of what he sees as injustice and is hell-bent to convert anyone who doesn't see it his way. We had a plaque on our parlor wall with the words from Deuteronomy painted on it: *'Thou shalt not deliver unto his master the servant which is escaped from his master unto thee.'* Pa said that was God's charter for the Underground Railroad. I think he thought that God spoke those words directly to Nathaniel Reid. But he's all right. I guess it's my stepmother as much as anyone who caused me trouble."

"What's she like?"

"Pretty good looking, if you don't know her. I can see how Pa would be interested in her. Must be pretty good in bed, too. I used to hear their old four-poster squeaking away. One night one of the slats broke and they came crashing down on the floor. I like to split my sides laughin'. I think they heard me 'cause Anna couldn't look me in the eye for a week after that."

David tilted his chair back and clasped his hands behind his head. "That's what I need, Sam, a good-looking woman. This job and this town are getting me down. Does Ellie have any beautiful girlfriends?"

"I don't think Ellie has ANY friends. At least I've never met any of them. It's probably her mother. I guess she scares everyone away."

"You have a girl back home, Dave?"

"No. When your daddy's the town drunk and your mother keeps the family together by taking in washings, there aren't many mothers who'll let their daughters take a second look at you. I guess they think being a drunk is hereditary. If I'm going to find a girl she'll have to come from somewhere more than fifty miles from Shelbyville, Indiana."

"I'll keep my eyes open, Dave. The first time I see a good lookin' girl who isn't wearing a wedding band I'll give her your name and put in a good word for you."

"That's mighty neighborly of you," David replied, smiling. "I guess there's always the chance I'll meet my dream girl on the train to Chicago tomorrow."

"Dave, if you do I'll wager it will be the only positive thing to come out of that trip."

"I agree. I guess my first job is to keep from getting killed like Felix Stidger."

Sam buttoned up his overcoat and started for the door. "Have a good trip, and get married while you're at it. You have a lean and hungry look. Like Shakespeare said, 'such men are dangerous.'"

David laughed and waved goodbye. Sam walked out the hallway and down the stairs. As he started out the front door he was almost knocked down by an out-of-breath soldier from Division V who excused abruptly himself and dashed on into the building.

Sam was already out of sight before the detective headquarters burst into a frenzy of excitement over the news the soldier had brought with him.

Chapter 6

Monday, February 13

When they were settled in Booth's room on the hotel's second floor the actor offered his guest a brandy and a cigar. "No thank you, Mr. Booth," G. W. Bishop replied. "I don't drink or smoke. But if you don't mind I think I'll have a chew." He looked at the wad of tobacco in his hand. "I'd prefer plug tobacco to this Yankee 'short cut,' you know, but I never come north with the plug. It's a small matter, I suppose, but I'd have a difficult time explaining to the Federal provost marshal why a Yankee would carry Rebel plug tobacco."

Booth laughed as he poured a glass of cognac. "Can't be too careful in this business, can we, Captain Bishop? Now sir, what's Secretary Breckinridge's order all about?"

Bishop leaned forward in his chair and spoke in a low tone. "Mr. Booth, what would you say is our nation's most desperate need right now?"

Booth swirled the cognac in his glass. "Men, arms, supplies, all these, I suppose. But men, soldiers in the field, I would say would be our greatest need."

Bishop nodded. "Exactly. The Yankees can throw hordes of German and Irish immigrants against us. They're cannon fodder perhaps, certainly not the caliber of our Southern men. But there are so many we're being crushed by the sheer weight of numbers. Of course Grant knows this and halted all prisoner exchanges last April. There are now over 60,000 Southern soldiers in Federal prison pens. The South needs those men."

Booth stared into his cognac. "Yes, and I think I know where you are heading. You are going to tell me that the South is planning expeditions against the larger camps. I've heard rumors."

"Well, yes, there are some plans of that nature. But I've nothing to do with them. My mission is much bigger and potentially more effective."

Booth tensed slightly and looked at Bishop, puzzled.

"You will remember, Mr. Booth, that under the prisoner exchange cartel which the Yankees have now ceased to honor, there was a table of equivalents established for exchanging prisoners of unequal rank. The table was based on the United States' agreement with Britain in the War of 1812. It provided, for example, that a lieutenant could be exchanged for four privates, a major for eight, a colonel fifteen and so on up to a general in command, who was worth sixty privates. Well, can you imagine what the President of the United States would be worth as a prisoner of war?"

Booth set his cognac down on the bedside stand, got up and crossed the room. He sat down on the edge of the bed opposite Bishop's chair, leaned forward and whispered dramatically, "Am I to understand, Captain Bishop, that you, or rather the Secretary of War, wish me to become involved in a plot to capture Abraham Lincoln?"

"Yes," Bishop replied softly, trying not to laugh at the actor's melodramatic behavior. "And so do President Davis and Secretary of State Benjamin. I met with the three of them in Richmond last week. This whole scheme is the President's idea. He had Secretary Breckinridge give me the orders you read earlier."

Booth drew himself up to full height, threw out his chest, and, with his brow furrowed deeply, said, "Sir, tell President Davis he will have my complete cooperation. We shall rid the world of this tyrant."

Bishop shook his head. "Sit down, Mr. Booth, we only want to capture Abe Lincoln, not kill him. A dead President will do us no good."

"If we make him our prisoner, we kill him politically. That's all I meant."

"Well, you're right there. If we capture Lincoln before he can be inaugurated, Andy Johnson will likely become President. And even if he doesn't, if the Yankees postpone the inauguration, Lincoln will have to resign out of humiliation and we'll be able to force a peace treaty on his successor. Either way, a captive Abe Lincoln is the key to Southern independence."

Booth sat quietly for a moment, blowing great rings of blue cigar smoke. "I like the idea. You can depend on me. What exactly do you want me to do?"

"You have contacts in the Rebel underground here and in Baltimore who can be helpful to us. I already have four men, not counting the two of us. I'll need two or three more. And they must be absolutely trustworthy."

"Of course. You shall have them. I know just the men you want."

"Not so fast," Bishop interrupted. "I don't want just ANY men. I'll need a man who knows how to use chloroform and has some knowledge of poisons. I'll need another man who knows lower Maryland like the back of his hand. And either or both of these men must know how to handle a boat. A large boat, big enough to hold a half dozen men or more. Finally, I'll need a man who knows no fear. A man who knows how to use weapons. When you have the men, I'll tell you more of what is expected of them."

"Very well," Booth replied. "I'll find the men you need."

"Good. Today is the 13th. I want you to have your four men here as soon as possible. When they are here and ready to act, place an ad in the *Personals* of the *Star*. It should read: "George. Mother died on the *blank*. Rosa." The date will be the hour of the day following the appearance of the ad when you want me to meet you and your friends here. Use the 24-hour clock, the European method of telling time. Do you understand?"

"Yes. If I run the ad on Monday the 20th and say that mother died on the 10th, you will know to meet us here at 10:00 the next morning, the 21st."

"Precisely. It's possible that I'll be unable to be here when your ad requests. In that case I'll send a friend in my place. But under no circumstances are you to mention me or our mission or your role as a Confederate agent until proper identification has been made. And for this particular project there will be a secret set of codes which will be known only to those involved. It's a set of three questions and three answers:

Q. "Excuse me can you tell me where to find the office of Wilbur Burroughs?"

A. "Wilbur Burroughs, what is his line of work?"

Q. "I believe he is a lawyer."

A. "No, the only Burroughs I know is a doctor."

Q. "Then perhaps he can heal our country."

A. "Only God can do that."

Bishop paused. "Do you have that, Mr. Booth?"

"Yes, I think so. I'm used to memorizing things, you know."

"Well, it mustn't be written down."

"Of course not."

"You'll notice, Mr. Booth, that the questions and answers are quite innocent and rather commonplace in the beginning. But they become rather stilted and artificial toward the end. It's all very deliberate. Anyone could ask the first question, so that if you ask it of the wrong person, you'll not arouse suspicion. But only someone who is privy to the code could possibly have all the questions or answers."

Booth nodded. "Quite so. Very clever."

"Well, Mr. Booth, I must be going. Thank you for your hospitality, and your willingness to help."

Booth took Bishop's hand. "It's an honor, sir, to be able to serve my country in such an important way and, I might add, in such distinguished company. I wasn't told I would be meeting you at Gautier's tonight, only to meet someone sitting alone at a table in the rear near the door, someone who would rise and introduce himself with the *Wilson/Baltimore* code. I'm quite sincere when I say that it is a great honor to be associated with the great G. W. Bishop."

Bishop's face remained impassive. "Good night, Mr. Booth," he replied, and started down the gas-lit hallway, ignoring Booth's compliment and his obvious effort to be friendly.

The man's a fool, a vain, posturing fool, Bishop thought as he went down the steps toward the lobby. But perhaps he's just the sort of fool we need to pull this thing off. As he reached the landing on the steps and began the final descent into the lobby, G. W. Bishop felt pleased with himself, even a bit smug. Despite his formal training in education and theology, he had risen to the top of the dangerous profession of spying, an unlikely consequence that was, he recognized, a tribute to his daring and adaptability.

At this moment he felt that he could do virtually anything, go anywhere and pull off any caper. He was the *Master Spy of the Confederacy*, perched securely on the edge of great fame. It was a good feeling.

The ancient grandfather clock in the lobby boomed out 10 o'clock as Bishop started for the door. The crowd had thinned out considerably in the hour or so he had been in Booth's room, a reflection of both the hour and the growing cold. Those still lounging on the worn Victorian furniture scattered about the lobby were for the most part "sunshine soldiers," those who wore gaudy uniforms covered with brass buttons and shiny epaulets but who had no need to rise early in the morning to help fight the war.

As he strode toward the door a soldier dressed in the pale blue uniform of the Veteran's Reserve Corps, the "Invalid's Corps," the soldiers called it, stepped out from beside one of the mammoth rubber plants that stood beside the door and walked nonchalantly toward the stairs. When he reached Bishop the soldier stared directly at him and, when he had caught the captain's attention, rolled his eyes toward the door and shook his head slightly.

Bishop tensed slightly but walked past the soldier without a visible display of emotion. After a few steps he turned and walked up to the desk, as if he had suddenly remembered something he must inquire about of the desk clerk.

"Your necessary? It's down the hall, isn't it?"

"Yessir," the clerk replied, inclining his head to Bishop's right. "Down that hallway and to the left."

As Bishop walked briskly out of the lobby and into the dimly-lit hallway he saw, out of the corner of his eye, a young cavalryman who appeared to have been dozing on the sofa at the foot of the stairs, spring to his feet and start toward the hallway. He was pulling a pistol from his holster.

Bishop's stomach tightened and a shiver of fear cascaded over him. Damn! He had walked into a trap! If the Yankee detectives were any good, and right now they looked damned good, the building would be surrounded. He couldn't go outside and there was nowhere to go inside the hotel. But there must be a way.

He quickened his pace and at the end of the hallway he turned left and stopped abruptly beneath a glowing gas jet. In one smooth motion he reached up, turned off the gas, and then backed up against the opposite wall and listened. The cavalry man was close behind. Bishop tensed as the footsteps grew closer.

The moment the cavalryman turned into the corridor Bishop hit him in the solar plexus. The soldier emitted a painful gasp and bent forward, his face a grotesque purplish-red blend of pain and surprise. Quickly Bishop grabbed the Army Colt revolver that the cavalryman had slapped across his stomach in reflexive reaction to the sudden blow, and swung the weapon at the side of his head. He uttered a soft, "oof" and crumpled to the floor. Bishop nudged him with his boot, but he lay motionless.

There was shouting in the lobby now, orders being barked out, and the sound of running men echoing through the hallways. Bishop raced down the length of the corridor and turned left again into the hallway that ran along the rear of the huge rectangular hotel.

About a third of the way down the corridor he stopped before a door on the right. He fished a skeleton key from his vest pocket, opened the door and stepped into the room. As he closed the door behind him a male voice boomed out: "I beg your pardon! What are you doing?"

Bishop leaped in the direction of the voice and jabbed his pistol into the soft body of a man sitting upright in the bed. "Keep quiet or I'll kill you!"

The men were in the hallway now, noisily stomping up and down the corridor. One man shouted: "Shoot the sonofabitch on sight!" From the tone of their voices Bishop guessed that the cavalryman he had disarmed was dead.

They were pounding on doors now and Bishop could hear them demanding to search the rooms. Like a slow ascent of a stairway the sound of the pounding on doors came closer, room by room, as the Federal detectives worked their way down the hallway. Occasionally, where they received no answer to their knocking, they were unlocking the doors themselves and going on in. Hell, Bishop thought, everyone must have a skeleton key these days.

His eyes having adjusted to the dark Bishop could see that the man in the bed was middle-aged, bald, beardless and fat. He sat bolt upright in bed and said nothing. His breathing was quick and shallow. The man was clearly scared. That, Bishop decided, was a big factor in his favor.

"They're going to want to search the room in a minute. Your life depends on keeping those blue-coats out of here." He pulled the pistol back from the man's soft stomach. "I'm going to slide under the bed. When the Yankees unlock that door and come in, you tell them you've got the smallpox and ask them to leave you alone. If you mess up, I'll shoot you through that mattress and splatter your guts all over the ceiling. Understand?"

The man nodded his head and grunted, "yes." Then he laid back down and pulled the covers about him. Bishop reached into a pitcher on the nightstand beside the bed and flicked water onto the man's face. "Sweat," he said. "Maybe they'll see the beads of water on your face and think it's sweat from the pox."

As Bishop started to slide under the bed his foot clanged against a porcelain chamber pot. After a moment's hesitation he grabbed the pot and carefully poured the liquid onto the bed about midway down the man's body. The pungent odor of urine wafted into the air.

"What are you doing? Are you crazy?"

"Tell them you pissed yourself, you were too sick to use the pot." Then he slid under the bed. "Remember, if anything goes wrong, I'm going to shoot you. I have nothing to lose. Understand?"

"Yes, goddammit, I understand," the man replied. His voice was tense, nervous. But he was fighting to maintain control.

There was a knock at the door, first soft, then louder, followed by the sound of a key in the lock. Then the door swung open and the room brightened with the light from the hallway. Bishop pulled his feet up from the bottom of the bed so he could only be seen by someone who deliberately looked under the bed. A pair of boots approached the bed.

"Yes?" the man in bed inquired weakly. "What is it you want? I'm awful sick, you know. Smallpox."

The boots stopped. "Smallpox? Jesus Christ! It smells like a pissery in here Don't you have a thunder mug?"

"I . . . uh . . . I fouled myself . . . couldn't get up out of bed . . . too weak . . . ." The man's voice trailed off. He was one hell of an actor, no doubt about that.

"Well, I'm supposed to search the room," the soldier said. "Lookin' for a Rebel spy who killed one of our boys."

Bishop shuddered at the word "killed." So it was true.

"Ain't noboby in here but me. Please don't strike any matches. I don't think my eyes could stand it."

The soldier backed away. "Well, all right. I don't reckon anybody could stand to be in here anyway, as pissy as it smells." He turned and started out the door. As he was closing the door another soldier asked him, "Everything all right in there?"

"Yessir, just an old man with the smallpox."

"That was a mighty good job," Bishop said as he crawled out from under the bed. "Now you just go back to sleep while I figure my way out of this mess."

The man pulled the covers tightly about him. There was no possibility of his going to sleep under these conditions. But he lay there quietly, his mind racing.

The wind whistled against the window frame, a low moan sliding into a high-pitched shriek, and the snow swirled in fanciful patterns on the street outside. As daylight came the snow let up and the wind died. But it was still cold outside, the icy temperature in the room evidenced that much.

There had been no noise in the hallway for over two hours, since around 5:30. But the blue-coats were there all right. They wouldn't give up that easily, not Colonel Baker's men.

The man watched as Bishop shaved his mustache and the upper part of his chin. The water was icy and the razor dull, so it was not a pleasant experience. When he finished only a narrow set of whiskers followed the line of his jaws.

The man spoke slowly, hesitatingly. "What are you going to do now?"

"*I'm* not going to do anything. *We're* going to go out *together*," Bishop replied.

"Whatever you say. That thing," the man nodded toward the pistol on the stand beside the shaving bowl, "makes you the boss."

Bishop opened the wardrobe at the foot of the bed and took out a shirt and coat. They were much too big but the sleeve length would do. After he had put on the shirt he took a pillow from the bed, stuffed it into the top of his trousers, and pulled the shirt down over the pillow, flattening the edges of the pillow under his suspenders. Then he pulled on the coat and looked at himself in the mirror. Not bad. He looked to be at least forty pounds heavier. And if he slouched over he could look shorter. It just might work.

"Get dressed, we're going out."

"Do I get my coat and shirt back?"

"I'm afraid not, Old Timer. Consider yourself lucky to come out of this with your life."

The man didn't answer but silently replaced his piss-stained clothes with a fresh outfit.. As the two of them left the room Bishop whispered, "Just remember my pistol and don't try anything clever."

The man nodded and thrust his hands deep inside his coat pockets.

At the end of the corridor a single door opened onto 4th Avenue. A soldier dressed in a disheveled blue uniform and wearing the chevrons of a corporal stood by the door, leaning on his musket. A gleaming bayonet extended beyond the end of the rifle. As the two men approached the door the corporal stiffened, picked up his musket and stepped in front of the door. Through the tiny beveled panes of leaded glass behind the soldier Bishop could see the traffic moving along 6th Street. "I'm afraid I'll have to have some identification, gentlemen," the soldier said in a flat midwestern tone.

Suddenly, the door swung open and the soldier was shoved against Bishop's companion, who looked around, startled.

The man who had opened the door was inside now. He had drawn a pistol and pointed it at the soldier. "Don't move. Hand me your musket and then start running down that hall," he said, inclining his head toward the corridor at the rear of the hotel. Then, without so much as a glance at Bishop, he murmured, "Let's go, G.W."

The soldier took off running down the hall, trying to put space between himself and these crazy men with all the guns. The fat man stood there, staring at Bishop and rubbing his forearm. Without warning, Bishop gave the man a hard blow in the abdomen. When the man bent over in pain, Bishop gave him a hard uppercut to the jaw that sent him sprawling onto the floor of the corridor. Then Bishop stepped through the door and out onto the street.

"Where in the hell did you come from, Noah?"

"Here, this is your horse," Noah replied, ignoring Bishop's question as he mounted one of two horses tied to a hitching rail by the side entrance of the hotel.

They rode in silence for two blocks or so. Finally Noah slowed his horse and let Bishop catch up. "When you didn't come back last night we got worried and came up here to the hotel. The place was all abuzz with how they had spotted you and how you'd got away. Since you hadn't come back and since the Yankees didn't have you, we figured you must still be hiding somewhere in the hotel. I put a man on each exit to help you. Been sitting on my horse by the door for over two hours now, acting like I was waiting for someone. I knew you the moment you walked up to the door, even with your disguise and the reflection of the glass. Damned good thing I did, too. You might have been a goner."

Bishop turned to Noah, "How did the Yankees know I was in the hotel last night? Who talked?"

"Don't have any idea yet. I guess we'll find out from Norton."

"Yes," Bishop replied, "we'll talk with Norton. And somebody's going to die for this - probably that Lieutenant Reid."

Chapter 7

Tuesday, February 14

Colonel Lafayette C. Baker was furious. His cold gray eyes flashed as he screamed at the two men standing rigidly at attention before his desk.

"You fools! You imbecilic, spineless, stupid jackasses! I ought to send you to the trenches before Richmond and let Lee's Virginians blow your asses off! You had the Confederacy's top spy in your net and let him get away. God Almighty, why do you think the government put you around the National Hotel that night?"

"You, young man, or perhaps I should say 'little boy.' Don't you know what it means to be in charge of trying to neutralize an enemy agent?"

Before Sam could reply the Colonel screamed into his face: "It means, Goddammit, to try to capture the sonofabitch! Where were you last night, anyway? Prancing about the city with your fancy lady friend? Well? Answer me!"

"Sir, I took Miss Ellie Richards to supper at Willard's around 4:30. By 6:30 we were at her home, in her parlor, where we chatted until around 8:00. After I left her house, I stopped by the office for a few minutes and talked business with Lieutenant Peterson. Then I went back to my room and went to bed. I regret that I did not stay longer or check with the Officer of the Day before I left but I was unaware of any compelling necessity to do so." God, Sam thought, was he really saying this? ". . . compelling necessity to do so?" What a way to talk.

He looked behind the irate Colonel to the maps of the South which hung on the wall behind him. The maps had tiny colored pins struck into them, purportedly showing the location of Federal agents in the Confederacy, though Sam had always thought they were fakes - hung there for show. He had no interest in the maps or what they disclosed. He was only interested in avoiding looking into Colonel Baker's eyes.

But the Colonel put his face right up to Sam's, so close that his coarse rust-red beard was a blur before Sam's eyes. Sam could smell the old man's breath, strong and somewhat sour, dominated by the pungent odor of tobacco. "Well, I hope you screwed your Miss Ellie Richards, Lieutenant. Because you sure screwed the United States Government. And I don't like it. Do you understand me?"

"Yessir, but I resent your slur on Miss Richards. She is a lady."

"Oh, shit, Lieutenant, some of the best screws I ever had were from ladies." The Colonel walked back toward the small walnut table that served as his desk and leaned his long, lanky frame against it. "Now you gentlemen listen to me and listen good. I want this Bishop fellow and I want him dead or alive. I don't give a good Goddamn which, but I want him. He's thumbed his nose at the National Detective Police one time too many. Major Wright, you fill Lieutenant Reid in on what happened last night and then you, Lieutenant, are charged once more with bringing Bishop in. And if you don't and if he does whatever he has been sent north to do, whatever that is, I will personally order your execution. DO YOU UNDERSTAND ME?"

"Yessir."

"Now, both of you, get the hell out of here!"

As they scrambled from the room Sam whispered, "What in the name of God is he so excited about? I can remember at least two other times when we heard Bishop was in town and didn't get him and the Colonel didn't go crazy then. What's so special about last night?"

Major Wright pulled a chew from his pocket, crammed it into his mouth and said, "Last night was different because this time we knew where Bishop was and what he looked like. Only we didn't put it together as soon as his friends did. As you know, Baker's command is scattered into offices all over town. It's hard to keep up with everything. Not catching Bishop is no one's fault and I reckon that pisses the Old Man off as much as anything."

They were out on the street now, threading their way through the bustle of early morning traffic on Pennsylvania Avenue. As he dodged the ancient negro who swept the snow and ice from the crosswalk to Willard's, Major Wright spoke. "Come on. Let's walk down to the river and look at the ships."

A long train of government wagons, bound for the arsenal at Greenleaf's Point and ultimately for Grant's army before Richmond, was rumbling down 15th Street. Sam and the Major dodged between the heavily-laden wagons and walked along the slushy path that bisected the President's Park behind the White House. At the far end of the park, where the path entered 17th Street, a dead horse lay stinking in the winter sun.

Sam watched the Major out of the corner of his eye. Major Wright was a short, dried-up, weather-beaten man who very well may have been the most unmilitary-looking officer in the army. Before the war he had been a fisherman off the coast of Maine. One day his boat went down in a violent squall and he swam to shore, five miles through the rough sea. Then he promptly got into a twelve-foot rowboat, persuaded another fisherman to accompany him, and the two rowed through the storm with a fisherman's sixth sense, to the spot where Major Wright's boat had broken up.

He found one of his mates clinging to the wreckage of the fishing boat, pulled him into the rowboat, and spent the rest of the day rowing about the area looking for the other three members of the crew. They were never found and only when dark came was Wright willing to row back to shore. He became a local hero, a fact which, in the true tradition of New England reticence, served only to embarrass and inconvenience him. But when the war broke out the local militia company remembered and elected him their captain.

At First Bull Run his company stood fast beside the Stone Bridge until the Union Army was safely across and then withdrew as coolly and deliberately as if they were a company of regulars. The word got around that Wright had been the last Federal soldier to leave the battlefield and he found himself a hero again.

He was promoted to Major and placed on the staff of the new Union commander, Major General George B. McClellan. His official job was Assistant Quartermaster but he found himself serving as assistant to Allan Pinkerton, the dapper little Chicago detective who served as McClellan's intelligence officer. When Pinkerton was fired because of his ridiculously high estimates of Rebel strength, Major Wright stayed on the General Staff of the Army of the Potomac, serving as operational assistant to whomever was the Intelligence Officer at the time. In the spring of 1862, when Colonel Baker was named chief of the War Department Detectives, Wright was assigned to head his Division II, Counter-intelligence.

The two got on well, largely because Major Wright was not afraid of Baker and Baker knew it. The Colonel might rant and rave and make nasty threats as he had just now but Major Wright knew he was just blowing off steam. Moreover, Colonel Baker knew that Wright had him figured out. It was a game that the two played. Others in the organization were vaguely aware of the situation but none, including Sam, felt safe when Colonel Baker began hurling his threats. It was good to have Major Wright on his side.

The sun was out at times today, peeking from behind the thick white clouds that went scudding by, driven by the brisk wind that swept the capital from the west. Some of the snow and ice had melted but there were still piles of crusty snow, dirty remnants of drifts that hugged the shadows of the ragged board fence that sealed off the President's Park. And the wind had a raw edge to it that forced Sam to dig his hands deeply inside his military overcoat and try to make himself smaller against the force of it.

Major Wright spit mightily into the wind and wiped his chin with the back of his hand.

"Yestiddy evenin' we got an anonymous message that Bishop was in Washington, dressed in a fine black suit of Northern cut and wearing a reddish-brown beard. Before you ask, there was nothing about WHY he was in Washington."

"Who took the message?"

"Corporal Pauley of Captain Summers' Department. You know, 'the tramps,' they're part of Division V."

Sam nodded at Wright's description of the disguise favored by Captain Summers' men.

"George Summers and three or four of his men saw the message," Wright continued. "Apparently they didn't consider it important enough to notify the Colonel right away so he could decide if the rest of us should have been told. My guess is Summers will have his ass chewed out by the Old Man for that."

"Anyway, about two days ago we intercepted a message in New York City from someone in Montreal to John Wilkes Booth, the actor. You know him?"

"Know *of* him, yes," said Sam. "Ellie and I saw him in *The Marble Heart* at Ford's last March. Is he a Rebel spy?"

"Don't know. But the message was suspicious, first because Montreal is the headquarters of the Rebel underground in Canada, and second because it told him to meet a 'friend' at Gautier's who would identify himself by a certain code. If I was you I'd look at both of these messages. Might give you some ideas."

They were at the river now and while no ships were tied up there a small commercial boat rode at anchor in midstream. Major Wright stared longingly at the sight of the tiny vessel rocking softly in the ship's channel. Directly in front of them was the 17th Street Canal lock which separated the C & O Canal, on their right from the City Canal which was officially titled the Tiber Creek in a highbrow salute to Rome. The murky, shallow City Canal was, in truth, little more than an open sewer. At the moment garbage and other debris was trapped in the canal's ice that formed against the lock gates, though Sam was relieved to find no bloated corpses of dead animals there now.

After a while Major Wright continued. "The message to Booth told him to meet his 'friend' at Gautier's last night so Summers had one of his men watching the restaurant. When Booth came out with his 'friend,' Summers' man followed them to the National Hotel where Booth keeps a room. After a while another one of Summers' men, Levi Banks, I think you know him, came up and asked what was going on. When he heard the description of the man who was with Booth, Banks remembered the message about Bishop, figured Booth's 'friend' might be Bishop and ran back to headquarters to get help."

"He was back about a half hour later with seven men and the nine of them set up around the hotel, with one man in the lobby watchin' the stairs.

The Major talked on, spitting into the wind occasionally, and described how Bishop had eluded the trap set for him and slipped out of the hotel the following morning.

"Why didn't they just go straight up to Booth's room and arrest him? With nine men they surely could have overpowered Booth and Bishop."

The Major coughed and spit. "They didn't know for certain that it was Bishop with Booth. Didn't want Booth to know we were onto him unless the prize was big enough. So they decided to wait and identify him as he came through the lobby."

"How'd Bishop know not to come out on the Avenue or the other exits?"

Major Wright looked at Sam. "Well, I reckon somebody must have warned him, somebody from our headquarters who knew what was afoot. What else would you think?"

Sam's mouth flew open in surprise. "Then there must be someone in our organization who is spying for the Rebels."

"Exactly, Lieutenant, exactly. Just like we apparently have someone working for us who is close to Bishop, close enough to tell us he's in town and what he looks like. It's one of the things you take for granted in the spy business, that the enemy will penetrate your organization. Your trouble, Lieutenant, is that you're too naïve. You trust everyone in a blue uniform. That kind of schoolboy attitude is liable to get you killed, like it did poor Felix Stidger."

Sam flushed at the sudden lecture. "How many people knew that Bishop had been spotted and that Captain Summers' men were staking out the hotel?"

"Well, that's one of the problems. Probably another half dozen men learned what was up by midnight, maybe more. The whole headquarters was abuzz with excitement. Your failure to stay around last night doesn't exactly leave you above suspicion either, Lieutenant, especially since you were supposed to be looking for the man."

"Now, just a minute!"

The Major cut him off. "No, you listen to me. I know you didn't have anything to do with warning Bishop and I'll wager the Colonel does too. But if I know Colonel Baker, someone is going to get blamed for this thing. You're a prime candidate right now. If I was you I'd get off my ass and grab this fellow Bishop before Colonel Baker decides to make an example of you. I don't think he'll hang you like he threatened, but they tell me that the food in the Old Capitol ain't so good."

Chapter 8

Tuesday, February 14

The old brick building at the corner of Ninth and Franklin Streets was cold. In the office a miserable stick fire sputtered and crackled and sent most of its heat up the fireplace chimney, offering little but the impression of warmth. With wood selling for $5.00 a stick in Confederate currency, being warm, like being well-fed, was an uncommon luxury in Richmond.

The Secretary of War, a commanding man of powerful physique who had been in office exactly eight days, came out of his private office and stood before the desk of his chief clerk, pulling on his gray kid gloves and jamming the fingers home. The steam rolled out from under his thick black handlebar mustache as he spoke.

"Mr. Jones, I'm going to the Executive Mansion to meet with the President. Don't disturb me unless we hear something from Captain Bishop. If that should happen, send a message immediately."

J. B. Jones nodded. "Yessir. But I doubt we'll hear anything more today."

"Just the same, if anything does come in from Bishop, I want to know about it."

Jones nodded again and readjusted the thick wool cap that covered his head and ears. When Secretary Breckinridge left, Jones sat for a while, idly toying with the ice in the ink pot. Then he stood up, walked to the window, and looked over the Capitol grounds. He shivered and began slapping his shoulders and stamping his feet for warmth.

The streets were deserted, no one in his right mind was out today unless it was necessary. Jones was about to turn back to his desk when Secretary Breckinridge came into sight. He was the very picture of self-confidence as he walked up the hill toward the Confederate White House, a confidence derived, Jones knew, not from his appointment as Secretary of War, but from a distinguished career that had seen him move from the U. S. Senate to the Vice Presidency of the United States to a major general's commission in the Provisional Army of the Confederate States, each position having been stamped with Breckinridge's special abilities.

As the Secretary strode out of sight Jones wondered what was so vital about this mission of Captain Bishop's, important enough, moreover, to interrupt a conference with the President. Only last Friday Bishop had been here, strutting about the office with his "Master Spy of the Confederacy" airs and meeting in whispered conferences with Secretary Breckinridge and Secretary of State Benjamin.

Secretary Seddon, Breckinridge's immediate predecessor, would have shared his confidences with his chief clerk, but this man Breckinridge was withdrawn and secretive. Apparently he trusted no one, not even a loyal chief clerk who had given the best years of his life to keeping the War Office operating under five different Secretaries.

Jones looked across the bare, forelorn grounds to the Capitol. Designed by Thomas Jefferson, it had been the pride of Virginia. Now it echoed to the cries of petty, provincial Confederate Congressmen who could agree only to disagree. These were desperate times that called for extraordinary measures and all that came out of the Confederate Government was bickering and back-biting. Jones shook his head. Extraordinary measures! That's what we need.

Abruptly he thought of Bishop again and Secretary Breckinridge's unusual concern about him. He turned and walked into the War Secretary's office and closed the door. The Secretary's desk was closed and the roll-top had been locked. But Secretary Seddon had insisted that his chief clerk have a key to his desk, a precaution that grew out of the frail Seddon's poor health and his concern that he might drop dead sometime and leave a locked desk full of important papers.

Smiling to himself, Jones removed the key from his vest pocket, unlocked the roll-top and quietly slid the rollers up. There were only a half dozen or so papers on the desk, none of them of any importance. Jones replaced them carefully and began going through the cubbyholes at the back of the desk. In the third cubbyhole from the left he found it - a small scrap of paper in the Secretary's hand:

> "G.W. Bishop - 12 men - relays of horses large boats (3) - Cawood/Mosby cooperate (will need order) - Terms of exchange: Immediate exchange of all prisoners of war - Grant withdraws north of Rappahannock -Sherman embarks from Charleston to North -Vicksburg/New Orleans evacuated - Last two items negotiable - Important no harm come to prisoner. . . . <u>ONLY</u> President, Secy. War, Capt. Bishop & Secy. State informed of plan."

Jones studied the paper for a full minute. Then he carefully replaced it in the cubbyhole and closed and locked the desk. He walked back to his desk in the big room outside and sat there for a long time, staring at the ceiling and mulling over what he had just read. Then he let out a low moan and rose to his feet.

Mother of God! There's only one thing that Captain Bishop could bring back from Washington that could drive the "exchange" bargain that

Breckinridge's note suggested. But surely they wouldn't try that. It wasn't sporting. Kidnapping a man and dragging him two hundred miles through enemy lines. Still, it just might be the thing the South needed. Might even bring France or Britain in on our side at last.

Jones shivered. The Devil with it! I'm building a fire. Got to think this over. Good thing, though, that I'm not one to talk about state secrets. Why if this got out . . . .

Chapter 9

Tuesday, February 14

The major's words still smarted as Sam studied the papers in his office two hours later. The letter from Montreal certainly appeared to be nothing to get excited about. Addressed to "Mr. J. Wilkes Booth, Esquire, National Hotel, Washington, D.C.," it told Booth to be at Gautier's on the 13th of February when a man would introduce himself by the "W/B" code. The letter had been written in Montreal on the 8th, and a copy which Sam read indicated that it was included in a pouch carried by a courier who had been compromised and who now showed all his mail, from Richmond or Montreal, to Federal agents in New York and Washington.

Sam knew of the courier. He was a 19-year-old boy from Boonsboro, Maryland. In the summer of 1864 he had been captured during a visit home and was released only when he agreed to cooperate with the North. Colonel Baker himself had given the boy the warning that kept him on the level. He told him that if Northern agents ever suspected a "double-cross," his whole family, father, mother, grandmother and two younger sisters, would die in a "tragic" fire. This story had been Sam's first indication of how totally cruel Colonel Baker could be.

Still, Sam could understand why no one got excited about the message. Sending a man to see who Booth was meeting and where they went was quite enough. On the other hand, the fact that John Wilkes Booth got a message from Montreal, in a Rebel Secret Service pouch, to meet someone at Gautier's under rather mysterious circumstances settled one thing. It meant Booth was a spy. That knowledge was, clearly worth something.

The other message was more troublesome and Sam sent for Sergeant Pollack. As he waited he read it again, stumbling over its labored childish script and bad spelling:

> Col. Baker, Nat'l. Det. Police, Wash. D.C.
>
> Captan Bishop will arive in the city Thursday Eve dressed in black business suit of northern Cut and wering a thick redish brown beard. He is short and heavy & has a deep clear voice.
>
> a Frend.

Sam was still puzzling over the letter when Sergeant Pollack arrived. He waved the Sergeant into a chair and handed him the message. "What do you know about this, Sergeant?"

The Sergeant wiped his brow with his sleeve. Sam noticed how he was sweating even though the room was chilly. His jacket clung to his skin in dark, stained wet patches and with his great bulk he appeared absolutely miserable. "Don't know nothin' 'cept what it says, Lieutenant. It was delivered to Colonel Baker's office by a darkie Thursday mornin'. Said a man on a boat had give it to him and paid him two cents to deliver it. I don't have no idee who sent it or why. Strange, too, you know. All the times Bishop has been in Washington, this is the first time we've had any warnin'."

Sam retrieved the paper and stared at it for a second. "Any chance this could be from one of our agents who has infiltrated the Rebel underground?"

"No. We checked that out right off. No, I've got a feelin' the letter is just what it 'pears to be, someone who knows Bishop and is sore at him and wants him out of the way. Either that or it's a set-up from the Rebs, tellin' us what Bishop looks like when he don't look like that at all. Only after last night we know he did look like the letter said. So the letter's real all right."

"How many of our people knew about this message and how many knew we had sent men to arrest Bishop at the National last night?"

The Sergeant stirred in his chair. "Prob'ly a dozen or so, by the time it all shakes down. You know, when word gets around that we're out to grab someone it spreads like wildfire."

"Is there any way you could get me a list of all those who knew?" Sam's voice was suddenly weary.

"Yessir, I'll try to put one together for you. But I don't think it'll do much good. It'll be hard for me to be sure I've got everyone who knew, and it'll be a pretty big list. But I'll do what I can." The Sergeant leaned forward, as if about to stand. "Is that all, sir?"

Sam nodded as he turned back to the papers on his desk. What a mess! A counter-spy in each camp. A Rebel spy in Washington on a vital mission and the Yankees don't know what it's all about and can't catch him. Shit fire!

Idly Sam began shuffling through the morning's mail on his desk. There wasn't much - the New York *Daily News* for Tuesday and three personal letters bound in red ribbon and wrapped in an explanatory note from the detective who took them off a farmer from Prince Georges County who was slapped in the Old Capitol the night before.

The letters were gibberish and double-talk, obviously with a hidden message but indecipherable at first glance. But something about the third letter caught Sam's eye. It seemed to weave in and out of a normal conversation, to make sense for a while and then to lapse into nonsense. And the handwriting was a bit bold. Sam tilted his chair back and studied it carefully.

Allens Fresh, Maryland February 10, 1865

Dear Martha,

It has been an exciting two weeks here at the farm. Tell my Great-Uncle David we saw the two dozen flocks of enormous geese today. Large geese, like fast horses bought are very exciting. Callie has several of them & placed according to our family custom. She asks about Jed & your plans. Send word quickly about her very fancy dresses and when they will be used. I will let Luther, Jed & all of the boys now move to buy the boats and see that they are very prepared for alternative crossings. Give our regards to David Witt and pleas do send word as soon as possible about any news about what is possible where crossing the mountains is to be tried. I hope that is to be made so we can settle those lands. Our blessings are on you all.

George

With a sigh Sam laid the letter down on his desk and took up the *Daily News*. Turning to the *Personals* he separated the front two sheets and laid them aside. As he did so the papers came to rest cater-corner on the letter from "George," covering the upper left corner of the letter and casting a deep shadow over the lower left corner. Sam stared at the letter for a moment with incredulity. It was a *grill!* The hidden message was a diamond in the middle of the page!

He grabbed a pencil, made a huge diamond on the paper, and read again the message concealed in the center of the letter.

"Clark!" he screamed. "Clark!"

The young orderly raced into the tiny office. "Yessir?"

"Get Sergeant Pollack up here immediately."

Sergeant Pollack huffed into the room, his face blotched and purple. "What is it, Lieutenant?" he gasped. "What's wrong?"

Sam shoved the letter at him. "Here, read this."

The Sergeant broke into a smile when he saw the penciled diamond in the center of the letter. He read slowly, moving his lips and murmuring softly to himself.

the two dozen
fast horses bought
& placed according to
your plans. Send word quickly
when they are to be used. I will
now move to buy the boats
for alternative crossings.
do send word as soon as
possible where crossing
is going to be made

The sergeant handed the letter back to Sam. "Congratulations, sir. You're gonna make a proper spy-buster yet."

Sam flushed at the compliment and then said hurriedly, "Now, let's see what we have. Captain Bishop is in town on a personal mission for Jeff Davis, a mission Davis thinks will end the war. One of Bishop's contacts is John Wilkes Booth, which means he is probably a Rebel spy. Someone close to Bishop is on our side, trying to get him caught. Someone in this headquarters is a Rebel agent, trying to help Bishop."

"Now someone from lower Maryland is putting together a chain of fast horses and getting boats together to cross the river. What does this all add up to? Have I left anything out?"

"Well," the Sergeant began slowly, "we don't know that the letter you just figgered out has anything to do with Bishop's business here."

"That's true," Sam replied. "And there's only one way to find out if there is any connection. I'm going to southern Maryland. But let's assume the two are connected. What does it mean?"

Sergeant Pollack squirmed about in his seat. "Fast horses and boats. Someone wants to get somethin' across the Potomac fast. Now if we knew where the horses were being placed we might know what they're after."

"You're suggesting a sort of hit-and-run raid, where they have to get away fast."

"Yes, that's a possibility. "Cept it's not a raid by a large group. Twenty-four horses, 'placed' accordin' to the letter from George. That means relays with whoever we're dealin' with switchin' horses several times. No, we're dealin' with three to six men at the most. 'Course, if it is six men, they can still do one hell of a lot of harm."

"All right. So it's a small group, say six at the most. Whatever they do they expect to be hotly pursued, so they have relays of fast horses. If I'm going to find out what they're up to I'd better learn where the horses are. I'm going to have dinner at Willards and then head for lower Maryland. Thank you, Sergeant."

The Sergeant stood up. "Sir, while you're in lower Maryland, you might stop at the Surratt Tavern for a meal and, if all else fails, talk with the postmaster at Bryantown. He's a Union man and can be trusted, at least as far as any man in that area can. Like all postmasters, he's nosy and knows what's goin' on. Name's Hugh Lowry."

"Good idea, Sergeant. I'll do that."

-o-

Dark storm clouds were boiling up in the west that afternoon when Sam rode across the Navy Yard Bridge heading south. He was smiling to himself, relishing the memory of the passionate, tearful farewell Ellie had given him when he told her he was off into enemy territory on a spy mission. By God, if her mother hadn't been there, they would very likely have made love, *right there in the parlor.*

Suddenly the wind howled and shrieked like a tortured demon, spooking Sam's horse and jolting Sam back into the present, turning his thoughts to finding shelter for the night.

The wind had picked up in Washington, too, causing Sergeant Pollack to glance up from his work and look at the blackening sky. Good God, *are we ever going to get any relief from this damnable weather?*

Then he turned back to the brief message he was drafting. ". . . I suggested that Lieutenant Reid also visit the Surratt Tavern and meet with the Postmaster at Bryantown, too. My judgment is that he will stop both places. He was to leave the city after the noon meal today, which should put him on the road by mid-afternoon. If I learn anything of his whereabouts in the meantime, I will keep you informed."

Then he folded the letter, scribbled a name and address across the front and called for the black boy who served as a messenger for the detectives.

Chapter 10

Tuesday, February 14

The room was cold but the sun's rays played brightly across the multi-colored quilt covering Bishop's bed. He exhaled quickly, watching his breath vaporize in the chilly air. Belle had risen earlier and her nightgown lay across the foot of the bed, a splash of pink and cream flannel that seemed strangely soft and feminine against the raucous quilt.

What had President Davis told him? "You've been selected for this job because you're one of our best men and you know your way around Washington. But, remember, this can also be a disadvantage. The Yankees know about you. They'll be waiting for you at every turn, especially if they ever learn what you're up to. So be careful."

Well, the President had certainly been right about that. Someone had set a trap. The question now was, do they know about our plans to kidnap Lincoln? Norton could tell him. Norton must have sent the boy from the Invalid's Corps to warn him, so Norton would be aware of how much the Yankee detectives knew. As the Confederacy's supervisor of clandestine activities in Washington, Edward Norton knew everything that was happening, and some things that had not happened yet. When in need, call on Edward Norton.

Bishop swung his feet to the cold floor and pulled on his trousers. He recalled how President Davis had outlined the plot that night in the White House in Richmond.

"We'll sneak you right into the heart of Washington, confuse the Yankees and steal their President right out from under their noses. Then we'll hold him in exchange for all our boys held in Yankee prison pens. We'll force General Grant to move from in front of Richmond. And we'll probably break the North's will to fight. It's our chance to win the war in one bold move."

"And you, Captain Bishop," Davis said as he jumped up excitedly, "you will bring home the bacon."

"Bring home the bacon." The phrase had struck Bishop as out of character for the polished, aristocratic Davis. But he had said it, eyes flashing with excitement.

Secretary of State Benjamin had broken into his enigmatic smile. "Mr. President, I don't think I've seen you so excited since First Manassas."

"Well, Mr. Benjamin, this is IT! This is our one big chance to win the war. We'll break the Yankee will to fight. With their President a prisoner of our government, they'll finally decide they've had enough. General Breckinridge here," he nodded toward the Secretary of War, "will issue the necessary orders."

Bishop pondered that meeting as he carefully donned the dark blue uniform of a Federal chaplain. When he had finished he tugged and straightened his coat, stepped back and admired himself in the mirror that hung beside the door and, just as the clock in the parlor was chiming twelve, descended the stairs to the dining room for the noon meal.

Two hours later, after a brief, whispered meeting with Norton among the display of models of old inventions and other curiosities in the basement of the Patent Office, Bishop walked briskly to a little boarding house on D Street near the city's dismal railroad station. There he was shown to a room at the back of the third floor where his old friend and co-conspirator, Noah Lewis Dyer, waited for him, huddled before a small coal fire.

After thanking Noah for coming to his rescue at the National Hotel earlier that morning, Bishop explained what he had learned from Norton a few minutes earlier. When he had finished complaining about the Yankees having learned of his presence in the city he said to Noah, "I know that Norton says Lieutenant Reid wasn't responsible for last night's close call. But, dammit, the boy knows too much! Right now he's on his way down into lower Maryland poking around among our people."

"G.W., you know he's not likely to learn anything down there," Noah interrupted. "Our people know enough to keep quiet. What harm can he do?" Noah started coughing, his chest racked by violent paroxysms.

Bishop waited until Noah had stopped."Who knows what he'll stumble across next. Even a blind pig finds an acorn now and then. I think we underestimated this fellow."

Noah sagged back in his chair, exhausted by the coughing fit. "There's another side to this, G.W. If we get rid of Lieutenant Reid, Colonel Baker's liable to put one of his best men on to this. Then we'll be in a real stew."

"Hell, Noah., we're *already* in a stew. This fellow Reid's better than we imagined he could be when we discovered he was assigned to this case. He's got to be put out of the way before he uncovers our whole plot. And remember, he killed Archie and we can't let that go unanswered."

Noah frowned, remembering their classmate at Franklin & Marshall College. "Yes, I agree we owe it to Archie. But how are we gonna do it?"

Bishop stood up and walked to the window overlooking the narrow alley. "Well, it would obviously be a lot less messy if we could dispose of him before he returns to the city. I think Tom Harbin just might be the man to do the job."

Noah thought for a moment, staring hard at the rough pine floor, weighing the possibilities of the Rebel underground's top man in southern Maryland killing Lieutenant Sam Reid. "Obviously he *could*. The question is, 'Will he?'"

Bishop turned back from the window. "Harbin knows how to follow orders."

"Do you think Reid will give him any trouble?"

"No. I know he's proved to be smarter than I expected when he was put on this case, but he's still nothing more than a Yankee shopkeeper. A hard character like Harbin will have no trouble at all getting rid of him. The poor boy won't even know we're after him until it's too late. Here, give me a piece of paper. Might as well take care of this now."

Bishop quickly scratched out a note to Thomas Harbin, describing Lieutenant Reid, explaining what was known of his itinerary in lower Maryland, and ordering him to "dispose of" him before he could return to the capital.

"Now," Bishop gestured as he folded the message, "this must reach Harbin by the safest means possible."

"The Doctors' Line?" Noah asked.

Bishop nodded. "There's one other thing I need you to do. Since I had better stay away from Wilkes Booth after last night's episode, I want you to take a message to him. He'll no doubt be watched so don't, for God's sake, carry ANYTHING on you that could give you away if Baker's detectives decide to arrest you. The message must be carried orally. And you'll have to use the six-part recognition code."

Noah nodded his assent and Bishop stood up, began pacing the room and continued talking. "Norton says Baker's detectives read all of our mail brought from Canada by one of our couriers. I want Booth to go to New York and find out the identity of the courier. John Headly can tell him who brought the message to Booth to meet me at Gautiers. Then have Booth send a letter to himself at the National Hotel that will suggest that his contact with us is something innocuous, like maybe the Confederate leadership is interested in him putting on a play in Richmond, or something.

You and Booth can come up with something that will get the Yankees off Booth's tail."

Noah looked up, puzzled."I'm not sure I understand."

"Well, it's possible the Yankees'll believe that Booth is playing a minor role if they're given some reason to think that. And if I can take attention off Booth maybe it'll take some off me. Anyway, we don't have anything to lose."

"All right," Noah replied. "I'll see that Booth gets your message. And I'll take Tom Harbin's note to Dr. Wyvill's and have him put it on the Doctor's Line. That's the safest and fastest way to send messages since doctors can be out in their buggies anytime day or night without raising suspicion. Anything else?" He started coughing again.

"No, Noah, that will be all." Bishop turned and smiled. "Times sure have changed for us, haven't they, old friend?"

Noah spit into the fire, thick sputum that sizzled and crackled in the coals. "Yes," he said, "can you imagine what Professor Grossman would think if he knew his two star pupils from 'Ancient Religions' class had just planned the death of an innocent man? His poor old Lutheran heart would break. In fact, the entire Franklin & Marshall faculty would disown us."

"I wouldn't call Lieutenant Reid 'innocent.' After all, it's him or us. And as I said earlier,

he did kill Archie." Bishop replied.

"Yes, I know. But we're still talking about killing another man," Noah said. "And sometimes I wonder if I'm not drowning in sin because I find this life so exciting, even downright enjoyable, despite the killing."

"Ah, Noah, you're too much of a worrier about sin. Take my advice. If it doesn't break one of the Ten Commandments, don't fret over it."

"Well, killing is one of the forbidden ten, G.W. Or had you forgotten?

"I don't' think killing your enemy in wartime is a sin," Bishop said softly. "Anyway, it's what we have to do, so no need to discuss this further."

Twenty minutes later as he crossed G Street Bishop hastily looked up and down the street to see if he were being observed. He casually dropped the small black Bible he was carrying. As he stooped to pick it up he glanced back down 12th Street. There were only a few people hurrying along in the cold. None of them had been there when he had last looked.

Recovering his Bible, he walked on up 12th Street, slowing his pace slightly. As he approached the third house on the left he looked intently toward the dining room window. The small fern in the red clay pot was sitting in the center of the window. It was safe to enter. With a sigh Bishop walked up the steps to the stoop and lifted the brass knocker.

It was nearly five when he came out of the house, flushed with excitement and rushed back to the Van Ness House at the foot of 17th Street. He was hungry but supper would have to wait. If he hurried he just might get his letter to Secretary Breckinridge off to the Confederate capital in tonight's "mail." Feverishly, he began to write.

"Washington, D.C. February 14, 1865
Hon. John C. Breckinridge, Secretary of War

I have just learned, from one of our agents in this city, a most incredible set of circumstances which may, I believe, be turned to our great advantage. The matter is far too sensitive to relate in a letter that must pass through the lines. Suffice it to say, however, that I will require a letter from you to the effect that Sergeant Richard Maynard of Battery Brooke (and formerly of Leesburg, Virginia) has been placed in "protective custody" pending the assurance of his father's cooperation with our agents in Washington.

I cannot reveal more except to say that it is of the utmost importance that Sergeant Maynard be placed in custody immediately.

With deep respect and in anticipation of the receipt of the aforementioned letter, I remain, sir

Yr. Obt. Svt.,
/s/ George Washington Bishop
Capt, 3rd Va. Cav."

"P.S.

I almost forgot to mention that, according to the same agent in this city, Lt. Samuel Alexander Reid of Col. Baker's detectives who has been assigned to uncover my mission and to foil it, is a devoted fan of our prey. He can, then, be expected to be especially sensitive to any dangers presented to him. For this and other reasons I have arranged for our man in Bryantown to rid us of Lt. Reid while the latter is in lower Maryland inquiring into our activities there. I have just this afternoon learned further details of Lt. Reid's suspicions and of his itinerary in lower Maryland which make it virtually certain that our man will come upon the lieutenant during his sojourn there.

G.W.B"

As he sealed the letter Bishop wondered if he should have given Secretary Breckinridge a few more details about this afternoon's exciting discovery. After all, the Secretary of War and the President would be most interested to learn that their secret service tentacles had at last reached into the very heart of the Lincoln White House.

Chapter 11

Tuesday, February 14

The lower peninsula of Maryland was technically a part of the Union. But in reality it was a hotbed of Secessionist activity and any Yankee soldier who found himself in that area in the winter of 1864-5 was bound to learn, sooner or later, that he was in enemy territory. Sam Reid was only three hours and twelve miles into the peninsula when he learned personally what he had heretofore known only second-hand, lower Maryland was a fine place for a Yankee spy to get himself killed.

It was dark, not good dark yet, but dark enough to call it night instead of day when he rode into the little crossroads village of Tee Bee on the old stage road between Washington and the lower Potomac. The weather had been terrible all day, with heavy, icy snow driven by harsh winds. He was miserably cold and shivering violently when he tied his horse to a rickety hitching rail in front of J. E. Huntt's general store and walked into the long, narrow frame building.

The familiar combination of odors, a mixture of brown sugar, tobacco, newly-dyed cloth, vinegar, ground coffee and dressed leather nearly overwhelmed him with a sense of nostalgia. Sam looked about the room with a professional eye. In one end there were a few bonnets, cheap ribbons and artificial flowers, with a pair of dusty wreaths propped up against a glass display case. Along the right side, in front of floor-to-ceiling shelves laden with bolts of spun wool, linsey and a little homespun cotton cloth, was a smoothly worn counter on which was displayed a small stock of earthenware and cheap crockery. At the end of the counter, near where Sam stood, was a display of tobacco, both the chewing and smoking variety. In front of the counter, by Sam's feet, stood a keg of whiskey and a jug of apple brandy.

Huntt's store was no match for Nathaniel Reid's "emporium" but then Tee Bee wasn't Steubenville either. Still, it offered the residents of Tee Bee a fairly decent variety of merchandise.

In the center of the room three men were seated around a potbellied stove. A fourth stood behind the store counter. A large light gray dog was curled up on the floor beside the stove. In the faint yellow glow of the kerosene lamp Sam could make out a fifth person moving about behind a cage that bore the raised brass letters, "U. S. MAIL."

He pulled off his gloves and stamped his feet. "Evenin'," he said, throwing a smile toward the men, "terrible weather, isn't it?"

One of the men spit toward the open stove door. He missed and the spittle crackled and sizzled as it ran down the side of the hot stove. But nobody spoke.

Sam walked up to the stove and held out his hands to warm them. "I've had a long ride today, all the way from the District. I'm tired and hungry. Do you gentlemen know of any place around here where a man can find a hot meal and a soft bed?"

"You'll not find much hospitality around here for Yankee soldiers," the man behind the counter replied.

Sam stiffened and stared at the man. "I'm Northern, from Ohio. But I'm not a soldier. I'm on my way to the prison camp at Point Lookout. My father's brother is interned there." He started pulling on his gloves. "Well, so much for Southern hospitality."

The man eyed Sam carefully. "If your uncle's in Point Lookout he must be a Rebel. What's that make you?"

"A Northerner. I don't hold with destroying the Union. But he's still my uncle, my father's brother, and I'm bound to see that he's all right." He turned and walked toward the door, proud of the lie he had told. As he made a final tug on his gloves he brushed the tobacco display and tobacco tumbled to the floor. The hell with it, he thought, let these Rebels pick it up.

Sam heard a woman's voice and he turned to see a girl who looked to be in her late teens walk out from behind the post office cage. She was talking to the man behind the counter. "It's cold out there, Pa, and the man's bound to be tired. At least we could let him sleep in the barn. I'd hate to have to answer on Judgment Day for turning him out on a night like tonight."

There was a long pause. In the flickering light of the kerosene lamps Sam could see his image reflected in the slanted glass case to his left. No wonder the girl felt sorry for him. He was a mess. His soft wool hat and long woolen scarf were covered with a crust of snow as were the shoulders of the heavy black overcoat which David had loaned him and which reached only to the tops of his knees. The whole effect, from the crumpled black wool cap, past his frozen, chapped face, to the scarf that looked as if it were holding his head up off his overcoat, was one of unfeigned misery. Seeing the image, he shook his head and chunks of melting snow flew off the cap. He looked down at his feet, painfully aware of the ill-fitting overcoat. At least the boots were substantial. For that he could thank Columbus Hall, the little boot maker on Pennsylvania Avenue. His boots were expensive, but at a time like this they were worth every penny.

The man behind the counter looked at the girl, and then at the three men sitting by the stove. Then he turned to Sam. "Well, I reckon it won't hurt none. You can sleep in the barn. Don't have no extra food, though. Can't give you supper."

"That's all right," Sam replied. "I packed a sandwich. You just show me where the barn is and I'll not be any more trouble."

He had unsaddled his horse and was wiping her off with a rag that hung over the side of the stall when he heard the barn door creak open. Instinctively, he reached for the saddle bag that held his pistol. The kerosene lantern lit up the doorway and as the door opened fully Sam could make out the figure of the girl from the store. Her dark green eyes reflected concern as she peered into the dimly-lit barn. She closed the door behind her and walked into the barn.

"When you're finished with your horse, come back into the store. Pa says you can bed down in the storeroom. It'll be a lot warmer there. Don't pay any mind to Pa. He thinks he has to talk Secesh to make up for being a Union man having the post office. But he's not so bad."

"Well, if you're sure it's all right. I don't want to be any bother."

"You'll be no bother at all. In fact if you stayed in the barn we'd only worry about you, so you'll be less bother in the storeroom."

A half hour later Sam was settled in the storeroom, stretched out on a pile of feed sacks and wrapped in his heavy wool blanket. As he lay there trying to fit together the pieces of the day there was a knock at the door. Sam groped in the dark for his pistol.

"Who is it?"

"Kate, Kate Huntt. May I come in?"

"Just a minute," Sam replied, as he fumbled for a match. He lit the candle and then moved the two wooden boxes he had leaned against the door so they would fall and awaken him if anyone should try to open the door in the middle of the night.

When he opened the door Kate was standing there holding a plate of food and a mug of coffee. The dog stood beside her, staring quizzically at Sam and wagging its tail. "I guess you don't trust us," she said, looking at the boxes. "Booby-trapped the door. Can't say as I blame you, though. Here, I brought you something to eat."

"You really needn't have. I've already eaten my sandwich," Sam lied.

"You need something warm on a night like tonight. Your mother wouldn't approve of your going to bed without a warm supper."

"My mother's dead."

"I'm sorry. But I guess I knew that. It shows in your eyes. May I sit here while you eat?"

"Sure, pull up a box. So your name is Kate. I'm Sam, Sam Reid."

Kate smiled. "My baptismal name is Catherine, but I've always been called Kate."

Sam nodded. "Kate's a nice name. It's a pleasure to meet you Kate Huntt."

Kate smiled again. "It's very nice to meet you, too . . . Sam Reid. We don't have very many nice-looking young men coming through this part of the country these days."

Kate sat down on the edge of a wooden crate. But when she sat, Sam noticed, her back stayed as stiff and straight as if the box were a piano stool.

"Are you really going to Point Lookout to find your uncle or are you another spy? It seems like that's all we have traveling through here these days."

Sam speared a boiled potato. "You wouldn't really expect me to admit it if I were a spy, would you? Anyway, I'm not. I'm in the mercantile business in Steubenville, Ohio. My father bought me a substitute so I've stayed out of the army. That's about it."

"Well, you don't look like a spy."

"What does a spy look like?"

"Like anybody else, I suppose, which rather contradicts my saying you don't look like a spy, doesn't it?" She laughed and Sam caught the sparkle in her eyes. "Still, the spies I've known have had a hard, outdoor look. You look like a clerk."

"How many spies have you known?"

"Not many. Half a dozen maybe."

"Who were they?"

"Why are you so interested?"

"When you're a clerk in a store that's nowhere near the war, spies sound pretty exciting."

Kate laughed again. "They just sound exciting. They're really not. Johnny Surratt, he's tall and thin and doesn't say much. And Richard Calvert, he's about forty, has a beard and uses snuff. Montgomery Taylor, we call him 'Monty,' he's small and fair-haired and laughs a lot."

"Are these Rebs or Yankees?" Sam interrupted as he chased a pea around his plate.

"Rebels. I only know one Yankee spy and I'm not sure he's a spy. That's Commodore Yancey. He's an old white-haired man who comes through here about every other month. He's very courtly and all, always driven in his carriage by a short shifty man who looks like a rat."

"How can you tell these men are spies?"

"Mostly from what I hear the men in the store say. I don't really know how they tell."

Sam finished his supper and leaned back against a sack of grain, sipping on the mug of coffee. "That's interesting. I've never seen a real spy, not that I know of. Oh, when I was in Washington last winter with Pa we talked with a man named Bishop and Pa thought he might be a spy. But he didn't look like one to me."

"There's a Parson Bishop who comes by here every now and then. They say he's a spy."

"What does he look like?"

"He's short and stocky. Has reddish brown hair and a thick beard. He was by here just a few days ago, going toward Washington. He usually travels with a big black man."

"Not the same man," Sam said. "The Bishop Pa and I spoke with was fair-haired. I wouldn't think a darkie would spy for the South, though. Or is your Bishop a Yankee spy?"

"No, he's a Rebel. And his slave is no ordinary darkie. He's part Indian. At least that's what Pa heard. When he's with the Parson he never says a word. Just stands back and watches and listens. He's big, about six feet, and looks like he could whip a mountain lion. I guess the Parson brings him along to do his dirty work."

"Well, I should have known. The spy business probably isn't any more exciting than the store business. I think I'll stay in the store business. What I'd really like to do is buy some horses and take them back home. Good horses are scarce back home. We could make a fortune off them. But I guess they're scarce everywhere. Haven't seen much sign of any around here."

You can't keep good horses around here. The Yankees are always grabbing them up for their cavalry."

Sam finished the coffee and set the mug down on his plate. "I wonder if this war will ever end. It seems so strange to think that Uncle Caleb and I are supposed to be enemies. I just can't accept that."

They talked for a while about Sam's fictional Uncle Caleb and Sam was pleased with the believable and occasionally touching story he was able to spin about his family being torn apart by the war. Long after Kate had left and he had rigged the boxes against the door and curled up in his blanket again, he lay awake wondering what he faced as he rode deeper into lower Maryland. He wondered if he should have pumped Kate more about Bishop or if he should have asked her about rumors of horses and boats. No, she'd said there weren't any horses about and Tee Bee is too far from the river to start asking about boats. Still, he couldn't escape the feeling that maybe he should have pressed her for more information. He had to find out about those horses and boats. Tomorrow, farther south, he would get his answers.

As he drifted off to sleep he tried to think about horses and boats and Rebel spies, but the image of Kate Huntt kept returning. It was in his dream that he first realized that her green eyes had changed their tint two or three times as they had talked in the little storeroom. And when she had smiled, tiny flecks of gold had danced about in her eyes, gathering up the available light and sending it back in sparkles.

-0-

Early the following morning there was a soft knock at the storeroom door and Kate's soft voice announced: "Please open the door. I've brought you some breakfast."

Sam lit a candle and moved the boxes away from the door.

"I'm sorry to wake you so early but we wanted you to have breakfast before the store opened and folks learned you had spent the night in the store. You can eat and then move back into the barn. Pa says it won't look as bad if it appears you had spent the night in the cold barn."

"That's very nice of you. I didn't expect breakfast. What do I owe you for breakfast . . . and last night's dinner?"

Kate smiled. "Don't be silly. You don't owe us anything. Don't you remember the Bible? 'I was a stranger and you took me in.' We're just doing our Christian duty. Besides, it's nice having a handsome stranger drop by like this."

Sam ate hastily while Kate watched him, smiling broadly. Kate Huntt. Sam hoped he would be seeing more of her.

Chapter 12

Wednesday, February 15

John Wilkes Booth put his glass down and pulled his watch out again. Eleven forty-five! Damn! Where was he? The letter said eleven. Has something gone wrong? He poured another glass of brandy and sat down by the window. Baltimore was as cold and dreary as Washington had been. Would spring never come?

Suddenly there were footsteps in the hall and a knock at the door. He stood up quickly, crossed the room and opened the door.

Michael O'Laughlen, small and seedy, his face dominated by large, sad brown eyes, sauntered into the room. "Hello, Johnny. Sorry I'm late. Stopped to have a glass with a couple of old friends and time just got away from me."

Booth closed the door and watched the little man as he settled into the overstuffed chair in the corner of the room. His bright maroon plaid trousers and vest were only slightly toned down by the black coat he wore and his two days' growth of beard served to accent his down-at-the-heels appearance. Mike O'Laughlen lived on the edge of respectable society, and most of the time it was on the wrong side of that edge. He looked around the room with the casual curiosity of a man who spent a lot of time in strange hotel rooms and then settled his gaze on Booth. When he smiled his teeth were stained, and one lower tooth was missing, left on the floor of one of Baltimore's cheaper saloons. If he was curious about why he had been called to this room his demeanor didn't indicate it. Mike O'Laughlen was used to having other men tell him to go or come or hurry or wait without explaining why. When you lived off handouts from other men, you learned never to ask why.

Booth poured his guest a glass of brandy, handed him an expensive cheroot, and helped him light the cigar. Then he settled back in his chair by the window. As he exhaled his cigar the smoke rolled out in a delicate blue cloud that swirled about his head and then drifted lazily across the room.

"Mike, I understand you're still helping your brother on his farm near here. Why haven't you been drafted?"

Mike took his cigar from his lips. "Come on, Johnnie, you know the answer to that. I'm a Rebel deserter. Left the South in June of '62. The Yankees won't have anything to do with me."

Booth raised his head in a gesture of understanding. "That's right, you're a Rebel deserter. I guess everyone knows that, don't they? Of course, what everyone doesn't know, Mike, is that your deserting is only a cover for the work you do for the Rebel secret service."

Mike sat bolt upright. Now wait a minute. Just what in the hell are you suggesting?"

"I'm not suggesting a thing, Mike. I'm *telling* you, you're a Rebel spy and your cover is that you deserted from our army. You work for the South. That's why I invited you here." His voice took on a harsh tone. "Don't bullshit me, I got the word from Richmond."

"*Our* army? You're a Rebel sympathizer?"

"More than a sympathizer, Mike. I work for the Confederate underground in Washington, New York and Montreal. I'm here today because I need a good man for an important job in Washington and I want you to be that man."

"What kind of a job?"

Booth noticed that Mike did not dispute the role he had just ascribed to him. "I can't say right now. It's too delicate. But it's one President Davis himself is interested in. It'll win the war for us, it's that big. When this war is over, Michael," Booth paused for dramatic effect, "you and I will be heroes throughout the South. There's fame and money in it, you can count on that."

"Fame and money, eh, Johnnie? I've heard enough. Whatever it is, count me in." He gulped down the rest of his brandy. "Here, Johnnie, I need a re-fill."

Booth took the glass and as he filled it, with his back still to his guest, he said quietly, "Mike, I don't mean to be stuffy about it, but it's not 'Johnnie' any more. I go by the name of 'John Wilkes Booth'. So it's 'John' or 'Wilkes.' Actually I prefer 'Wilkes.' John Wilkes, an English reformer and member of Parliament back in the last century, was an ancestor of mine."

He turned and smiled at his guest who was crimson with embarrassment. "It's not terribly important, but I just wanted to get it straight."

Michael sat still for a few seconds. Finally he spoke. "I'd like to know more about this business before I say yes for sure. Ah . . . how do I know you work for the South?"

"Well, I haven't any documents with me, if that's what you want. But I can get you some proof. Don't blame you for wanting to be sure. Why don't you just come to Washington for a few days, a week at the most. I'll introduce you to some people and we'll fill you in on the whole plan. Then you can decide whether you want to join us."

"All right. I'll give it a try."

"Good." Booth put his glass down and smiled at Mike. "Good to have you aboard."

The little man stood up, aware that the meeting was over, and started for the door.

"I'd like you to be in Washington by the day after tomorrow. Bring a pistol and watch the *Personals* of the *Star*. When you see an ad reading

"George. Mother died on the – and there'll be a date - Rosa." come to my room at the National the following day at the same hour as the date given for 'mother's' death. Do you understand?

Mike looked puzzled and Booth repeated his instructions.

Finally Mike smiled weakly. "All right, I've got it." He looked at the floor. "Ah . . . I'll need some money to set up in Washington. I still have six dollars out of the twenty you sent me. But I'll need some more."

Booth frowned at the little man. "Fourteen dollars in just a little over a day? What in God's name did you do with it, Mike?"

Mike shuffled and cleared his throat. "Well, I drank a little of it up and there was this woman, I owed her some money, you see, had to pay her."

"A bottle and a whore," Booth replied as he reached into his pocket. "Well, Mike, here's ten dollars more. But if you drink and screw this away we'll see about having you replaced in this business. And you know what that means."

"Yessir, uh . . . Wilkes, I'll straighten up. You'll not have no trouble with me." His words were soft and his eyes never left the floor.

Three hours later Booth was on the train to New York City. The car was miserably cold and damp and by the time he arrived in New York in the early morning hours of Thursday and endured the open hack ride to the Astor House, he was chilled to the bone. He went to bed immediately, wrapped in the thick down coverlet that lay at the foot of the bed, and sipped on the remains of the bottle of brandy he had shared earlier that day with Michael O'Laughlen.

Mike O'Laughlen worried him. There was something about the man, a seedy sense of unreliability, that didn't fit with a mission as important as this one. Yet he needed the man.

Booth decided he'd have to keep a sharp eye on him. If Mike proved to be a problem, he'd have to be eliminated. It was that simple. Captain Bishop wasn't playing games. And neither, Booth decided, was he.

Chapter 13

Wednesday, February 15

By noon Sam was in Bryantown, the cultural and commercial center of St. Mary's County, Maryland. Not that either of those titles meant very much for St. Mary's County was backwater country, a land of over-worked farms and shabby villages that saw too many shady characters running back and forth on the clandestine road between Richmond and Washington and too little of the pre-war commerce the area so desperately needed.

Sam tied his horse to the hitching rail in front of the Bryantown Hotel, a shabby two-story building with peeling paint and loose, rotting siding, and went inside for the noon meal, half hoping he'd meet another Kate Huntt. There were only about a dozen men in the stuffy little dining room, most of them obviously locals. The conversation ran to fishing and spring planting, with an occasional comment about some local who was obviously known to most of the men in the room. The man who sat at Sam's right, a fair-haired, red-faced man the others called "George," asked Sam what business brought him to Bryantown. Sam said he was a government agent, looking for horses for the cavalry, and asked if anyone in the room knew of any horses for sale.

George looked up from his plate and asked, "Which government?" and the room grew quiet as the others sitting nearby waited for the answer.

"*Our* government. The *United* States. I wasn't aware that the so-called *Confederate* States even pretended to exist on this side of the river."

The man went back to his brown beans and cornbread. When his mouth was full he mumbled, "'tain't always so clear around here. But it don't matter, ain't a decent horse left in the county."

An old man who sat at the head of the table laughed. "Mebbe he oughta go see John Wilmer and buy his jackass. He'd teach the Yankee cavalrymen a thing or two."

The others laughed. Then the man opposite Sam ran his tongue over his front teeth, cleaning them, and looked up, eyes narrowed and jaw set. There were cornbread crumbs hanging from his thick, brown mustache as he spoke. "I never knew a government agent to travel alone. The ones I seen before always traveled in pairs."

"We're short-handed, Mr. . . .1 didn't get your name?"

"Jones. Thomas Jones."

"We're short-handed, Mr. Jones. We've had to abandon that policy."

Jones looked at him for a while, his gray eyes registering disbelief, and then went back to eating. The room grew quiet again, and the silence was punctuated by the ticking of the Seth Thomas clock on the mantel. Sam sensed that he was in a room populated by the enemy. It was getting to be a habit.

After the meal had mercifully ended Sam paid the man at the desk fifteen cents and asked directions to the post office.

The postmaster was a large, burly man with hard callused hands who would have appeared more at home behind a blacksmith's anvil than a postmaster's cage. There was no one else in the room so Sam introduced himself.

"My name's Reid, Lieutenant Sam Reid of Colonel Baker's detectives. I'm down here on some important business and I was told you might be of some help."

"I'm just the postmaster, sonny. Don't get involved in this war one way or the other. As for my loyalties, I'm a Union man obviously, otherwise wouldn't have the post office. But I mind my own business and I expect others to do the same."

Sam looked directly at the man. "Sergeant Pollack said I was to talk to you. He said you'd help me."

The man laughed. "Angus Pollack? That fat old fart? He sent you here? Why, hell yes I'll help you. How is old Angus?"

Sam relaxed. "He was fine when I left yesterday."

"Well now, why did Angus think I'd know anything?"

"He said you were nosy," Sam replied, adding, "like all postmasters."

Mr. Lowry let out a big laugh. "He did, did he? That fat old fart. Called *me* nosy? Well, let's see how right he was. What do you want to know?"

Sam explained about the messages dealing with boats and relays of horses. He told Mr. Lowry about Bishop's visit to Washington and his suspicion that Bishop was somehow tied to the boats and horses.

Mr. Lowry sat down. "Last week there was a man through here asking about horses. I heard later that the same man was down along the river a couple of days earlier looking for boats large enough to hold eight to twelve men."

"Was anything said about Bishop?"

"Yes. I don't recall who told me now, but I heard this fellow was supposed to be representing Captain Bishop.

"What did he want the boats and horses for, Mr. Lowry?"

"Don't know. He didn't say. There've been rumors that the Rebels were going to try to free the prisoners at Point Lookout. But there are several thousand Rebs penned up there. With two or three boats carrying eight to twelve men apiece it would take 'til Judgment Day to empty the place. No, those boats must be for something else. Why don't you go to Port Tobacco and look around? That's where most of the river traffic comes across."

"I think I will. Anyone I should talk to there? What about the postmaster?"

"Don't know about him. But if I was you I'd be careful about revealing myself to anyone at Port Tobacco. That's Rebel country through and through. Worse than here."

While they were talking a man walked into the post office. Sam recognized him as one of the diners from the hotel. He picked up his mail and after he had left Sam spoke again.

"What do you know about Captain Bishop?"

"He's a hard man, Lieutenant. A hard man. He does what has to be done. Doesn't fool around. If that means killing someone, he doesn't hesitate to kill.

"What about his darkie?"

"William? He's been with the family all his life. Him and Bishop grew up together. William's mother was a cook for Bishop's folks. She got in trouble with an Indian from a circus - a full-blooded Cherokee. They say William took after his father, that he's more Indian than darkie. He runs Bishop's camp at Boyd's Hole, Virginia, just across the Potomac from Maryland Point, when Bishop's not there. I've only seen him once or twice. He didn't strike me as a man who would stay a slave. But he's fiercely loyal to his master. Sleeps on the floor at his feet, cooks for him, blacks his boots."

After a few more questions Sam was on his way to Port Tobacco. The weather had cleared somewhat and he found the ride across the gently rolling countryside a pleasant change from the day before. After about three miles the road crossed Kerrick's Swamp Run and Sam stopped to let his horse drink from the slow-moving stream.

Four miles of hard riding later brought him to the little village of La Plata, a stage stop on the road to Port Tobacco. The stage was just pulling out from a disreputable-looking tavern and the driver was laying the lash to his team. Sam rode up beside the swaying vehicle and shouted to the driver."Going to Port Tobacco?"

The man nodded.

"How about hitching my horse to the rear and riding along with you?"

"You got fifty cents?"

Sam nodded and the stage ground to a stop. After he had tied his horse to the back of the stage he mounted the metal step to the door, stepped into the stage and settled back for the jolting ride to Port Tobacco.

The stage was a light six-passenger Concord coach drawn by four horses. It took off with a jerk as the horses lunged forward and the body of the coach heaved backward and then violently forward. The rocker-bottomed body of the coach was hung on thoroughbraces, wide, multi-ply leather straps that held the coach above the wheels but offered little protection from the jostling and jolting along the rough road. Including Sam only four of the six hard wooden seats were taken which at least reduced the crowding. It was an uncomfortable ride, but nonetheless better than by horseback.

They approached Port Tobacco by way of Port Tobacco Creek. The valley of the creek was broad and flat and the course of the stream was traced by a line of willows and birches. As they neared the town, where the creek became Port Tobacco River, the stream widened out in places, forming pools that reflected the barren trees growing along the banks. Occasionally a marshy spot would hold a stand of cattails, now beaten and scarred by the winter's storms.

Port Tobacco was a sleepy little village whose economic influence as a shipping center on the lower Potomac had long ago ceased to matter for much. Now it squatted, forelornly and somewhat down-at-the-heels, at the end of a broken-down wharf at the head of the Port Tobacco River, a river which was less a river than a short, wide inlet of the Potomac.

From the letters and messages he had read for the past four months Sam knew the town to be a center of Rebel activity. Its location made it a perfect way station on the underground road between the two warring capitals. Through here passed the messages, clandestine supplies, secret service gold, and the dandies and horse thieves who carried it all.

Sam dismounted the stage before Brawner's Tavern, gave the driver a dime tip and untied his horse from the rear of the stage. Then he walked the horse to the post office, which was in the back of a small general store. A stout woman with a thin black mustache greeted him icily. He asked about accommodations for the night, and was directed to a boarding house run by a Mrs. Knight. There he was led by an unsmiling middle-aged woman to a small, musty room at the top of the stairs from the kitchen where he laid his saddlebags across a cane-bottomed chair and stretched out on a narrow cot. He clasped his hands behind his head, stared at the sloping ceiling, and pondered what he would do next in this town where nobody smiled.

He spent the next two days riding about the countryside, asking where he could buy horses and inquiring about a large boat for a river crossing. He learned absolutely nothing about horses or boats. Nor did he notice the small man with one eye who recorded his comings and goings in the little town from the upper window of the house on the town square.

It was the people in this area who bothered Sam. They were obviously Rebels and they made little effort to conceal their feelings. The fortunes of war had made them suspicious of anyone wandering about asking questions, especially about river crossings and horses, so they told him nothing. And when *they* began asking *him* a lot of difficult questions, Sam decided it was time to move on.

On Saturday, February 18 he ate a leisurely breakfast and left Port Tobacco after he had paid Mrs. Knight for the two nights lodging and his meals. About five minutes after his passage through the town square had been recorded by the one-eyed man in the house overlooking the square, a message was delivered to a short, thin man who had been waiting by the stove in the post office. The message suggested Sam's destination. The man wrapped it in a small leather pouch and sent for his horse.

Sam rode all day in a freezing rain, hunched over in the saddle, trying to keep as dry as possible under his rubber slicker. The roads were deserted except for occasional church-goers and one or two horsemen riding purposefully toward Washington, or in the opposite direction toward the lower Potomac.

The rain had turned to snow and it was getting dark when he rode up to Huntt's store in Tee Bee. When he had visited earlier Mr. Huntt kept the store open until ten o'clock but tonight it was dark. A large sign in the front window read: *CLOSED.* One of the glass panes in the door had been broken out and a small piece of wood covered the space. The store appeared to be out of business, not just shut down for the night. Sam wondered about Kate, if she was still there in what appeared to be an abandoned building. But there was no one to ask, no way to know. And he had one more official stop to make and so he rode on.

Sergeant Pollack had suggested that he stop at the tavern in Surrattsville and take a meal. Sam had decided to spend the night there as well. No telling what a man might learn there. And there shouldn't be much risk involved. After all, the Rebels didn't know he was in lower Maryland, much less that he planned to stop at the tavern in Surrattsville.

Chapter 14

Saturday, February 18

It was nearly noon when Booth awoke and gathered the courage to face the icy city. He left his hotel and walked briskly toward the decrepit, run-down section of New York City known as Five Points. An icy wind whipped up the street, scattering trash and filthy snow and howling a mournful, depressing combination of low moan and high whistle.

Building by building the structures became more dilapidated and the neighborhood more sinister. Because of the bitter cold the streets were nearly vacant, but here and there some poor creature shuffled along, head down and hands dug deep inside coat pockets, a picture of abject misery. As he passed one dingy brick building Booth noticed a small girl, wearing only one shoe and wrapped in what appeared to be part of a filthy rug, huddled in the recess of the doorway, gnawing like a young dog on a piece of bone.

He thought of his niece, Edwina, living in relative splendor just two miles north of where he now walked. In all her four years she had never wanted for anything and here this poor child could probably not recall when she had seen her last full meal.

Suddenly he heard a piercing scream and a great commotion. The door of a rickety house flung open and a black woman, blood gushing from her nose, staggered out onto the sidewalk and collapsed on the frozen pavement where she commenced rolling and pitching about like a catfish in mud. In a moment or so a drunken beast of a man appeared in the doorway, shouting at the woman in a thick Irish brogue.

"You filthy, drunken slut of a whore!" Then he saw Booth. "What are you starin' at, you swaggering Broadway dandy?"

Booth quickened his pace and left the raving man behind.

He crossed the street, dodging a mound of horse manure that had been piled at the corner for collection by the city sanitation department, and passed into a narrow alley between two shabby frame buildings.

As he left the street he reached inside his cape and pulled a slip of paper from his jacket pocket and looked at it. He wadded the paper up and threw it onto the pavement and walked up to a rickety flight of stairs on the right side of the alley. He stepped under the stairs and followed garbage-littered steps to the basement and rapped softly on the door.

A thin, mousey woman answered the door. Her ragged dress was covered by a filthy apron that showed no sign of ever having been near water and her hair hung down in greasy rivulets across a neck that badly needed washing.

Booth removed his hat. "Good afternoon. Is Mr. Clarke at home?"

The woman stared at him, never changing her expression. "Come in."

Booth entered and was somewhat taken aback by the sour smell of dampness mingled with the odor of a pot of potato soup simmering on the stove at the back of the room. His eyes hadn't adjusted to the darkness when a man's voice behind him said sternly. "What do you want?"

"Good afternoon," Booth replied quickly. "My name is Wilson."

"Of the Annapolis Wilsons?"

"No, my family is from Baltimore."

"All right. What do you want?"

As Booth watched, the man put away a pistol he had obviously been pointing at him since his entry into the room. There is a time for ceremony and idle chatter and a time to dispense with it. This, Booth knew, was no time to waste words. He went immediately to the point.

"About the Eighth of February a message left Montreal addressed to John Wilkes Booth, in care of the National Hotel, Washington, D.C. That would put it through here on the Ninth or Tenth. It arrived in the District on the Twelfth and I got it. I'm John Wilkes Booth. I want to know the name of the courier who brought it to Washington. "

"Why?"

Booth started to tell the man it was none of his business but thought better of it. "Because he's apparently letting the Yankees read our mail. If we know who he is we can use him, let him carry messages we want the Yanks to read. But we have to know who he is."

"I'll have his name by tomorrow morning. Where can I reach you?"

"The Astor House."

"It figures. All right, you'll have his name before noon tomorrow. Anything else?"

"No. I'll be going now." Booth started for the door. "Thanks for your hospitality" he said.

The man laughed. "Didn't think the likes of you would want to stop and have a pot of soup with us. We're not quite as fancy as the Astor House. Besides, we're running a courier service, not a restaurant."

Booth didn't answer but walked back out into the bitter cold. As soon as he was out of the alley and into the relative safety of the street he reached inside his coat and took out a cigar. He struck a match against the wall of a grimy brownstone and lit the cigar, shielding the flame in his cupped hands. Booth inhaled deeply of the cigar and exhaled the blue smoke through his nostrils, covering the smell of the dingy room he had just left with the pungent odor of good tobacco.

He had gone but a few paces when a bleary-eyed man, hatless but with his overcoat collar drawn up about his beard, came shuffling out of an exposed doorway and headed straight for Booth.

"Sir, can you spare a dime for a hot meal? I ain't ate for over a fortnight."

Booth raised his cane in front of the man and stopped him. Then he tossed him a coin, taking great care not to touch the man. "Here's a quarter. Now go clean yourself up."

"God bless you, sir," the man mumbled and disappeared into the narrow passageway between two houses. Booth shuddered and continued on his way, puffing vigorously on his cigar.

At Bowery Street Booth finally allowed himself to relax. He slowed his pace and, oblivious to the cold, began to peer into the windows of the tiny shops. Ahead of him was a brightly painted candy store, its windows filled with candies of an enormous variety of substances of different sizes, shapes, colors and flavors. Booth knocked the ashes off his half-finished cigar with his gloved forefinger and turned into the store. The warmth of the small shop was a welcome change from the bitter cold outside and the enticing sweet smell of the candy whet his appetite.

Booth looked into trays filled with spice drops, jaw breakers, and marshmallow confections in the shape of bananas, rabbits and eggs. There were chunks of Turkish Taffy, sticks of licorice, and wide strips of paper a foot and a half long dotted with candy buttons.

After a period of delicious indecision Booth settled on a box of Whitman Samplers.

Then, with his purchase wrapped in a copy of the *New York Times* tucked inside his coat pocket, he went back out onto Bowery Street and hailed a cab for the mile and a half ride to Gramercy Square.

-o-

He rapped on the door knocker three times and stamped his feet and clapped his gloved hands to generate warmth. Finally his brother's face appeared in the frosted-edged door glass.

"Wilkes! Come in, my boy, come in! What are you doing in the city?"

"Had to see a man about my oil speculations, Edwin." He pulled off his gloves and blew on his hands. "Have you any brandy?"

"Did you ever know a Booth NOT to have some brandy about the house?"

"No, thank God, never. Where's Edwina?"

"She's up town with Mary, shopping for some little trinket or another."

"I'm sorry I missed her. Here, give her this copy of my heart from her Uncle Johnny." He handed the box of chocolates to Edwin.

"She'll love them, Wilkes. She always loves what you bring her."

The two brothers drank and chatted for nearly an hour. Finally Wilkes stood up to leave. "It's good to see you looking so well, Edwin. You always were father's favorite."

"And you were our mother's pride and joy. We're a lucky family, Wilkes. So many have lost sons and brothers in this useless war."

Wilkes bristled. "I'd not call a war for independence 'useless.' Edwin. The South fights for the right to be free . . . nothing more."

Edwin smiled. "Still carrying the Southern banner, are you? I've always wondered why you didn't join up with Bobby Lee. Unless you're afraid of spoiling your pretty face . . . ."

Wilkes' voice suddenly became harsh. "I promised Mother I'd stay out of the army, Edwin. And a promise to a dear old mother is one you don't break lightly. Besides, there are other ways to serve the South, you know."

-o-

It was nearly eleven the next morning when Booth watched a man approach the front desk of the Astor House and hand a message to the clerk. The clerk consulted the register and then placed the message in a box on the wall behind him, about where the key to Booth's room was kept. Booth got up from the thick divan where he had been enjoying his cigar and crossed the lobby to the desk.

"Any messages for J. Wilkes Booth?"

"Yes, one was just delivered, only a moment ago."

Booth opened the folded paper and read: "Raymond Key. Boonsboro, Maryland. Red hair, no beard, scar on back of left hand. Stutters. Next trip South next week." When he had finished reading, Booth paid his bill, returned to his room and picked up his bag and took a hack to the train station.

The train arrived in Baltimore a little after nine that night. It took nearly an hour to locate a hack and find his way to Mr. Brennan's house on Paca Street. Considering the weather, the hour, and the fact that Booth had rousted him from bed, Mr. Brennan was remarkably cheerful and friendly.

"I need to send a message," Booth said after the recognition code was finished. "Won't keep you up long." He motioned toward the street. "My hack is waiting."

"Certainly," the man replied.

"But I'll need you to write it for me."

The man looked puzzled.

"Oh, I can read and write," Booth added hastily. "I just don't want the letter to be in my hand."

"Very well. What should I say?" The man sat at a table at the edge of the parlor. He took a quill pen from the table and dipped it into a small bottle of black ink, carefully breaking the skim of ice that had formed over the surface of the ink.

> "Dear Wilkes, that's W-I-L-K-E-S," Booth began. "Dr. Bailey will deliver the next shipment of quinine sometime after the 15th of March. The price continues to soar in the South, so you should make another fortune. Take care to protect your

line of distribution and I will exercise equal caution on this end with regard to the source of the drug. Perhaps together we can become rich - if only the war lasts long enough.

Webley."

"Got that?"

"Yes, every word. But let me read it back to you just to be certain."

When the man had finished reading Booth said, "Have it delivered to 'J. Wilkes Booth, Esq., c/o National Hotel, Washington, D. C.' And this is most important. It is only to be carried by a courier named Raymond Key. He's a red-haired fellow with no beard. He stutters and he has a bad scar on the back of his left hand."

"I know just the man you mean. I'll see that he gets the message."

"Fine. He'll be through here next week. Only don't let him know we've held the letter for him. Here's five dollars for your trouble."

The man smiled and took the coin. "Thank you, sir. That's most generous of you."

An hour later Booth was in the bar of the Barnum Hotel, Baltimore's finest hostelry. He spent nearly two hours there, sipping on good brandy and chatting with a group of young men who had recognized him and praised his work on the stage. Amid all the excitement of showing off for his young fans he failed to notice a large dark-haired young man who sat alone at a table in the corner sipping from a glass of corn whiskey and carefully watching Booth. When Booth left the bar shortly after midnight, the man paid his bill and quietly left the hotel.

Chapter 15

Saturday, February 18

The James River, which flowed from Richmond into the Chesapeake Bay, was broad and deep and offered a tempting route by which the Federals could threaten the Confederate capital. But, fortunately for the Confederacy, the river bent and curved around all degrees of the compass, beneath steep bluffs, past rich meadow lands and alongside forbidding swamps.

To hold the U. S. Navy at bay the Confederates placed artillery batteries at every significant vantage point along the river. Huge guns, cast and bored in Richmond, swept the twists and turns of the river and threatened certain annihilation to any Federal gunboat that tried to rush the capital.

Battery Brooke was one of the more recent of these defenses, a battery of home-made naval guns that had been constructed after cock-eyed old Benjamin Butler had been bottled up in Bermuda Hundred between the Appomattox and the James in his weak-spirited drive against Richmond in May, 1864. The battery overlooked the Dutch Gap Canal, a by-pass of the river which Butler's men had dug to try to get the Federal gunboats past some obstructions which Butler himself had sunk in the James. On New Year's Day, 1865, the canal was finished and the dam between it and the James was blown up. But Butler's bad luck had held. The twelve thousand pounds of powder raised the dirt into the air and it fell back into the opening. Under the fire of the guns of Battery Brooke the dam could not be dredged away.

Battery Brooke was a powerful work. Its trenches were lined with wicker-work bastions reinforced by tiers of sandbags or boarded up with stout timbers. Here and there bomb-proofs, underground shelters covered with twelve to sixteen feet of earth, provided shelter from enemy shells. The gun positions were boarded in by heavy fences of timber set behind thick walls of earth and the gunners serviced their massive weapons on solid wooden floors that kept them out of the Virginia mud. These guns were obviously here to stay and the crews that served them were among the most confident and highly motivated soldiers in the Southern army. Here, at least, the Rebels had the upper hand, and they meant to keep it.

It was nearly noon on Saturday, February 18, 1865, when the three men from Richmond, two young officers and an older civilian, rode up to the battery headquarters. After a brief whispered conference with the commanding officer, a short pot-bellied major, the three were led through a maze of deep, well-maintained trenches to a large brass naval gun with a reinforcing band shrunk around its breech. The gun looked out over a bend of the James nearly a half mile away through a slit in the neatly carpentered wall that surrounded the emplacement on three sides.

The major stopped a few feet from the entrance to the gun emplacement and, after returning the salute of the members of the gun's crew, motioned for one of the men, a Sergeant with a heavily pocked face and a slight limp, to come over.

"Gentlemen, this is Sergeant Maynard. Sergeant Maynard, these men are from the War Department and need you to accompany them back to Richmond."

The sergeant looked puzzled. "Is something wrong?"

The civilian spoke up. "No, sergeant. We just need you to accompany us back to Richmond and remain there for a few days. It's fairly important so we really can't waste much time talking about it."

"Could I see your orders? I'm not leaving here without orders."

"Certainly." The civilian nodded to a thin, one-armed lieutenant who handed a piece of paper to Sergeant Maynard.

"War Department Richmond, Feby. 17, 1865,
J. B. Jones, Chief Clerk War Department

You are directed to take two armed officers and proceed to Battery Brooke overlooking the James River and there arrest and return to this headquarters Sergeant Richard Maynard of that battery. This letter will serve as your authorization to make this arrest and will also confirm that neither you nor the two officers accompanying you are privy to the reason for Sergeant Maynard's arrest.

/s/John C. Breckinridge
Secretary of War."

"Arrest? Just what's that supposed to mean?" He looked at the civilian. "Are you Jones?"

"Yes, but as the letter states, I know nothing beyond the fact that I have been ordered to arrest you. Shall we go?"

The sergeant looked at his commanding officer. "Major . . . ?"

The major shrugged his shoulders. "You've seen the order, Dick. I guess you'd better go along."

The sergeant sighed deeply and then nodded. "All right. I guess I have no choice."

The little party rode off through the scrub pines toward Richmond.

-0-

J. B. Jones was in the kitchen, sidled up to the stove while his wife poked at the miserable- stick fire and tried to coax the pot of turnips to a boil, when the door knocker began to rattle. His wife looked at him.

"John, you'd better answer the door. It might be that crazy Van Lew woman. She likes you and maybe if we invite her in and she sees how poorly we're eating we can buy an egg or two from her. Be your charming best, dear."

Jones put the newspaper he had been reading on the supper table and headed toward the door to the hallway. He was back in a minute, followed by a frail, stoop-shouldered woman with frizzled brown hair that hung greasily in all directions at once. She was carrying a small basket covered with white cloth.

"Good evening, Miss Van Lew," Cora Jones said.

"'Evenin' ma'am. Whatcha cookin' fer supper?"

"Turnips. That's all we have. Won't you join us?"

Elizabeth Van Lew's face screwed up and she shook her head. "Turnips ain't a fittin' meal for the Chief Clerk of the War Department. Here, you wanna buy some eggs?" She pulled the cloth back from the top of the basket to reveal four pale brown eggs.

"How much, Miss Van Lew?" J. B. Jones asked.

"Five dollars each, Confederate bills, or ten cents each, hard money."

Jones sank down in his chair by the stove, a disgusted look on his face. "You know we don't have that kind of money, Miss Van Lew."

The woman cackled and skipped around the kitchen. "Ain't it somethin'. The South don't have nothin'." Then she stopped and looked at Jones. "What kin you pay? I like you folks and want you should eat good. Not many folks'll talk to old Crazy Bette."

"I can give you two dollars Confederate for all of them," Jones replied.

The woman grinned. "Sold! You got your eggs! Better eat 'em up, though. Grant's gonna come stormin' into Richmond any day now. The South is finished. Done fer." She stared at Jones. "You think the Yankees'll hang you when they get here?"

Jones smiled smugly, ignoring her taunt. "Excuse me, Miss Van Lew. I need to go upstairs to get money to pay you."

After Jones left Cora smiled. "You shouldn't count your chickens before they hatch, Miss Van Lew. My husband knows a thing or two about our government's plans and he tells me a great many people are going to be surprised very shortly. In fact don't you be too surprised if Grant goes packing back up north and all our Confederate prisoners are returned to us."

"Bah! Talk. Big talk. How we gonna do that? Grant ain't afraid of us."

"There are other ways of making the enemy do what you want him to do besides overpowering him on the battlefield, or so John tells me. Before a month passes we may well have our hands on the one thing that will make the Yankees deal with us on our terms. John says Mr. Lincoln in particular is going to be a mighty unhappy man."

The woman shook her head. "The South is going nowhere and doing nothing, Mrs. Jones. We're FINISHED!"

The two women were staring silently at each other when J.B. Jones came into the room holding out two Confederate greenbacks. "Expensive eggs, Miss Van Lew, but it's nice to have something better than turnips. We sure appreciate your sharing them with us." He started the woman toward the door.

When Jones came back into the kitchen he was frowning. "What was that all about? Why was she so worked up?"

Cora smiled and patted him on the shoulder. "She just gets very excited when she hears people say the South is doomed. But, thank goodness nobody pays any mind to Crazy Bette Van Lew."

Chapter 16

Saturday, February 18

Booth was back in Washington by 10:30 Saturday morning. He went straight to the office of the Washington *Star* and placed an ad in Sunday's edition announcing that "Mother died on the 11th." Back at his hotel he wrote a brief note and dispatched it from the front desk by messenger. After supper that evening he waited in his room. A little before seven there was a soft knock at the door.

"Come in, Davy, come in," Booth said to the boy who stood grinning in the doorway. "How's everything with the Herold family?"

"Fine, I reckon. When you're the only boy among eight kids you don't stay home that much."

"Would you like a glass of brandy?"

"No, but I would like one of them seegars over there, if you don't mind."

"Certainly, I'll light up with you."

Booth lit the cigars and then sat back on the edge of the bed watching the pale blue smoke roll up to the ceiling. "What have you been up to lately, Davy?"

"Not much. Huntin' a little in lower Maryland."

Booth made no comment. After a few seconds of awkward silence Davy added, "Helped in Doc Ward's drugstore a couple of days last month. Don't like that much, though."

"You used to work for him regularly, didn't you?"

"Yessir, for almost a year."

"What did you do?"

"A little everything. Deliveries, waited on customers, mixed drugs. You know, whatever there was to be done when we got busy."

"You know anything about poisons, Davy?"

Davy looked puzzled. "A little, why?"

"What about chloroform? Ever use it?"

"No, but I seen Doc Ward kill an old dog with it once."

"Could you put a man to sleep with it - and not kill him?"

"Sure. Ain't nothin' to it. Why you askin' me about this?"

"I need your help, Davy, in a project that will bring us a lot of money and make us very famous. The only problem is there are some risks and we'll have the government after us."

"This involve helpin' the South?"

"Yes." Booth stared hard at the boy. "And from what I hear that won't give you any trouble."

"No sir. I don't care nothin' about politics. I'm for lettin' the South do what it wants to. Carried a few messages in lower Maryland for the Rebs last summer, in fact."

"Yes, I heard. Then you'll join us?"

"In what? You ain't told me what we'll be doin' yet."

"Trying to capture someone important here in Washington and sneak him off to Richmond."

"That what the choloform's for? To knock him out?"

"Yes."

Davy grinned. "And the poison. What's it for?"

"Frankly I don't know. I have my orders, too."

"Who we tryin' to sneak out?"

Booth caught the "we" for the second time. "We'll talk about that later, after you say you'll join us."

"Sure. I'll join you. Ain't doin' nothin' else anyway. Who is it? Old Abe?"

"Yes. How'd you guess?"

The boy's smile was gone. "My God. That was just a wild guess. I never really thought about it. You serious about capturing the President?"

"No Davy," Booth lied, "but we are after someone big. I'll tell you later when it's safe." Booth stood up, walked over to the boy and put his arm on his back. "You just be here at eleven Friday morning and you'll learn what this is all about. In the meantime if you talk too much, you'll join that old dog Doc Ward took care of. You understand me?"

Davy stood up and looked at Booth with a serious expression on his face. "Mr. Booth, I won't say nothin' to nobody. Don't you worry. You can trust me."

"All right. That's fine. Oh, just a minute." Booth grabbed a handful of cigars from the dresser. "Here. Enjoy a couple of smokes."

"Thank you, Mr. Booth. Them's fine seegars. Fine seegars."

After the boy had left Booth put on his cape and walked up to Etta Starr's place on 14th Street. The girl was busy with a customer and Booth had to wait in the gaudy parlor for nearly an hour. He amused himself by flirting with the other girls waiting there in their low-cut gowns. Finally Etta was free and Booth went up to her room.

"Wilkes, darling. Where've you been? It's been days."

"Had to go out of town for a few days. Nothing important. Your customer sure took a long time. What's the matter, couldn't he keep it up?"

"They always keep it up with me, Wilkes. You know that. He just wasn't in any hurry. It was his money so I let him take his time."

"How about me. Do you have time for me tonight?"

Etta smiled. “Sure honey. I always have time for you. Let me go tell the girls I don’t want to be disturbed. You go ahead and get undressed.”

Booth slipped into the warm bed and pulled the covers over him. Outside heavy sleet was drumming against the window pane. He shivered and drew the covers closer about him. “Come on, Etta,” he shouted. “I’ve waited long enough.”

-0-

When he emerged from Etta’s place it was after 4:00 a.m. The sleet had stopped but the streets and sidewalks were sheets of bare ice. Several times Booth was glad he had brought his gold-headed cane for it broke what could have been a nasty fall.

At the corner of C and 9th Streets he stopped and glanced back down C Street. A man, his shoulders hunched against the cold and his hands shoved deep inside his overcoat, was coming up the street in an unsteady gait. Booth paid him little notice but when he crossed Pennsylvania Avenue opposite the City Market he peered into the window of the Dexter House. In the reflection of the glass he could see that the man was still there. He studied him as carefully as the poor light and distorted reflection would permit. He was dressed in rags, a shabby overcoat several sizes too big and a moth-eaten woolen cap pulled down over his ears.

Booth fought his growing suspicion. He recognized that, most likely, the man was just a drunk who happened to be going his way. Then, despite the hour and the unpleasant weather, he decided to test the man.

He turned left on 7th Street and walked north for three blocks, past the Post Office Department, then turned right on E Street. After one block he was at 6th Street, by the Chase-Sprague Mansion. There he stepped into the shadows and waited. After a few minutes the man appeared at the corner of 7th and E Streets, no longer walking unsteadily.

Booth walked down 6th Street and entered the National Hotel by the side entrance. As he closed the door he glanced up the street. The man was still there. Booth was certain now that he was being followed.

My God, he thought. I've got a meeting in my room at 11:00 Monday morning. If I'm being followed the Yankees are likely to capture the whole band.

It was nearly 7:00 a.m. before he finally fell asleep, confident at last that he had figured out a way to shake his pursuer.

Chapter 17

Sunday, February 19

Lloyd's Tavern, which until the past November had been known as Surratt's Tavern, stood in a patch of small pine trees to the right of the road from Tee Bee, a large, nondescript rust-colored building that had sheltered many a Confederate agent on his way to or from Washington. When Sam arrived there it was already dark and the snow was thick and heavy. He entered the bar and inquired about supper and a room. Told that he could spend the night and that the cook would set supper out for him, Sam led his horse to the barn out back. By the light of the kerosene lantern that hung near the door he could make out six horses stabled there. A small black boy came out of the dark and took Sam's horse.

"Looks like Mr. Lloyd's got a full house tonight," Sam said to the boy.

"Nawsir. Three of them horses is bein' kept here by Mr. Lloyd. Ain't nobody stayin' in the tavern tonight 'cept a tinker and the man what come here today from Bryantown."

"How about showing me whose horse is whose."

"How come you want to know?" The boy stared at Sam, suddenly wary.

"I trade in horses. Maybe I'll want to offer to buy a horse while I'm here."

The boy led Sam through the barn pointing out which horses were which. The three horses that Lloyd was "keeping" for someone were beautiful, high-spirited animals.

"These are fine looking horses," Sam said to the boy. "Who's Mr. Lloyd keeping them for?"

"Don't know for sure. Some big darkie brought 'em here. Massa Lloyd said to take good care of them. Said they'll be gone before the fifth of March. Anything happens to them before then, he'll whip my ass for sure."

Sam reached into his pocket. "Here's a nickel. I don't want you to tell anyone about our little talk. If I decide I want to buy the horses I'd just as soon the owner didn't know I asked you about them. Just tell anyone who asks that I paid you the nickel to take care of my horse. All right?" He smiled and winked at the boy.

Inside the tavern Sam ate alone in the dining room which was situated in the room behind the bar. When he was about finished the cook told him, "Why don't you take your coffee in the parlor with the other gentlemens? There's a good fire there and you'll be more comf'tble." "Thank you, I will," Sam replied. "Who are the other guests?"

"There's a tinker, Roscoe Simmons, and a Mr. . . er . . . Harbin, a friend of Mr. Lloyd who is spending a few days here."

Sam glanced at the door and beckoned the cook to come closer. "Are we alone? Can I ask you something without anyone knowing about our conversation?"

The cook walked over to the table. "Yes, we're alone. Why? Who are you? Massa Lloyd don't like me to talk much to strangers. He gets awful mad ..."

Sam ignored her questions. "Do you know a Rebel Captain named Bishop?"

The cook wiped her hands on her apron. "Yes, he stops by here regular. Been stoppin' here since early in the war, on his way to and from Washington. Why do you want to know?"

Again Sam ignored her question. "What's he like? What's he look like? Is there anything different about him?"

"He's short and heavy-set. Dark brown hair, almost reddish. An' he's cocky. Popular with the women, though. But I never thought much of him. Too cocky, like a banty rooster. Them's his horses out in the barn, leastwise his man William left 'em there."

"What are the horses for?"

"'Don't know. But it must be awful important. William told my boy Jonas he' have a hole blowed clean through him if anythin' happened to them horses."

"When was the last time you saw him?"

"Who? William or Captain Bishop?"

"Captain Bishop."

"Las' Monday. A week ago tomorrow. He stopped here on his way into the District."

"Was he alone?"

"Yes."

"What's he up to now?"

"Don't know. Onliest thing I know is he's got horses scattered from here to the River. William told Jonas he gonna see some fancy ridin' some night." The innkeeper, John Lloyd, a bloated, red-faced man with three day's growth of beard, came through the door, smiling broadly. "Well, sir, have you finished? Why don't you join the others in the parlor."

Sam nodded and rose from the table. "Thank you, Mr. Lloyd, I think I will." He walked into the hallway and stopped for a minute, listening. Lloyd was questioning the cook. What did he want? What was he asking you?

"You tell me, or I'll beat your black ass."

"He was just makin' talk, Mr. Lloyd. Wanted to know about my boy Jonas. Asked did he like horses, was he a good boy. That's all."

Lloyd grunted and Sam continued on into the parlor.

He took a vacant chair before the fire, nodded toward a ragged-looking man who was placing a pinch of snuff under his lip and trying to keep his eyes on a chessboard set before the fire.

He turned and looked at the other guest who was seated across the chessboard from the tinker, intently studying the board. Sam tensed slightly. It was the man who had come into the post office in Bryantown while he was talking to Mr. Lowry, one of the men in the dining room at the Bryantown Hotel. The man looked up and smiled.

"Evenin' sir. Our paths cross again. Small world, isn't it?"

"Yes," Sam replied. "I saw you last in the post office in Bryantown, if I'm not mistaken."

"Yes. Thomas Harbin. Pleasure to meet you." He held out his hand.

Sam took his hand. "Sam Reid. My pleasure, sir."

The door opened and John Lloyd came into the parlor. "Can I get you gents a drink from the bar?"

Mr. Harbin spoke up. "Yes. I'll have a bourbon, Mr. Lloyd. You other gentlemen care to join me? I'm treating."

The tinker nodded yes quickly. "No thank you," Sam replied. "I'm having coffee brought in."

Harbin moved a knight and sat back in his chair. "Did you have any luck finding horses for your cavalry?"

"No, no luck at all. Seems the area's been pretty well cleaned out. Of course there are some horses here and there." He looked at Harbin, but the man was studying the chessboard again. "There's talk that horses and boats are being gathered to do something about freeing the Rebels from Point Lookout. You gentlemen hear anything about that?"

Harbin looked up at Sam. "No, I've heard nothing of the sort. It would take a great many horses and boats to free that place, though." Harbin's face was impassive.

What the hell, Sam thought, might as well throw everything at the man. "There are rumors that the South plans to force the North to exchange prisoners again." Harbin's eyes flickered for an instant. Sam had struck a nerve.

The tinker spoke up, exposing a set of broken and snuff-stained teeth. "I've heard queer talk of that, too. Wonder how the Rebs would do it?"

Harbin cut in. "There's lots of ways if they set their hands to it."

Sam's coffee had arrived and he took a sip of it. "Just what would some of those ways be, Mr. Harbin?"

Harbin ignored Sam's question. "Why does this interest you so, Mr. Reid?"

"It was just a question that caught my fancy, a puzzle. I wondered how they could do it. I mean, the North is obviously so much stronger and I can't see how the South can force them to do much of anything." Again Sam had struck a nerve. Harbin's face was red.

Lloyd was back, grinning nervously and rubbing his grimy hands together. "Maybe the North ain't as strong as it thinks."

Sam turned around and looked at him. "What's that supposed to mean? I'm only a government purchase agent but it looks to me like the South is all but finished."

Harbin picked up a captured bishop and turned it around in his hand. "In chess the game isn't over until the king is captured. 'Checkmate.' The word is from the Persian 'Shah Mat,' meaning 'the king is dead.' The South isn't done yet. Not by a long shot."

Sam stood up. "Well, politics is not my business. Whatever happens will happen. Mr. Lloyd, if you'll show me to my room, I think I'll retire. Good night, Gentlemen."

In his room, which was situated at the head of the stairs in the corner of the building overlooking the road to Tee Bee, Sam placed his saddlebags on the bed and pulled the drapes. Then he tried to lock the door. But the lock was broken, the door couldn't even be closed securely. Fortunately the house had settled so that the door stayed closed sufficiently for privacy. But it could be opened without so much as a telltale 'click.'

Sam reached into his saddlebags and removed a small leather-bound diary. He leaned it against the door and placed a silver dollar atop the book. Then he pulled the blankets and a pillow off the bed and made a bed on the floor of the room, alongside the wall where the door was located. Finally, he placed his Army Colt under his pillow and lay down, fully dressed, between the blankets.

There was something about this fellow Harbin that disturbed him. The way he kept staring with those hard eyes. And his showing up here after being in Bryantown. But then how could he know Sam would stop here? It could only be a coincidence. Best to think of better things - like Ellie.

He pulled the blanket tighter about him. Ellie. Those beautiful eyes. Those lovely breasts. But as he thought about Ellie the image of Kate Huntt kept returning. Those green eyes, flecked with gold. And the way she smiled, with her whole face, not like Ellie whose smiles encompassed only her lips. It was strange, too. Ellie was decidedly more beautiful but there was something about Kate that made her in some ways more attractive than Ellie. Sam was wrestling with that puzzle when he fell asleep.

The clock in the parlor below had just struck 2:30 when the silver dollar clattered to the floor and the diary fell with it, waking Sam. He tensed and reached under his pillow for his pistol, eyes on the door. There was nothing, no movement, no sound for at least five minutes. Still Sam kept his eyes glued to the door.

Then silently the door opened and the figure of a man crept into the room. Sam could make out a knife in the man's hand as he walked quietly toward the empty bed. When the man was almost at the bed, with his back to Sam, Sam pointed his pistol at the man and cocked it.

"I have you covered from behind. What do you want?"

Instantly the man bolted from the room. Sam threw the covers back and stepped to the door. He pointed the pistol at the fleeing shadow and pulled the trigger. The pistol roared and its flash lit the hallway for an instant. But he had missed and the man kept on going down the stairs, past the gaping hole Sam had blown in the plaster at the stairway landing, and on out the back door into the night. Sam stood in the doorway for a few minutes and then closed the door and "re-set" his alarm at the foot of the door.

A few minutes later there was a soft knock at the door. John Lloyd's voice inquired softly, "You all right in there? You fire that shot?"

"Yes to both questions," Sam replied, irritated.

"Well, you shot a powerful hole in my stairway wall. I'll need at least five dollars to fix it."

"The hell with your stairway wall," Sam snapped. "Somebody tried to kill me. You just better hope I don't cause the Federal government to close this miserable place."

Lloyd didn't reply and Sam heard him padding back to his bedroom. After a few minutes Sam moved his bed to another corner of the room, and after a tense hour or two, fell asleep again.

At breakfast John Lloyd was sullen and morose and Sam didn't mention the commotion of the night before. Harbin was gone, he said. He had planned to leave for Washington at 4:00 a.m. The tinker was totally unconcerned about the previous night's activities and wanted to talk to Sam about duck hunting, though he could not get an answer from Sam. Finally the table lapsed into silence and the three ate their breakfast. It was nearly 8:00 a.m. when Sam sent for his horse.

A few yards north of the tavern the road to Washington was intersected by the Woodyard-Robeystown Road. Sam reined in his horse for a moment and sat there thinking. If anyone were to set an ambush for him it would be on the direct road to Washington, the most obvious way for Sam to go. They could never cover every road into the city. It was unlikely they would even consider a roundabout route. He decided to take the long way and nudged his horse onto the road to Woodyard.

It was about 2:30 that afternoon when he crossed Benning's Bridge over the Anacostia River and rode into the city toward his boarding house. The weather was growing worse. Though it was only mid-afternoon the sky was dark and the lamps in the houses along the street were lit. The Avenue was nearly deserted. In the distance Sam noticed a carriage approaching with a driver and a lone passenger.

Sam was nearly even with the carriage before he recognized the familiar figure of President Lincoln, huddled beneath a heavy shawl and a lap robe. Sam reined in his horse, came to rigid attention, and saluted the President. Lincoln's right hand came out from beneath his lap robe and he touched the brim of his stovepipe hat in response.

Sam turned in the saddle and watched the carriage until it faded away up New York Avenue in the swirling snow.

An hour later, after changing into dry clothes, Sam was back in his office, reading the Sunday *Star*. On page three he read a small announcement:

> "President Lincoln will attend a performance of the Soldiers' Home Patriotic Chorus at 3:00 o'clock this afternoon."

Sam's mind flashed back to the empty street and the lonely ride out to the Soldiers' Home. *Checkmate! The king is dead!* It all fit. Sam began yelling for Sergeant Pollack whom he had passed in the hallway on his way in.

Chapter 18

Monday, February 20

The telegram from Chicago was blunt and to the point. "Camp Douglas plot part of larger effort against all prison camps planned for Inauguration Day. Some curious talk of forcing prisoner exchange by bold stroke, not just raid on camps. I am being followed. My presence here no secret to Rebel underground. David."

Sam read it over again, sucking hard on the piece of maple sugar in his mouth. "This business of the 'bold stroke' to force a prisoner exchange, it fits. Don't you see, Sergeant Pollack. I heard the same thing in lower Maryland. And capturing President Lincoln fits into the picture. Look at it. He rides around the city without an escort. He goes out to the Soldiers' Home on that godforsaken lonely Seventh Street Road. Last summer, when General Early attacked the city, the President was out at Fort Stevens with only his driver. All the Rebels have to do is pick him up on one of his jaunts and head south for the Potomac. They change horses every few miles and leave us behind as our horses tire and then cross the river on their large boat. With Lincoln in their hands we'll have to agree to resume the prisoner exchange and God knows what else."

"And there's more than that, Sergeant. Bishop is involved in this horse and boat business, your friend Lowry in Bryantown told me that. We know Jeff Davis sent Bishop here to pull off something that he thinks will end the war. Well, by God, this is it! They plan to kidnap President Lincoln."

Sergeant Pollack rubbed his beard and read the message again. "I'll admit that it makes sense in a way. But the only thing is we don't know they're after Lincoln. We're guessing that. Colonel Baker doesn't like guesses. He likes to know."

"Well, shit fire, I can't get him a sworn affidavit from Jefferson Davis. But it seems to me that it's too likely a possibility to ignore. Who's going to be hurt if we decide to provide a little protection for the President for a few weeks? Tell me that."

"All right. But you tell that to Colonel Baker. And we got another problem. How'd the Rebels learn Lieutenant Peterson is in Chicago?"

Sam looked hard at the sergeant. "It's simple. Somebody in this headquarters is spying for the South. The same person who warned Bishop we were on to him at the National also sent word that David is in Chicago and why."

Sergeant Pollack coughed and scratched his beard. "Any idee who it might be?"

"No, but the list is narrowing. I'm going to think about it some more. I hope to have a solid suggestion by noon tomorrow."

"How you gonna to do that?"

"Well, you've already prepared me a list of those who knew Bishop was in the National Hotel and that we were after him. I'll make a list of all those who knew David was in Chicago. There'll likely only be a few names on both lists. Then we begin to zero in on each one of those names."

"Don't forget the two of us will be on both lists."

"Not me, Sergeant. I didn't know we had Bishop cornered until the next morning. And I don't think you're our man."

Sergeant Pollack laughed and stood up. "Well, we can't afford to overlook anyone, or trust anyone. Sir, you've had a long hard day, what with almost gettin' killed and all and ridin' the long way into Washington in a snowstorm. Why don't you get some supper and go to bed. You can trap our Rebel spy tomorrow."

"I'm more interested in seeing Ellie than getting supper right now. I have some cheese and summer sausage back in my room. I think I'll call on her and just take a snack before I go to bed."

"Lieutenant, anytime you'd rather call on a lady friend than take a good meal at Willard's, you're in love."

Sam grinned at the Sergeant's suggestion. "Yes, Sergeant, I am. And right now that fact is just about the only thing that makes any sense in my life."

After the Sergeant left Sam looked at the list Sergeant Pollack had prepared of all those in the headquarters who knew about the move against Bishop at the National Hotel. First he eliminated those who couldn't be the traitor for one reason or another, Major Wright, Captain Freeman, Sergeant Pollack. They were all "solid," no need to suspect them, despite the Sergeant's warning to trust no one. Then there were the six men who were on surveillance duty that night, they hadn't any opportunity to leave their posts to warn anyone. That left Sergeant Henry, the duty sergeant that night, Corporals Olen and Gatens, who were on another "tail" that night but had learned of the Bishop caper, and Private Selvern, who just "happened" by and then didn't stick around for the finish.

Selvern. He was the man! Had to be. A Maine man, from along the coast, a fisherman. Quiet, aloof, no real friends in the organization. Yes, it had to be Selvern. Now if he is just on the list of those who know David is in Chicago and why.

He began compiling that list. Sergeant Pollack, Major Wright, Lieutenant Arnold, who took care of tickets and other transportation matters; Captain Freeman, the paymaster who would have provided David with expense money; Sergeant Post, Captain Freeman's assistant; and the clerks in the adjutant's office who cut orders and kept the duty roster, Privates Selvern, Cappadocia and Cantley. There were four names on this list which were also on the first list: Sergeant Pollack, Major Wright, Captain Freeman and Private Selvern. It had to be Selvern! Tomorrow, Sam decided, he would go after Selvern with a vengance.

Twenty minutes later Sam was standing on the stoop at Ellie's house, rapping on the door knocker. Her mother answered the door and it seemed to Sam that she was actually glad to see him.

"Good evening, Lieutenant Reid. Ellie has been wondering where you were. In fact, she's been quite concerned about you. Come in."

Ellie shouted down the stairs. "Is that Sam? Is he all right?"

She burst into the room and grabbed Sam. She was sobbing. "Oh, Sam darling. I was so worried about you. So afraid something might have happened to you. Oh please, let's get married. I can't wait any longer!"

Mrs. Richards broke in. "Ellie! There will be no talk of a wedding until this war is over or Lieutenant Reid is discharged from the army. It is out of the question."

Ellie was clinging to Sam. "Oh, Mamma. You don't understand."

"Yes I do. I know how you feel. But you've no business getting married to a soldier." She turned to Sam. "You've had a difficult trip I imagine. Have you had supper?"

"No ma'am. But I'm really not hungry. I'll grab a bite back at my room."

"Nonsense. I'll warm up something for you."

When Mrs. Richards left the parlor Ellie pulled Sam down on the horsehair sofa and kissed him passionately.

"What if your mother should walk in?"

"She'll see us. That's all. I'm sure she doesn't think we're sitting in here holding hands and discussing Shakespeare. Come here."

Again and again she kissed him, her mouth soft and moist as she sought out Sam's. After a while Sam ran his hand down inside her dress and caressed her breasts softly. Soon her nipples were hard and tense and Ellie was breathing deeply and rhythmically. Then she began to moan softly. "Oh Sam. Oh that feels so good I can hardly stand it. Oh, please don't stop. Don't stop!

They parted abruptly at the sound of Mrs. Richards' footsteps coming through the dining room. Sam's supper was ready, she said, and he could take it in the kitchen where it was warmer.

It was ordinary fare, but as hungry as Sam was it seemed like the best of Willard's meals. He speared a thick slab of sugar-cured ham, dipped in the "soppings" that had settled at the bottom of his plate, and placed it in his mouth. Next he scooped up a forkful of fried potatoes mingled with thinly-sliced onions fried in butter. Occasionally he washed the food down with a swallow of the thick milk from the gray ironstone pitcher that sat in the center of the table.

Ellie watched him adoringly, touching him occasionally with her soft fingertips as if to assure herself he was alive. From the living room they could hear the soft clacking of Mrs. Richards' knitting needles.

Sam told Ellie about his journey through lower Maryland, leaving out the brief episode with Kate Huntt at Tee Bee and glossing over the nighttime visit by the stranger at Lloyd's Tavern. Then he stopped eating and took her hands.

"But I think I've put it all together. I think I know what the Rebs are up to. They're out to capture President Lincoln! And tomorrow I'm going to ask Colonel Baker to get a warning to the President."

"But why would they want to capture President Lincoln?"

"So they can force us to resume prisoner exchanges with the South. It's their only hope to raise more men."

Ellie smiled. "I hope Colonel Baker appreciates what you went through to find all this out."

"Colonel Baker never appreciates anything. He's a grabber. He takes what comes his way. If he likes it he grabs it and says it's his. If I'm right, or if he thinks I'm right, he'll take my warning to the White House and pretend it was all his idea. But that's the way things are. If I'm right I don't care who gets the credit."

Ellie leaned over and kissed him warmly on the lips and in a moment they were standing, locked together in an embrace. Sam's hands sought out Ellie's breasts again and in his haste he scratched her slightly.

She jerked backward and then fell against him, laughing. "Sam, you poor awkward dear. You'll probably fall out of bed on our wedding night."

Sam grinned, embarrassed.

The door knocker's raucous pounding interrupted them. "Damn," Ellie said. "Damn such timing." Sam looked at her with surprise. She grinned. "I'm sorry, darling. Forgive my language. But I wanted you to get back in my dress again."

Private Jesse McKenzie of Major Wright's staff was at the door with a message for Sam: "Lieutenant Reid, you'd best return to the office at once. Urgent!" It was signed, "Sergeant Angus Pollack."

Sam followed Private McKenzie back to the headquarters at a slow run. Once inside the building he vaulted past him and bounded up the stairs to Sergeant Pollack's office. The Sergeant was seated in a rickety chair with a broken cane bottom. He was ashen-faced.

"Bad news, sir. Here, read this." He handed Sam a telegram.

"Headquarters, Nat'l. Det. Police
Washington, D. C.

Provost Marshal,
Camp Douglas, Illinois
February 22, 1865.

The body of Lt. David Petersen was discovered late this evening in his room at the Palmer House. He had been stabbed several times by an unknown assailant. Please notify where body is to be sent. Personal effects will be returned to your office for examination before delivery to next of kin.

Charles R. Elliott
Captain and Provost Marshal"

Sam handed the paper back to Sergeant Pollack and walked slowly down the hall to his office. He sat down at David's desk and stared at the wall. The image of the knife-wielding man in the corner bedroom at Lloyds Tavern kept flashing before him. He shivered and drew himself up. If there had ever been any question, it was now settled. The Rebels were playing a fast game, and they were playing for keeps. Poor David had paid with his life. Now, by God it was the Rebels' turn to suffer. In this painful moment he felt a little better about having killed Captain Archie Miller.

He shouted for the messenger. When the boy appeared, Sam spoke softly but with a voice tinged with anger. "Get me Private Louis Selvern's file. And if you tell anyone that I've asked to see it, I'll have you in the Old Capitol within an hour."

The boy blanched. Everyone knew that the Old Capitol – the building that had served as the nation's capitol after the British had burned Washington in the War of 1812 – was now a harsh prison maintained to house anyone who fell on the wrong side of the federal government. He shook his head.

"I ain't tellin' nobody nothin'. No sir!"

"Good," Sam replied. "Now get on your way."

Chapter 19

Tuesday, February 21

Booth looked again at the ad in the Washington *Star*. "George. Mother died on the 11th. Rosa." Simple. And very effective. They'd be here at 11:00 a.m. If he were to throw off his Yankee pursuers he had best move fast.

He walked to the lobby with a small carpetbag and sent one of the bellmen for a hack.

Often if he were going out of town for only a day or so, he didn't bother to check out of the hotel. So the hotel clerk thought nothing when he saw Booth enter the lobby with his luggage.

Neither did the small, balding man who had been reading a paper near the stairs, where he could see anyone coming down from the second floor and could follow him from the hotel.

The train station was dark and cold and its new inauguration coat of paint added little cheer. Booth bought a one-way ticket to Baltimore from a bored clerk whose neck bore the evidence in cinders of the past twelve hours' arrivals and departures of the monstrous wood-fired steam engines. A lame newsboy was swinging through the waiting room on crutches and Booth bought a *National Intelligencer* from him. The news was all bad. Sheridan was heading up the Shenandoah Valley again, this time with a force of ten thousand men. Against him the South had only Jubal Early with two weakened brigades and a few pieces of artillery. If Sheridan should push Early aside, as seemed probable from the *Intelligencer* account, he would be at Lee's rear and Richmond would surely fall.

Lee needed every man he could get. It was so bad that the Confederate Congress was debating using slaves as soldiers, granting freedom to those who fought. Who would have thought it four years ago?

Booth folded the newspaper and stuffed it into his carpetbag. If General Lee can just hold on a little longer, he thought, he'll soon have all the men he needs. The very possibility buoyed him and he whistled softly as he stood by the track.

Shortly before 7:30 he boarded a dingy wooden car and took a seat near the coal stove that squatted in the aisle in the center of the car. At precisely 7:30 the train chugged out of the station. At that moment Booth looked back toward the train platform. The man who had been following him since he had left the National Hotel was walking back into the waiting room.

One mile north of the city the train stopped at the little village of Ivy City. Just as it was pulling out of the station Booth stepped off, entered the tiny depot, and inquired of the stationmaster where he could rent a horse. The community had no stable but at the undertaker's shop at the corner of Central Avenue and Main Street the owner was willing to rent a small bay mare for two dollars. Booth removed the old newspapers from his carpetbag, stuffed the bag into a saddlebag, and rode off for Washington followed by the undertaker's son who was to lead the horse back to Ivy City.

Back in the city he tied his horse at the 6th Street entrance to the National, tipped the undertaker's son a quarter, and walked up to the second floor, keeping out of sight of the front desk.

As he turned the corner at the head of the stairs and walked toward his room, which was only a few steps from the stairs, Booth heard voices coming from his room. Without hesitating he walked past the room to a broom closet about halfway down the hall. He opened the door, stepped in and pulled the door closed, leaving just a crack through which he could keep watch over the door to his room.

After about fifteen minutes three men in uniform, one an officer and the other two enlisted men, emerged from the room and went down the stairs. Booth stood quietly for another five minutes and then slipped out of the closet and walked directly to his room.

He was in Baltimore now as far as the Yankees knew. They had undoubtedly finished searching his room and would not be likely to return, so that in a strange way this room was now the safest place in all Washington for the conspirators to meet. Booth almost laughed at the thought that the Yankees had themselves "consecrated" his room as a safe meeting place for the little band of plotters who were going to bring down their government.

He looked about quickly. There was nothing suspicious in sight. Even yesterday's *Star* was not open to the *Personals*, though if it had been it would have told the northern detectives nothing.

Booth hastily cleared away the newspapers he had strewn about and by the time Michael O'Laughlen arrived shortly before eleven the room was ready for the meeting. Within five minutes or so Noah Dyer and Davy Herold had also shown up. Booth introduced Dyer around and Noah immediately took over.

He quickly sketched the plan to kidnap the President on the road to the Soldiers' Home, described the relays of horses that were waiting in lower Maryland, and showed them a small map of the Potomac on which the three possible crossing sites were marked. The others were quiet and there were no questions. Booth watched Mike O'Laughlen as the plan was revealed to the group. The seedy little man never changed his expression. Either he had figured it out for himself or he had long ago ceased being surprised by anything. Booth decided it was most likely the latter.

Noah had folded the map and was talking again. "There are still three men to join us. When they're all ready you'll be called together again. You'll receive a message reading 'Dr. Ashley will see you at such and such an hour.' When you get that message, go to 541 H Street, that's a boarding house run by Mrs. Mary Surratt, and ask to see 'John.' Be there one hour before the time stated in the message."

Noah stopped talking and began coughing violently. When he finished he spit into a brass spittoon that sat at the foot of the bed. "At our next meeting we'll run through the final details of the plan and you'll each receive your assignments. Any questions?"

There were none.

"All right," Noah continued, "in the meantime I want you all to stay out of trouble. Don't do anything to draw attention to yourselves."

Mike O'Laughlen spoke. "Ah . . . when will we be getting some money to support us while we wait?" He looked at Booth. "I still have some money Wilkes gave me but with the prices in this city it won't last long."

Noah reached into his pocket and pulled out a small leather pouch. He untied it and dumped a pile of gold coins into his hand. "Here's a $20 gold piece for each of you. It's Confederate Secret Service funds, so go easy." Everyone but Booth took a coin.

Chapter 20

Tuesday, February 21

"Louis A. Selvern, Pvt., Company K, 20 Reg't., Maine Infantry (Lafayette Rifles). Enrolled July 16, 1861, Bangor, Maine, for three years. Injured (gunshot wound, thumb of right hand) December 13, 1862, Fredericksburg, Virginia. Treated in hospital there until December 27, 1862, when transferred to army hospital in Philadelphia, Pennsylvania. Reported absent without leave February 19, 1863. Restored to duty, April 18, 1863, assigned to National Detective Police."

Sam looked up from the file and stared into the fire. "Absent without leave. Paydirt! A deserter. The sonofabitch ran away. Obviously he can't be trusted."

He turned back to the file. There was a letter in Selvern's hand, addressed to a Captain J. A. Collins.

"Ellsworth, Maine, March 2, 1863

Capt. Collins Dear Sir -

Knowing it to be an impossibility to get near you to speak to you, I have thought I would do the next best which is to write to you. I am a member of Co. K, 20th Maine Vols, & was wounded at Fredericksburg, had my right thumb shot off at the first joint - was sent to Philadelphia Hospital & while there I was sick all the time. While lying there on a sick bed I heard of the death of my youngest brother, from wounds rec'd, at Bull Run. Also of the death of another bro, from wounds rec'd, on the peninsula, and yet another bro, sick in the Hospital at Washington. Do you wonder that I got discouraged & that I came home? I had no influential friends to get me a furlough or discharge & so I came without, & did not leave the hospital because I was a coward & did not want to fight (for I have been in Eight battles & done my duty). But because I knew I should never get well so long as I staid in the hospital. I have been feeling better since I came home, but I am not fit for duty now & I am afraid I never shall be again. I cannot use my hand yet, & I have a terrible pain in my side & chest.

I have written this much because I knew you could not understand my situation without. I would like to have you tell me what to do, if you will. Had I not better come down to Philadelphia & be examined by Surgeon General Dale? I hope to receive a note from you if you are not too busy.

Yours Respectfully,
/s/ Louis A. Selvern
Ellsworth, Maine

Capt. J. A. Collins
Washington City

Sam thumbed through the rest of the file. There was nothing but the routine listings of "Present for Duty" and a medical certificate describing Selvern: "Born in Ellsworth, Maine, is 22 years of age, 5 feet 6 inches tall, Sandy complexion. Blue eyes, Light hair and by occupation when enlisted a freight master. Wounds received: gunshot wound right thumb. Not disabling."

Sergeant Pollack was writing something when Sam entered his office. The Sergeant turned the paper over and started to stand up. Sam motioned for him to stay seated.

"What do you know about this man, Sergeant?"

The Sergeant took the file from Sam and opened it."Oh, you mean Private Selvern? Well, actually not too much. He's been pretty quiet since he came to work here. Why?"

"Well, for one thing, he's on both of my lists."

"What lists?"

"The list of those who knew Bishop was with Booth at the National Hotel and that we were going to try to catch him and the list of those who knew David was on his way to Chicago."

The Sergeant thought for a moment. "You think he's our man? Why don't you ask Major Wright what he thinks. Company K of the 20th Maine, that was his old company."

Major Wright's old company? Sam took the file from the Sergeant and walked back up the hallway to the Major's office. Captain John Lynburn, another Maine man and Major Wright's assistant, was, as usual, guarding the way into the Major's office.

Lynburn was, in the minds of most of the officers and men of Department II, a perfect ass. He was competent enough in his narrow field of endeavor, as a stockbroker before the war, but he was totally at sea in any situation that called for grace or tact or even minimal understanding of human nature. As a soldier he delighted in calling men of subordinate rank to task for the most trivial of infractions. Moreover, he took special pleasure in conducting his "dressing down" sessions in front of others. Sam never saw Captain Lynburn without recalling the time he had stopped him and Ellie on the street and pointed out that one of Sam's uniform buttons was unbuttoned.

"Good evening Captain. Is the Major in?"

"Yes, but he's very busy. What do you need to see him about?"

"Something I've been working on for the Major. A confidential matter."

"Confidential? Come, come. There are no secrets among us. Is it about Bishop?"

Sam raised his voice so the Major would hear him. "No, it's not. But it is important and I do have to see the Major."

Captain Lynburn's smile turned to a hard glare. He spoke softly but with a tone of harshness. "Lieutenant, you'll not see Major Wright until I decide . . . ."

The door flew open and Major Wright leaned his head out. What's the problem here?"

"No problem," Sam said quickly. "I was just explaining to the captain that I needed to see you."

"Sure, come on in." The Major swung the door open and Sam walked into his office, throwing a superior smile at Captain Lynburn.

Major Wright sat quietly and chewed on a huge cud of tobacco as Sam explained his concern about Private Selvern. "Sergeant Pollack told me to come see you about Selvern. He said Company K of the 20th Maine was your old company."

The Major spit his cud into the brass cuspidor at the side of his desk and wiped his chin on his shirt sleeve. "That's a pretty good piece of detective work you did there, son. Only Selvern ain't your man."

"Well, sir, he's on both lists and he deserted once, he can't be too loyal and trustworthy."

"Deserted? Selvern? He didn't desert, he ran away home. There's a hell of a difference between running off home and deserting. Look at that medical report. Notice anything funny about his wound?"

"It's minor, not the sort of thing you'd think would lay you up for long. It says 'not disabling.'"

The Major took out a fresh chew and crammed it into his mouth. "It's self-inflicted! The boy did it to himself. He shot his own thumb off!"

"Why that's a court-martial offense."

"Yes, I suppose it is. But not to anyone who was with the 20th Maine at Fredericksburg. Those poor devils were part of French's Division that crossed the Rappahannock on the pontoons on the 12th of December. They spent that night trying to sleep on the frozen ground, huddled up beside what was left of the town's houses after our artillery had helped drive the Rebel sharp-shooters out. The next morning they lined up in the streets and when the fog finally lifted that stupid jackass Burnside marched them straight out of town and up towards the stone wall where the whole goddamned Rebel army commenced picking them off one by one. And the ones that weren't picked off by rifle fire were blown to hell and back by the Rebel cannons."

"Them that weren't killed right off dropped to the ground and laid there 'til dark when they could finally crawl back into Fredericksburg. Out of over two hundred men of the 20th Maine who went against the stone wall that morning, only seventy-six weren't killed or wounded."

The Major stood up and pointed at Sam. "Can you calculate that, boy? That's better'n sixty percent casualties."

"Was Selvern one of them?"

"No. He was right there, in the thick of it like he had been in seven battles before, but he wasn't hurt. Boys all about him were blown to bits, guts shot away, faces smashed in, heads ripped off, but he wasn't touched. That night was as cold as a well-digger's ass again and the boys had to sleep on the cold, frozen ground like the night before. Late that night the rumor spread that Burnside was sendin' them back against the stone wall again the next morning."

The Major turned and picked up the poker and stirred in the fire. "It was too much for the boy. He took his musket and walked out into the dark and shot his right thumb off. They put him in a hospital set up in a warehouse in Fredericksburg and a week or so later he was shipped off to the army hospital in Philadelphia. There he got some kind of fever and when he wasn't getting over it he just up and left, took the train to Bangor and walked home to Ellsworth."

"I'd just been assigned to duty with Colonel Baker when this happened. The boy's pa, Moses Selvern, I've known him all my life, he didn't know this Captain Collins who took over command of Company K, so he sent me this letter Louis had wrote for his pa to send to Captain Collins. I wired back to send Louis to Washington to see me and I'd fix him up."

He put the poker back and sat down in his chair. "And I did. Got him assigned here and he's been here ever since. Maybe that's not much to go on but, take my word for it, Louis Selvern ain't your traitor. He's quiet and he's moody and I reckon he's still ashamed of what he done. And he don't have any friends. But he's no traitor."

Sam took the file from off the Major's desk and closed it. "Your word's good enough for me, sir. If you say he's no traitor, I believe it."

"But you still think he's a coward, don't you?" The Major was staring at Sam.

"Yessir, I guess I do. I mean, well . . . he disabled himself on the night before a battle was expected and then he ran away from the hospital .What else would you call it?"

"I'd say he just might be the bravest man in this headquarters, Lieutenant. He's seen more fightin' than anybody else here. Most of us here are re-cycled clerks or worn-down cops or, at the most, veterans of one or two battles. You ever hear about my great heroism off the coast of Maine?"

Sam nodded. "Yessir, I heard."

"You know why I was so brave? 'Cause I was scared shitless that if I didn't find those fellows off my fishing boat they'd string me up in town for skippering a boat that sank. So I stayed out there all day, wore my hands raw rowin' back and forth and bawled like a baby. When the fellow that was with me told about my bawlin' everyone said it was a sign of how deeply I felt for those poor damned bastards that drowned. Well, maybe so, but mostly I was bawlin' because I was scared."

"When the war broke out I joined the 2nd Maine and at Bull Run, you know why I didn't break and run like hundreds of others did that day? Because I was too scared. I knew if I ever started running I'd never stop 'til I got to Maine. So I stayed and they made me a hero. Then, when the 20th Maine was organized in August '62 I raised a company and joined the regiment as a captain. A hero. Hah!"

"No sir, Lieutenant, bravery ain't cooly stayin' behind and takin' on the enemy single-handed. Bravery is bein' so scared you piss yourself and you try to run but your legs won't work. When the poor sonofabitch who ain't as scared as you runs and is called a coward and you stay behind and become a hero, pissed-in pants and all."

"Well, son, the difference between Private Selvern and me is he ain't as scared as me. Don't underestimate him. He's no traitor and he ain't no coward. No, I reckon you'd best look somewhere else on your list for your traitor. Truth is, it's probably someone you least suspect and someone who may not even be on your list. That's the trouble with this spy business, son. It ain't like runnin' a store. Neat little lists and logical conclusions don't count for much. The man we want is probably someone you wouldn't suspect in a thousand years. That's why we ain't caught him yet."

Chapter 21

Tuesday, February 21

Noah was cold by the time he arrived at the high-walled mansion at the foot of 17th Street where Bishop kept a safe house. As always, the cold aggravated his lungs and intensified his coughing. This time it was so bad that he had to stop at the gate house and rest for a few minutes before walking the last few feet to the main house.

Bishop was waiting for him, pacing the floor anxiously. "Thank God, you're here, Noah.

I was afraid the Yankees might have gobbled all of you up. Are you sure you weren't followed?"

"No, we weren't followed. The Yankees didn't even know what we were up to. Wilkes Booth is a bit more clever than I gave him credit for." He explained to Bishop how Booth had "left town" and shaken his "tail."

Bishop laughed. "Good. Very good. Now, what about the others at the meeting, the men Booth's brought into the plot?"

"There were two," Noah began. "I stayed for a few minutes after everyone had left and asked Wilkes about them. I think he was very clever in who he picked, that is if they're everything Wilkes says they are."

He stopped and coughed. "This blasted consumption. It's about to get me down. Where was I? Oh, yes. The two men. There is Davy Herold, a short fellow, stocky, about your size, G.W. Dark hair, quiet. At least he was quiet today. Smokes cigars. I gather he got his cigars from Wilkes. At least

Wilkes gave him a handful as he was leaving. He used to be a pharmacist's apprentice so he knows something about chloroform and poisons. Also knows the roads in lower Maryland. So we got 'two for one' with Davy, a guide through Maryland and a man who can handle chloroform."

"And then there's Mike O'Laughlen. He looks like a drunk to me. A short, thick-chested Irish banty rooster. Frankly, I think he's the weak link. Just the sort of man to get drunk and blabber everything. I complained to Wilkes about him. Wilkes says he does drink and whore around but he'll keep his mouth shut. Says he's been active in the underground in Baltimore the past two years with no problems. His cover is that he's a deserter from our army. I'm still not sold on him but Wilkes says he's more reliable than he looks."

"Where's Davy Herold from?"

"Here in Washington. Grew up near the Navy Yard. His father was a mechanic there before he died."

"What's your over-all impression, Noah?"

"They'll do, G.W. I'd just as soon not have Mike O'Laughlen involved but Davy will be fine. And I suspect Mike is probably harmless."

Bishop stretched out on the bed, hands locked behind his head, and stared at the ceiling. "I'm not so sure I like the sound of Mike O'Laughlen either. Let's keep an eye on him and if we have to, we'll remove him."

"Remove him?"

"Yes. We're playing for big stakes. A drunk like Mike O'Laughlen is not very important in the overall scheme of things."

"G.W., you're talking about a human life. First you order Lieutenant Reid's death, now you off-handedly talk about 'removing' Mike O'Laughlen. Doesn't it bother you?"

"No, not at all. I do what I have to do. This is war, Noah, not a theology class. And we can't ever forget that Reid took the life of Archie Miller – never forget that. Which brings me to another problem. I have learned that

Lieutenant Reid outsmarted Thomas Harbin in the Surrattsville Tavern the other night. Harbin tried to stab him but Reid was ready and nearly shot Harbin. Reid's back in the city safe and sound."

"That's bad for us, isn't it, G.W.?"

"Well, Reid knows I'm in town, that I've got relays of horses between here and the Potomac, and that we're after big game. But he doesn't know we're after Lincoln. And Lincoln's too much of a democrat to want to travel about surrounded by a cavalry escort. Remember the beating he took in the press when he slipped into Washington in the middle of the night in 1861?"

"Yes. I see your point. But I still don't like it."

"Neither do I. And what we're going to do is this. First we - you and I - are going to get rid of Reid. Then, we're going to lead the Yankees to believe we're up to something else instead of capturing Lincoln."

Noah raised his hands in protest. "Now, wait a minute, G.W. I'm no killer. I'm not certain I can help you do away with Lieutenant Reid . . . I just don't know, G.W."

Bishop stood up and walked to the window overlooking the courtyard of the estate. "Noah, I have it all figured out. We really won't have much to do with it. We'll just lead him to kill himself."

Noah stared at him with a puzzled look.

"Reid's no dummy," Bishop continued. "He wants to solve this puzzle and he wants to capture me. So, we'll just concentrate on his desire to grab me and lead him into a trap. We'll invite him to come to Lizzie Walker's house at 13th Street and the City Canal. The letter we send him will invite him to come if he wants to 'learn something about the whereabouts of Captain Bishop.' If we write the letter like the one Baker's detectives got telling them I was in town, you know, the one signed 'a f-r-e-n-d,' I think Reid will be curious enough to come."

Noah lay back on the bed. He closed his eyes and coughed three or four times. "What if he shows the note to others in the headquarters and the whole force comes out to greet us?"

Bishop turned toward the bed. "We'll be across the street in the Wolf's Den, watching Reid come up. If my plan works we won't even go into Lizzie's until he's dead."

Noah opened his eyes. "The Wolf's Den?"

"You know, the whorehouse run by Mrs. Wolfe. The boys from General Hooker's Division nicknamed it the 'Wolf's Den.'"

"Well, how you going to kill him?

Bishop stared at Noah. "We're going to poison him."

"Poison him. You're not serious."

"Yes I am. You just watch what happens."

-o-

It was quiet at Lizzie Walker's house when Davy Herold knocked on the door the following afternoon. Lizzie herself answered the door.

Davy flashed a simple grin at the large blowzy-haired woman. "Cap'n Bishop said I was to come here and talk with Mrs. Walker and Miss Western."

"Oh, yes. I'm Mrs. Walker. Come on in, but be quiet. Most of the girls are still asleep."

His eyes opened in amazement as he took in the flashy, overdone elegance of what was one of the city's "finer" whore houses. He had never seen such richly-done furniture as the crimson satin settees and chairs that were scattered about the large parlor on his left and the smaller sitting room to his right.

And the paintings. They were supposed to be copies of works by Titian and Peter Paul Reubens. But to Davy they were merely "neckid women" whose pink skin added a welcome light touch to rooms dominated by red satin upholstery, dark floral striped wallpaper and ornately carved rosewood and mahogany.

Mrs. Walker nodded toward the smaller parlor. “You can wait in there. I’ll get Katie.”

A few minutes later she was back with a younger woman who had obviously just crawled out of bed. “This here’s Katie Western. I don’t think I ever got your name.”

Davy stood up, grinning. “I’m Davy, ah David Herold.”

Mrs. Walker gestured toward the sack Davy was carrying.

“That the stuff?”

“Yes’m. White arsenic. ‘Nuff to kill a horse.”

“Well, lets go to the kitchen and get this over with.”

In the kitchen Davy took the 6-ounce bottle of poison and poured it into a crock of sasparilla. He stirred it carefully, then sniffed the crock. “No smell. Hardly got no taste, either. Here, see for yourself about the smell.”

Mrs. Walker sniffed the crock, then Katie leaned over and took a deep breath. As she did so Davy could see down her robe where two large white breasts swung freely. His eyes were riveted on those breasts. When Katie straightened up Davy was grinning broadly and his face was blood red.

Finally he spoke. “Now, you’d best put this in a safe place where no one else will drink it by mistake.”

“We’ll put it outside,” Mrs. Walker said.

Quickly Davy picked up the crock and handed it to Katie. Then he followed her across the room and opened the back door. He watched grinning as Katie bent forward and set the crock on a flat rock by the back stoop. When she had straightened up Davy told her, “You’d best cover the crock with something heavy.”

“Yes, you’re right.” She walked back into the kitchen and returned with a heavy saucer which she bent forward and placed atop the crook as Davy stood, transfixed, staring at her breasts.

Back in the kitchen Katie asked Davy: "How much will it take to kill him?"

"A glass. Maybe two. Give him two if you can get him to take it."

"When will he begin to feel the effects?"

"Maybe after an hour."

"How do we know he'll stay here that long?"

Davy quickly reached into his pocket. "Here. I forgot. Give this letter to him when he gets here. It tells him the man he was to meet here will be late and he is to wait for a while. Actually we don't care whether he stays here and dies. All we care about is that he gets enough poison in his innards to do him in. He can die in Lincoln's bedroom for all we care."

"How am I expected to keep him here if he won't wait and doesn't want to drink a sasparilla?"

"Well, ma'am," Davy began awkwardly. "You . . . ah . . . you might bend over and show him your tits, sort of 'by accident', you know. Bet he'd want to stay around then." Then he added hastily, "That was Captain Bishop's idea. He said to tell you."

Katie laughed. "Show him my tits, huh? Well, if that's what Captain Bishop wants, that's what I'll do. Why not? Anyone can see them for two dollars anyway."

Davy was grinning as he walked out of the house and up 13th Street. He was now in the midst of "Hooker's Division," so named because the men of General Joseph Hooker were the most infamous clients of the low life there. As he walked among the whore houses and cheap dives of the region he was surprised to see Noah Dyer walking toward the City Canal.

Noah was dressed in an elegant fur-trimmed overcoat and carried an expensive silver-headed cane. He was, to the casual observer, a wealthy young man out for a bit of sport among the fleshpots of the capital. Davy nodded and smiled at Noah, who returned the greeting with a barely perceptible nod and a soft-spoken "Good evening." Davy turned and watched as Noah walked to the end of 13th Street and entered the "Wolf's Den," a whore house situated directly across from Mrs. Walker's house.

Mrs. Wolfe was a short, fat little woman who smiled nervously and preened herself constantly, patting her hair and brushing at her robe in short, spasmodic gestures. She walked unsteadily on tender feet, complained of her ailments and drank to excess.

But she knew how to please a man and her girls were instructed in all the arts of carnal pleasure. She nodded at the elegantly-dressed young man who stood in the doorway.

"Please come in. Shall I call the girls down?"

"No. I want to arrange a private party for later tonight."

"A private party. What do you have in mind?"

"I want to rent the two rooms overlooking 13th Street from 9:30 to 11:00 tonight."

Mrs. Wolfe looked puzzled. "Two rooms? How many girls?"

Noah blushed. He thought for a moment. Best to have a girl in each room, in case the place were raided. "Two. One in each room. I'll leave the choice to you. How much will the rooms be? I'll pay you now."

My girls get two dollars a throw. Takes about a half hour each. You'll be using the rooms for three half hours. That'll be six dollars for each room. If you want drinks or anything, that'll be extra."

Noah broke into a coughing fit. When he had finished he handed Mrs. Wolfe two Twenty Dollar gold pieces. "That should take care of it, Mrs. Wolfe. The extra Ten Dollars is for your silence. I'd rather no one knew about our little party."

"Sir, I won't tell no one. Come 9:30 them rooms'll be yours with a girl in each. Won't you have a drink before you go?"

Noah started coughing again. "No thank you," he gasped and hurried into the street. Thank God for that coughing fit, he thought as he hurried to put Hooker's Division behind him. At least it got me out of that wicked woman's parlor.

-0-

Around 7:30 that evening Bishop walked to a streetcar stop on Seventh Avenue where Norton was waiting.

"He hasn't told anyone in the headquarters about the letter," Norton said softly. "He left for supper around 5:30 and said nothing about coming back."

Bishop nodded. "Good. It looks like he's coming alone." Then he looked at Norton, searching out his eyes in the dim flicker of the gas street light. "You're sure no one knows about the letter?"

Norton stared back, eyes hard. "Of course I'm sure. Don't you think I know my business? If the boy had told anyone I would know about it."

Bishop turned and walked away, out G Street to 12th, and then turned left. As he neared the third house on the left he slowed down and looked toward the dining room window. The fern in the red clay pot was sitting on the left side of the window. It wasn't safe to enter! He quickened his pace and walked past the house without as much as a glance.

After he had gone fifty feet or so he crossed the street and walked back up the opposite side to where he could see the dining room window with the red clay pot and fern. There he stepped under a pair of wooden stairs leading to a second story entranceway and watched the house across the street. After about a half hour a shadowy figure emerged and walked briskly down the street. As Bishop watched the fern in the window was moved to the center of the window. When he was certain that the street was empty, Bishop quickly walked across the street and rapped with the door knocker.

The door was opened and Bishop stepped into the tiny hallway. "I'm in quite a hurry," he said without ceremony. "Has Lt. Reid told anyone at Baker's headquarters about his invitation?"

"No, not a thing. Were you expecting something specific?"

"Not really," Bishop replied. "In fact since you don't have any news for me, that tells me what I wanted to know."

He left abruptly and hurried to the "Wolf's Den." Noah and Davy were already there in the rooms overlooking Mrs. Walker's place, along with two painted girls who were quite curious about what was going on - or what wasn't going on. Davy was staring at the girls, grinning broadly, but Noah was obviously uncomfortable.

"Well," Bishop announced, "he's told no one. He'll be here alone." He looked at the two girls, then at Noah, and smiled.

"What are they doing here, Noah? You have a little fun planned for later?"

Noah blushed. "For God's sake, G.W., you know better than that. I thought it would be less suspicious if we had girls up here. They're paid for."

"Paid for? Sort of a shame to let them go to waste, isn't it? But we have work to do. Why don't you girls wait in the next room."

When the girls were gone Bishop turned to Davy Herold. "Davy, I want you to go outside and wait at the edge of the canal where you can see up 13th Street and up and down the canal. Take this cigar and when you see him coming light it and walk back into this house. Don't let him see that you're watching him."

Davy went outside and stood where Bishop had told him. Around a quarter after ten he started motioning toward the window.

"I'll go see what he wants," Noah said. He walked outside the Wolf's Den and came over to the edge of the canal.

"What is it, boy? What do you want?"

"I'm cold, Noah. Freezin' my ass off. How long I got to wait here?"

"Not much longer, Davy. He'll be along soon. Just remember to light your cigar when you spot him. Then you can come on inside."

"And if there's time, can I screw one of them girls?"

"We'll see," Noah replied as he headed back into the house.

Davy blew on his hands and rubbed them together.

Then, far up 13th Street, barely discernible in the gay lights playing out of the fleshpots of Hooker's Division, was the figure of a young man. Davy reached for his match and cigar.

Chapter 22

Tuesday, February 21

The boy was around nine or ten, black, shabbily dressed, and he was very scared.

"Don't be frightened, son," Sam said quietly. "I'm not going to hurt you. I just want to ask some questions. Why don't you come up here and sit by the fire where it's warmer."

The boy moved a little closer to the fireplace, not close enough to make any difference in warmth but close enough to be considered obedient to the Lieutenant's request. But he did not sit down.

"What's your name?"

"Thurston Humes."

"Where do you live, Thurston?"

"With my grandmammy in Hooker's Division, near the Ma'sh Market."

"Who gave you this letter?"

"A man."

"What did he look like?"

"I dunno. Just like a man, a white man."

"Had you ever seen him before?"

"No."

"Where did he give you the letter?"

"On the Avenue, near the Market."

Sam sighed. It would be hard to get anything out of this boy. "Did he have a beard?"

"No. "

"Mustache?"

"Yes."

"Was he short or tall?"

"Tall, and skinny."

"What color was his hair?"

"Light, or dark. I don't remember. He wore a hat."

"What else was he wearing?"

"Dark suit."

"Was there anything unusual about the man?"

"No."

"What did he say when he gave you this letter?"

"He said to bring it to the War Department Annex on 17th Street and give it to Lieutenant Reid. Nobody else. Had to go to Lieutenant Reid. Made me repeat it."

"That's all?"

"Yeah. Oh, and he gave me a nickel."

Sam smiled, reached into his pocket and pulled out a quarter. "Do you see this, Thurston?"

The boy nodded his head.

"Know what it is?"

"Un huh. It's a quarter." "Thurston, I'm going to give you this quarter *if* you can remember anything about this man that was different."

"Different?"

"Yes. Like he had a bad eye or no left hand or walked funny, something like that."

"Well, he didn't have no bad eye or nothin' like that. But he coughed a lot."

"He coughed a lot?"

"Yeah, like he was sick."

Sam held out the quarter. "Anything else you remember?"

"Uh uh. Just that he coughed a lot."

"All right, here's your quarter."

The boy grabbed the quarter and dashed from the room. Sam sat down and read the letter again.

"Lt. Reid,

> Captan Bishop nos you are on to him so be careful. but if you want som information that will lead to his whereabouts, be at Lizzie Walker's whorehouse at 13thStreet and city canal in hookers Division at ten tonite. I warn you - you must com alone for my safty. If anyone else from Baker's detectives is seen in hokers division tonite our meeting is off.
>
> a Frend."

Sam took the first letter from "a Frend" out of the file, the one that told about Bishop being in the city, and compared the two. The handwriting was different but they were signed the same way. And the first letter had been accurate. Bishop was in the city, and his appearance was as the letter had said. Moreover, both letters were awkwardly done, with poor spelling and the characters laboriously done, as if the writer were not at home with a pen and paper. Sam decided that he could not afford to miss this chance to capture Captain Bishop. Ignoring the difference in handwriting, he stuffed the letter into his uniform jacket and mentioned it to no one.

After supper he called on Ellie. He tried to keep the conversation light and trifling, but Ellie quickly sensed that he was preoccupied.

"What's wrong, Darlin'? Why are you so quiet?" Ellie ran her fingers up the back of his neck and played with his hair.

"Nothing's wrong. I've just had a long, hard day. I'm tired. That's all."

Ellie drew back and her lips formed into a pout. "No, something's bothering you. I know you too well for you to fool me. And I don't appreciate being kept uninformed if the man I love is troubled."

Sam leaned forward and kissed her on the cheek. "Ellie dear, if anything were bothering me, you'd be the first to know it. The fact is I've had a long, mind-numbing day where nothing much happened but I'm tired. That's all there is to the 'mystery' you're worrying about." He took her hands in his. That had been such an easy lie. He remembered the bold-faced lie he had told Kate Huntt about his mythical uncle in Point Lookout. There must be something to the old saying that each lie you tell makes the next one easier.

Back in his room he changed into a dark wool sweater layered over two wool shirts. He removed his .44 caliber Army Colt from beneath the wool underwear in the bottom drawer of his dresser and checked the pistol carefully. It was a good weapon, solid and dependable. Like most Northern officers, Sam would have preferred the smaller .36 caliber Navy Colt. Still, you took what you were issued or you bought a substitute. As seldom as he had use for a pistol, Sam wasn't about to buy one just because it was one inch shorter and one ounce lighter than the perfectly good one he had been issued.

Then he brought out a small, single-shot derringer that he had purchased shortly after joining the Detectives. He remembered how serious and purposeful he had felt carrying this tiny weapon in his first weeks on the job. Lately, however, he had left it in the drawer.

After checking the derringer thoroughly he stuffed it into the inside top of his left boot and slid the revolver into his trouser waistband. Then he pulled on a soft felt cap, a joke gift from one of Captain Summers' "tramps", and started to leave the room.

He stopped at the door and took the letter out of the pocket of his trousers and lay it carefully across the bed, where it would be readily seen if someone should miss him and come looking. Then he closed the door behind him and headed for the ramshackle part of the city known as Hooker's Division.

As he made his way down toward the Canal an old sense of excitement gripped him, a feeling he had not experienced since the days before the war when his father's place outside Steubenville had served as a stop on the Underground Railroad. For a moment he imagined himself back there again, standing on the bank of the Ohio signaling to a boatload of runaway slaves coming across the river from Virginia's Northern Panhandle.

He remembered the advice his father had always given him: "Always approach a secret rendezvous from an unexpected direction." Tonight Pa would be proud.

At the boat basin at the foot of 11th Street the grubby little German was waiting with the boat Sam had rented just before supper.

"Ach. Here you are. Vot you vant vis dis boat I don't imagine? But here it is. You got the udder two dollars?"

Sam paid the man the remainder of the rent for the boat and shoved off into the canal. Quietly and invisibly, in the pitch black of the moonless night, he rowed toward the foot of 13th Street. The whore houses and saloons of Hooker's Division were ablaze with gas lights, tinkling pianos and raucous laughter.

Near the foot of 13th Street he glided his boat up to the brick wall that lined the canal and carefully peeked over the side toward the house kept by Lizzie Walker. A few feet away two men were talking, their gestures punctuated by the steam that rose from their lips and faded into the chilly night air.

Sam could only hear part of their conversation. The tall man, who wore a thick, drooping mustache and was elegantly dressed, called the shorter man "Davy." Davy was obviously taking orders from the tall man for he kept nodding his head and saying "yessir." The tall man pointed up 13th Street and said something that sounded like "light a signal when you see Lieutenant Reid coming." That didn't make sense to Sam but the fact that HE was the subject of this particular conversation stunned him.

The tall man began coughing violently. He motioned to Davy that he was leaving and walked into the house across the street from Lizzie Walker's. Davy remained at his post, watching intently up 13th Street for any sign of Sam.

Sam thought for a moment. A tall man with a mustache who coughed a lot sent the invitation to Lizzie Walker's. Now a tall man with a mustache who coughed a lot has a man watching here for him. Whoever was waiting for him was now watching this Davy for a signal.

Sam pushed softly against the wall of the canal but the boat was caught up in the current of the stream. Frantically he pushed against the slime-covered brick wall of the canal, trying to stop the boat's steady drift toward Davy. But it was no use, the boat was drifting closer to Davy. The boat was almost even with Davy when it slapped hard against the canal wall.

Davy turned instantly. "What the hell . . . !"

Without hesitation Sam lunged at Davy. He grabbed him by the ankles and pulled hard. Davy tried to jerk away, lost his balance, and flipped over the edge of the canal, crashing into the boat. Sam dived at him. Davy was still off balance and a bit dazed. He swung at Sam, a feeble blow that didn't come close to landing. Sam got his right hand under Davy's shoulder, threw himself down in the boat and pushed with all his might.

Davy rolled away and sat up, sideways in the boat. He grabbed for Sam and his left hand caught Sam's sweater. Now Sam was off balance, being pulled toward Davy. Davy swung his right fist and caught Sam in the temple with a staggering blow that sent him reeling backward in the rocking boat. Then Davy leaped for him and Sam brought his knees up to his chest, and planted his feet in Davy's chest as the boy lunged forward. With a mighty effort Sam straightened his legs and Davy was sent rolling out of the boat in a backward flip, a great plume of water rising as he hit the surface of the canal.

Quickly Sam sat up, grabbed the oars and started rowing furiously toward the Potomac. Behind him Davy was screaming, "Help! I can't swim! Help!"

Someone yelled at Davy: "Stand up, you dumb sonofabitch! The canal ain't that deep." Still the boy splashed about and continued screaming.

Suddenly Sam was aware of someone running alongside the canal. Ahead of him, at 14th Street, a wooden bridge crossed the canal. Since a man on foot could make better time than Sam could in the boat he realized he would be cut off at the bridge. So he suddenly veered toward the island. When the boat banged against the brick wall of the island, Sam scrambled over the wall and disappeared into the bushes.

He crashed through the underbrush, half crawling at times, until he was fifty yards or so from the canal. Then he burrowed under a low bush and lay still, curled up in a ball, suppressing even his body's desire to breathe deeply. He lay there for at least a half hour, shivering violently and listening to the sounds of men searching the bushes and shouting from over in Hooker's Division.

Gradually the commotion died down. Still Sam waited silently. Finally he stood up and began walking quietly up the island toward the Capitol. On his right the red-turreted castle of the Smithsonian Institution loomed against the night sky.

He had gone about a hundred yards when he heard a twig snap. Before he could reach his pistol a voice said: "Stop where you are or you are a dead man," and a shadowy figure stepped out from behind a low shed in front of him.

Chapter 23

Tuesday, February 21

The heavy, sodden atmosphere of the deep of night had long since settled over Richmond when Elizabeth Van Lew slipped out of the rear door of her family's elegant mansion on Church Hill. Quickly she made her way down the gravel path, past the garden and the family privy and out onto 24th Street. Only the soft crunch of her feet on the frozen, rutted street betrayed her presence.

Behind her, his small frame wrapped in a ridiculously oversized overcoat, came Joshua Dancey, seemingly oblivious to the noise of his shuffling boots. Josh had been a slave until Elizabeth Van Lew and her mother had freed all the family's slaves shortly after the death of Elizabeth's father in 1860. He had gone north immediately but returned to Richmond in 1861 at Elizabeth's request to help in the spy network Elizabeth had established in the Confederate capital. As a "free black" Josh had the run of the city and he became a familiar sight in the wartime capital, his diminuitive body dressed in clothes too large for him and his outfit topped by a badly-worn high silk hat that sat down on his ears. Elizabeth herself had picked out his clothing, aware that the more outlandish he looked, the less the citizens of Richmond would be likely to take him seriously. Ostensibly he was the Van Lew servant, a comical caricature of a "darkey" to whom no one paid attention. But beneath his grinning, outrageous facade, Josh was, like his former owner, a clever enemy agent who was content to be thought a fool so long as it meant he got the job done.

As they crossed Broad Street Elizabeth stopped and leaned up to Josh's ear. "For Lord's sake, boy. Lift your feet. Do you want to wake up the entire city?"

"Yes'm," Josh replied without changing expression.

From the southeast came a low rumble, like the sound of rolling thunder. Artillery. They both looked in the direction of the sound. But they could see nothing.

At the brow of the hill Elizabeth stopped again. Josh approached and put his head near hers. "You sure the paper's still in your heel?" Elizabeth asked.

Josh nodded. "Yes'm. That heel won't come off less'n I pry it off."

"All right. And if you lose your boot or if the message is ruined somehow and you have to deliver it personally - what is the message?"

"'Steadfast' says Cap'n Bishop's mission in Washington is to kidnap President Linkum."

"And if they ask you how I know this for certain?"

"I tell 'em you got it from a 'high official in the War Department.'"

"Good," Elizabeth said softly. She put her hand on the boy's shoulder. "Now remember what I told you. Follow Osborne's Old Turnpike until where it crosses Allmound Creek. That's about a mile south of here. Then follow the creek away from the river. You'll be heading east - toward the sunrise. The creek is broad and deep and it passes between our works. After about two miles it comes onto the Darby Road - what we used to call the Central Road. You know the road I mean?"

Josh shook his head vigorously. "Yes'm. I knows the road. Used to go out that road to Cornelia's Creek to gig frogs."

"Well, take that road south. You should come on a Yankee patrol before too long. Ask to be taken to see the general in command. They'll likely make fun of you but tell them you have a message from a Union spy in Richmond. Act dignified and insist on seeing the general. That way you'll at least get to see an officer."

"If you move fast you could be on the Darby Road by noon. If any of our people stop you, you know what to say."

"Yes'm, I'm Captain Walker's servant, from Drewry's Bluff Battery. He sent me into Richmond and I got lost comin' back and now I can't find the James River no matter how far east I go."

Elizabeth nodded her head. "Yes. They'll laugh and carry on and tell you you're already east of the river. Play the dumb darkie role. When they send you back toward Richmond, double back and keep going southeast. Now, be on your way, Joshua."

"Yes'm. Don't worry about me none. I can make it."

Elizabeth looked at the boy, trying to discern the outline of his face in the dark. "You have to make it, Joshua. I've never sent a more important message out of Richmond. It's so important I can't wait until my next contact from General Grant."

The boy nodded and then turned and walked down the hill toward Cary Street and Osborne's Old Turnpike.

Elizabeth watched him as long as she could see him. Then she stood for a while looking in the direction of the sound of the guns. After a while the guns grew quiet and Elizabeth wearily made her way back to the big mansion on Church Hill.

It was all up to Joshua now. Somehow, Elizabeth thought, it was fitting that a black boy, born to slavery, should be the one to carry the message out of Richmond that might save President Lincoln.

Chapter 24

Tuesday, February 21

Sam froze in his steps at the man's command and raised his hands slowly, trying desperately all the while to assess the situation, to learn if the man were alone, how he was armed - anything that he could use to his advantage. Suddenly a second man stepped up behind him, frisked him quickly, pulled his revolver from his waistband and shoved him roughly to the ground.

The night was dark but the island received enough light from "Hooker's Division" across the canal for Sam to make out a ragged man holding a short club menacingly over him. He couldn't see the man who had shoved him from behind but the two were probably members of one of the gangs of toughs who lived on the island and preyed on each other and on any outsiders who ventured near. There appeared to be only two of them. That was a break.

The man in front spoke. "Give us your money, your watch and anything else you got on you that's worth anything."

"I don't have any money," Sam replied softly.

"Don't give me that shit!" the man screamed at him. He swung the club fiercely and Sam raised his left arm to deflect the blow. A searing pain surged through his arm as the club struck and Sam rolled back under a thick bush. The man flailed at the bush with the club, beating it apart savagely.

Desperately Sam pulled his legs up and drew himself further under the bushes. His left arm was throbbing now and practically useless. There was a flash of light and a loud crash. The man behind him had fired the revolver! Sam could smell the gunpowder and feel the heat of the explosion but, miraculously, the man had missed him.

With his right arm Sam frantically tore at his left trouser leg. He reached the boot top and clawed for the derringer. His hand closed around it and he withdrew it. The swings were getting closer. A piece of the disintegrating bush slapped him in the face and Sam instinctively grabbed at his face with his right hand. At that moment the derringer went scooting off under the bush to the right. Desperately, he crawled after the gun.

The man with the revolver fired again. Once more he missed, but the muzzle's brief flash reflected off the shiny barrel of the derringer. Sam grabbed the weapon, screamed out, and lay motionless, keeping the derringer tightly in his right hand.

"You got him, Jake," the man with the club said. "Hurry up and search his body and see what he's got on him. Then let's get the hell outa here."

The man with the pistol leaned forward, grabbed Sam by the sweater and rolled him over onto his back. In one quick movement Sam cocked the derringer, swung his hand toward the man and pulled the trigger. The man was only inches from Sam when the derringer exploded in his face. He screamed, dropped the revolver, grabbed his face and fell backward. Sam dropped the derringer, grabbed the revolver with his right hand and turned toward the man with the club. He had vanished.

Sam crawled back under the bush and waited for a moment, listening for some indication of where the other man could be. Off in the distance he could hear someone running, crashing through the brush in a great hurry. That would be the man with the club.

Flooded with a sense of relief, Sam was aware for the first time of the great pain in his left arm. He felt it and moved his hand and wrist. Thank

God it wasn't broken, just horribly bruised. Slowly and painfully, Sam dragged himself out of the bushes and started back up the island toward the Capitol. By the time he had reached his room his arm was so swollen Sam could hardly move it.

-0-

The Colonel was angry. It seemed to Sam that was the only emotion he ever saw Colonel Baker display these days. "Well, how's my 'master spy' this morning? Or would you rather keep it to yourself like you did you brilliant plans for Saturday night." He fixed a hard eye on Sam and pointed his finger at him. "Lieutenant, you're lucky you didn't get your ass shot off the other night. I know about the two bullet holes in your clothing. And, of course everyone knows your left arm is practically useless. You can't hide that. You're lucky. DAMNED lucky!"

"Yessir, I know that. But I'm fine, considering the circumstances. And as to why I didn't tell anyone about Saturday night, someone in this headquarters is spying for the Rebs. I thought the only chance I had to get Bishop would be to keep my own counsel." ("Keep my own counsel." Sam liked that. Maybe he was getting better at standing up to Colonel Baker.)

"Keeping your own counsel doesn't work in this business, Lieutenant. I know we have a leak in our headquarters - anyone but a simpleton would know that - but the way to find the leak is to give different information to different people and see what gets out. Now you've bummed up your left arm, we've lost our chance to catch whoever was after you and some poor bastard on the island is dead with your derringer bullet buried behind his face."

Sam's eyes dropped to the floor. "Yes, I know he's dead. I guess that shouldn't bother me, being a soldier and all, but it does. I don't know that I'll ever get comfortable killing."

"Well, you have killed two men now. It will get easier with each one. Sit down, son."

Sam sagged slowly into a thick, battered leather chair by the window overlooking Pennsylvania Avenue. Outside he could see a dreary line of Rebel prisoners, dressed in shabby butternut and bits of captured Northern uniforms, shuffling up the Avenue toward the Old Capitol. Most of them were officers, captives from Lee's army. They looked despondent - the way Sam felt.

"Lieutenant, you've been given a very important assignment. Just how important we don't know because you haven't been able to find out what Captain Bishop's up to . . . ."

"Sir, I'm convinced he's . . . ." Sam interrupted.

The Colonel raised his hands, palms toward Sam. "I've heard your ridiculous theory. Just shut up until I'm finished. I'll tell you when you can talk."

Sam sank further down into the chair. "Yessir."

"You spent, how many days was it? Four, five, it doesn't really matter, in lower Maryland, almost got yourself killed, and learned what? That Bishop's gathering boats and horses for some unknown mission that is probably set to come off here in Washington. We already knew that before you left."

"You openly revealed yourself and your mission to the postmaster at Bryantown, right in the heart of the most Secesh country in Maryland. The rest of the time you wandered about snooping so obviously that only a child under the age of three would not have known you were a Federal spy. Now you come back with some fanciful theory that the Rebs plan to kidnap President Lincoln, a theory based on nothing but your own wild imagination."

The Colonel leaned back in his chair, clasped his hands behind his head, and dropped his voice to a whisper. "What am I going to do with you? Your imagination can cook up Rebel plots at will but doesn't seem to be any help at all in helping you learn how to do this job."

There was a long silence. The Colonel obviously expected a comment from Sam.

"Sir, I can understand why you may be reluctant to accept my theory that President Lincoln is the target of the Rebel plot. But, even if I'm wrong, what do we lose by warning the President and providing him some protection? He oughtn't go about unprotected anyway."

Baker leaned forward in his chair and jabbed his index finger at Sam. "What we lose, Lieutenant Reid, is my credibility with the President. I'm his top spy. I don't feed him a bunch of misleading, outrageous bullshit like that little fool Allan Pinkerton used to give McClellan. When I go to him, it's with facts, not wild-ass theories!"

"Well, Colonel, it seems to me that at times a good spy will have to theorize - based on the facts mind you. That's what I've done. I may have fumbled all over lower Maryland but I stand by my facts and my theories. I think the President is in danger." Sam was proud of the way he had stood up to the Colonel. Now he braced himself for the Colonel's response.

It was surprisingly mild. "And I don't think he's in danger, Lieutenant. But if I was you and felt the way you do, I'd get me some facts to back up my theories. Because I'm not going to the White House with any half-baked warning for the President. Do you understand me?"

That was a statement, not a question. But Sam nodded his head in response.

Out on the Avenue again, Sam threaded his way through the crowds of business men, soldiers and early morning shoppers who filled the sidewalks. On impulse he walked up 15th Street to Lafayette Square and strolled in front of the White House. He stopped and stared at the building for a long time. Like the nation itself, the White House made itself out to be a bit more than it was. White-painted and pretentious, it was surrounded on three sides by low-sided sheds and greenhouses which straggled out toward the War and Navy Department buildings that shared the President's Park. The park was fenced but the fence was little more than an ornament to keep Tad Lincoln's goat from wandering off. There were no guards at the gates and anyone who wished could stroll at will across the grounds. The leader of the most powerful nation in the New World sat inside that building virtually unprotected, a perfect target for an enemy who was determined and willing to take a minimal risk.

Sergeant Pollack was waiting for him at the office, aware that he had just been called before the irate Colonel. "Sir, Lieutenant Petersen's things arrived from Chicago. I know you probably don't feel like it, but you should go through them and see if there's anything we can learn."

"Yes," Sam replied flatly. "I'll do that now." His arm hurt again, throbbing and aching where he had taken the club's blow. Thank God, however, it wasn't broken. That was all he needed now, to have an arm amputated.

David's effects were wrapped in a small bundle and laid on his desk. Sam untied the bundle and moved the contents, item by item, to his own desk. The clothing told him nothing. There was $12.86 in gold and silver and a $20 Greenback. A small map of Chicago was marked in ink showing, Sam supposed, David's routes around the city. Finally, there was a tiny, leather-bound diary. Sam opened the book and commenced to read at the point where David had left for Chicago.

"Feby. 17. Pittsburgh. Took evening train for Chicago. Cold, damp, altogether dreary ride. Feet nearly froze. Passengers mostly soldiers on leave and a few wives obviously on their way to or from a visit to a wounded husband, sat silent and morose. Cold and miserable, I fit right in."

"Feby. 19. Chicago. The wind off Lake Michigan makes this the coldest, most uncomfortable city I've ever been in. Lodged at Palmer House on arrival at 7:00 p.m. Elegant hotel - puts Willards to shame. Dined tonight on Lake Michigan bass. Feet warm and stomach full at last. Things are getting better."

"Feby. 20. Chicago. Unsatisfactory meeting with commandant of Camp Douglas. Rumors abound that Rebels plan 'something' against the camp. But the commandant, a short, swarthy man named Marantz, declines to take them seriously. Told me his small garrison from the Invalids Corps could withstand any rabble the Rebs could throw against him. Maybe so. But I doubt it. After dinner I visited the city's police chief to see what he knew of the rumors of Rebel activity in the city. I think the chief was offended that I would ask him such a thing - as if I were attacking him personally. He claimed not to know of a single Rebel in the city."

"Feby. 21. Chicago. Back at Camp Douglas again today. The Provost Marshal there says Rebel prisoners are talking of uprisings in camps all across the North to coincide with the inauguration. The prisoners are excited, confident. They talk of going home soon - of a resumption of prisoner exchange. My room was searched today while I was out. Professionally done, but they didn't replace my stockings the way I had them. They could have found nothing but I wonder why it was done."

Sam looked at David's cluttered desk. It was hard to believe that David could have been orderly enough to keep track of how his stockings were stored. Maybe it was the strange city and his sense of being alone there. It probably brought out the professional in him. Still, the thought of David as a professional spy made Sam smile.

"Feby. 22. Chicago. Washington's Birthday. The city is decked with flags and bunting, whipping in the wind, but I don't feel very cheerful. I am being followed by at least two men, maybe more. Telegraphed Sam of my findings and inquired of other suspicions. I am now convinced that what I suspected when I left Washington is true - Sam is our 'leak.' He is being betrayed. He will be reluctant to believe it but the proof is on my desk. I leave tomorrow for Washington, thank God."

The diary ended there. Sam stared at that last entry dumbfounded. *I am the leak?* How could that be? He took the diary and placed it in the saddlebags that hung on the coat rack by the door. Then he sat down at David's desk and began to study everything there, item by item. Dinnertime came and went and Sam never moved from the desk. By mid-afternoon he had read everything there at least twice.

Like his own desk, David's desk was cluttered with papers and memorabilia. There were pages of *personals* from the New York *Daily News* and Washington *Star*, many with ads circled in red pencil. Sam read every item that David had marked. Some were pure gibberish, like the one from the December 2, 1864, *Daily News;* "Courageous. The flag of splendor has been sent away. Forthright." Others, like the one from the February 14, 1865, *Star*, were clear messages but might hold a double meaning: "Eleanor. Your old teacher will call on you next week." And still others had obvious military meaning, if that meaning could only be deciphered. An ad from the February 4, 1865, *Star* was typical of this sort: "Paul. The movement will commence the day after your birthday. The objective is the third name on the list. Edwin."

Then there was an ad in the February 6, 1865, *Daily News* that intrigued Sam: Andrew. Our man suspects nothing. Shall I send him to the well again? Robinson." THAT might be it.

There were also the intercepted letters. Sam carefully scrutinized all of them - there were twenty-four - paying particular attention to the possibility that they might contain a hidden message decipherable by a grill, as had the letter about the horses and boats in lower Maryland.

Finally, Sam read again every scrap of writing in David's handwriting, paying particular attention to his working papers and David's notes to himself about the probable meaning of this message or that letter. Still, there was nothing, unless the message to "Andrew" was what he was looking for.

Around 4:00 he gave up, leaned back in his chair and stared at the ceiling for a long time, trying to think about what, in all the mass of papers he had just studied, might point toward him as the department's leak to the enemy.

It was there somewhere. David had said it was and David was precise about those things. The question *was*, which item?

At 4:30 Sergeant Pollack strolled by. "Find anything important in Lieutenant Petersen's belongin's, sir?"

Sam thought for a moment. No, Sergeant Pollack could not be the leak. "Yes," he said. He walked over to the coat rack and pulled out the diary. "Something very disturbing. Here, read this last entry in his diary. Then you see if you can find what he's talking about on his desk."

Slowly and deliberately the Sergeant read the diary entry, lips moving and murmuring softly. As he handed the book back to Sam a frown crossed his face. "Why don't you go on to supper, sir. I'm not hungry and I'll go over his desk myself while I'm all alone here. If'n I find anything, I'll send for you."

When Sam had gone Sergeant Pollack wrote out a brief note describing what Lieutenant Petersen's diary entry had said. He ended the note with, "I will go over Lieutenant Petersen's desk with great care to see if I can learn what evidence he refers to. It is, of course, most important that this information not fall into the wrong hands." Then he sealed the paper, wrote an address on the outside, and called for the messenger boy.

When the boy had left, Sergeant Pollack began a careful and methodical search of David Petersen's desk.

Chapter 25

Wednesday, February 22

It was about 2:00 p.m. when Bishop crossed over Rock Creek into Georgetown, the oldest inhabited section of the District, and strolled casually out Bridge Street, the city's main thoroughfare. After a bit of maneuvering he arrived at Dumbarton Street where he turned left and walked among the fashionable red brick homes to the narrow three-story brick dwelling of William Poindexter.

He rapped softly at the door and as he waited on the narrow stoop he looked up and down the tree-lined street, admiring the handsome homes and the neat, orderly setting that made this one of the most sought-after and fashionable residential areas in the District of Columbia.

A young girl, around fifteen, answered the door. Yes, her father was in. She would go get him and Bishop could have a seat in the parlor.

While he waited Bishop walked over to a small piano and glanced at the sheet music. Someone had been playing "Listen to the Mockingbird," the hauntingly beautiful melody that had been dedicated to Miss Harriet Lane, former President James Buchanan's niece and his hostess when the bachelor Buchanan was President. Idly, and somewhat unconsciously, Bishop began humming the tune under his breath.

"I see you like that piece, too," a voice said from the parlor door. "It's our family's favorite."

Bishop looked up to see a small, slightly built man in his late 50's. "Good afternoon," he said as he extended his hand. "I'm William Poindexter."

"Richard Milburn. Pleasure to meet you, sir," Bishop said, taking the man's hand. "Yes, it's a beautiful song. I think I'd rather be able to create something like that than do almost anything I can imagine."

Poindexter motioned Bishop to a settee by the piano and seated himself in a chair beside the settee. "What can I do for you, sir?"

"Are we alone?" Bishop asked, glancing toward the door.

"Yes, quite. My family is in the kitchen. It's the only room we heat in the winter. Is it too cold in here for you?"

"No, I'm quite comfortable, thank you. I want to talk with you about a matter that I suspect you may not wish to share with your family. That's why I asked if we were alone."

Poindexter's eyes narrowed. "Please come to the point."

"I understand that you are the Chief Usher at the White House."

Poindexter nodded.

"And you work from seven in the morning to seven in the evening, with Sunday's off."

"Yes, that's right."

"You're very close to the Lincolns, then. You would know something of the President's habits, would have access to his plans, would know something about those surrounding him?"

"Yes, I suppose so. But I maintain my confidences. It's the very least one should expect of the Chief Usher at the Executive Mansion. If you're here to learn anything personal about the President, I'm afraid you're wasting your time . . . and mine," He stood up to signal Bishop to leave.

"Sit down, Mr. Poindexter. I'm not finished. I want to talk about your son."

Poindexter stiffened. "You're mistaken. I have no son. Two daughters, but no son. I don't know what you're trying to do . . . ."

Bishop raised his hand, motioning Poindexter to stop talking. "Please, Mr. Poindexter. I haven't time for games. I know all about you and your son, facts I'm sure Mr. Lincoln would be shocked to learn." He pulled a piece of paper from his pocket.

Poindexter was ashen-faced. He sat back down in the chair. "Really, Mr. Milburn, you are mistaken. I have no son."

Bishop ignored Poindexter's protests. "Your son, Richard Maynard, was born in Leesburg, Virginia, on March 14, 1845. His mother was Anna Maynard, the daughter of a Baptist minister in Leesburg. When you discovered that Anna was pregnant you wanted to marry her but her father forbade it because you are Catholic."

"The birth caused quite a scandal, what with her father being a prominent clergyman and all, and you moved here to Georgetown when your son was about six weeks old. You have, to your credit, supported the child financially over the years, and have maintained as close a relationship as has been possible under the circumstances. But, so far as I can tell, no one here in the District is aware of the fact that you have a son . . . or of the much more interesting fact that your son is now a Sergeant in the Confederate States Army. I'm not even certain that your wife knows."

"She knows. And as far as I am concerned everyone who wants to can know. I'm not ashamed of Richard. I'm sure Mr. Lincoln would understand that I could have a son in the Rebel service and still be loyal to my President. After all, several of Mrs. Lincoln' family are in the Rebel army."

"Mr. Poindexter, I'm involved in a little enterprise in which I will require some inside information regarding President Lincoln.

Poindexter stood up abruptly. "Never. I would sooner die than betray the President."

Bishop looked directly at Poindexter. "You're not going to die, Mr. Poindexter. But, unless you help us, it's very possible that Richard may die." He handed Poindexter a small slip of paper. "Read it."

Poindexter unfolded the paper and read:

"War Department
Confederate States of America
February 17, 1865.

This is to certify that Sergeant Richard Maynard has been placed in 'protective custody' pending his father's cooperation with the Confederate States Secret Service.

/s/ John C. Breckinridge
Secretary of War."

He put the paper down and glared at Bishop, his nostrils flaring with anger. "Secret Service. You bastard. You thoroughgoing bastard." Tears welled up in his eyes. "What exactly do you want and what guarantees do I have that Richard will be spared?"

"What I want is complete cooperation from you in answering the questions I have and giving me the information and materials I request. As for the guarantee of your son's safety, well, my word is my bond."

"Your word, Mr. Milburn, means nothing to me. Anyone who would threaten my happiness as you just have would do anything."

"I don't think you have much choice, Mr. Poindexter. My word is the only guarantee I can offer."

"And if I let him die? Where are you then? With Richard dead you won't have anything to hold over my head."

"Ah, but Richard is not dead and I DO have that fact to, as you so quaintly put it, 'hold over your head. Now, shall we proceed to business?"

Poindexter looked at the letter from Secretary Breckinridge again. Then he spoke softly to Bishop, his voice tinged with resignation. "All right. What do you want?"

"A number of things," Bishop replied. "A dozen or so sheets of the President's stationery, a sample of Mrs. Lincoln's handwriting, a list of all White House employees and the days and hours they work, a key to the White House, a map of the family quarters in the White House and, finally, a warning if the President or any of his aides begin to suspect that the President may be in danger."

"Mr. Milburn, are you planning to assassinate the President?"

"Oh, no, not that, Mr. Poindexter. You can rest assured that no harm will come to the President because of my plans."

"When will you want all these items?"

"Tuesday evening will be quite fine. I'll be here or send someone. All you need to hear is that 'Mr. Milburn sent me.' Then it will be safe to pass the information."

Bishop stood up. "I must be going. Thank you, Mr. Poindexter, for agreeing to cooperate."

"Don't thank me. I'm cooperating ONLY to protect my son. But if ANYTHING happens to Richard, I'll follow you to the end of the earth to get my revenge. And that is not a threat, sir. That is a solemn promise."

"I quite understand. But you needn't worry. Richard is safe so long as you cooperate."

"He'd better be. He'd just better be."

-0-

When he returned to the Van Ness Mansion Bishop shaved his mustache and clipped his hair shorter. It was unlikely that Poindexter would go to the Federal detectives but there was no sense in letting them have an accurate description of him. In the future he would send someone else to pick up the information and make the demands on Poindexter.

As he was cleaning his razor and putting it away he heard a familiar voice downstairs asking for "Cap'n G. W."

Bishop rushed to the head of the stairs and called out: "William! Up here."

A tall, muscular black strode into the room, smiling broadly. He took Bishop's outstretched hand and clasped it firmly. In an age when most American blacks, slave or free, kept a low profile and always acted subservient to whites, William Noble stood tall and radiated the confidence of a man who could take care of himself under most any circumstances, and knew it. He was Captain Bishop's body servant, a slave who was owned by his master like a domestic animal. But he was no man's toady. Three times in this war and twice before it William had saved his master's life and between the two men there was a strong bond, forged in a hundred close calls and tested in a war that was about slavery itself. And when they spoke it was more like two colleagues conversing than a master and his slave.

"Cap'n., you been well?"

"Yes, William. What do you have for me?"

"A message from Mosby. His man will be in the city tonight. You're to meet him at Mrs. Surratt's boarding house. He goes by the name, 'Mosby.'"

"'Mosby'? That's not very subtle, is it?"

"That's what the man tole me, Cap'n."

Bishop nodded his head. "Any news from my folks?"

"No sir. Nothing. I reckon your pa must be all right or we would have heard."

Bishop heard Belle's footsteps coming up the stairs. He turned toward the door. "Belle, come in, sweetheart. You remember William. He's just arrived with a message from Mosby."

William nodded toward Belle. "Miss Belle, I think I met you in Richmond last winter. It was right after the big Yankee raid."

Belle looked at Bishop.

"The Dahlgren-Kilpatrick Raid. You remember, dear, they found those papers on Colonel Dahlgren's body directing him to kill the President and his cabinet."

"Oh yes. You spent most of your time consoling Mrs. Patrick Campbell, whose husband was killed in the raid." She cast a perfunctory smile at William. "Hello, William. So nice to see you again." Then she walked over to a chair by the window and sat down.

"Well, William," Bishop said, "why don't you go downstairs and let Mrs. Lomax show you to your room in the cellar. I'll talk with you later."

When the black had left Bishop turned to Belle. "Well, my pet, what have you been up to today?"

"Precious little. I strolled about for a while with Virginia, but I got tired of her silly questions. Mostly I've just been bored."

Bishop reached down and kissed the girl's pouty lips. "How about an 'afternoon delight'? We've time before supper."

"Is that all you ever think about?"

"No. I think of other things when I have to. But now I can't think of anything better." He reached inside her low-cut dress and squeezed her breast.

"Ouch! Not so hard. You're hurting me."

"There's not much room to maneuver down there, Belle. You'll just have to undress to protect yourself."

Belle stood up and put her arms around Bishop. "All right. But it had better be good."

Bishop backed away and began undressing. "Have you ever known me not to be good?"

Belle's dress dropped to the floor. "No, you're a regular stallion."

-0-

It was a clear star-lit night, cold and crisp but not uncomfortable, as Bishop walked jauntily toward his rendevouz with Mosby's man. He smiled at the memory of the afternoon's romp with Belle. That girl moaned more with pleasure than any woman he'd ever known. Everyone in the house must have heard her today. Sort of nice, though. Good advertisement in a way. Mrs. Lomax's niece, Virginia, kept staring at the two of them during supper. Maybe she's interested. Perhaps he'd best pay a bit more attention to Virginia. It shouldn't take much if the way she looked at supper was any indication.

At 541 H Street he climbed the stairs to the second story entrance. A young man with a mustache and a pompous air answered the door.

"I'm here to see a gentleman named 'Mosby.'"

"Yes, come in. I'm Louis Weichmann. I clerk at the War Department. Whom shall I tell Mr. Mosby is calling?"

Bishop looked at Weichmann. The nosy little snip, he thought. "Just tell him a friend is here. He's expecting me."

"Yes, of course. I'll tell him right away."

At that moment two women walked into the hallway. Ignoring Weichmann, Bishop turned toward the older woman and nodded slightly. "Milburn. Richard Milburn. Pleasure to meet you Mrs. Surratt."

Then Weichmann interrupted and gestured toward the younger woman. "And this is Miss Anna Surratt, the jewel of the household."

Anna shot Weichmann a "drop dead" look and nodded politely to Bishop. They were a plain pair, this mother and daughter. Mrs. Surratt was in her mid-forties, fashionably plump and wore the air of a woman who had spent too many years trying to make ends meet. Anna was in her late teens or early twenties, it was hard to tell, thin and somewhat on the "mousey" side. Bishop threw her a smile.

"I was told to meet a gentleman here tonight but I had no idea I would meet two such lovely ladies."

"That's a nice compliment, Mr. Milburn, but I'm sure my daughter alone is worthy of it," Mrs. Surratt said softly.

Before Bishop could answer Weichmann was back, announcing, like a stiff-necked butler, that Mr. Mosby would receive him in his room.

Bishop followed Weichmann down a darkened hall and up a flight of stairs to a small room under the eaves where he was introduced to his contact from Colonel John S. Mosby's command in northern Virginia. The man was large - over six feet tall - and he had the build and the bearing of a classical warrior.

He shook Bishop's hand formally and motioned for him to sit down. Then he looked directly at Weichmann, who was standing in the doorway. "You may close the door after you as you leave, Louis."

Weichmann fumbled about awkwardly for a moment and then closed the door softly and walked down the steps.

"Nosy little bastard," Mosby's man said. "Has to know everything going on in this house."

Bishop nodded. "Yes. I got that impression. Well, Mr. Mosby, what word do you bring?"

"The Colonel said I'm to be at your service, to help you in any way I can. Said I might be needed to guide a party through northern Virginia to our forces."

"Did he tell you what we would be up to?"

"No. I didn't get the impression that he knew."

Bishop quickly filled in "Mr. Mosby" on the broad outline of the plot. "Mosby's" eyes never left Bishop during the entire discussion. It was a chilling sensation. The man seemed utterly devoid of emotion.

"What's your real name, Mr. Mosby? At least you must have a more fitting name than 'Mosby.'"

"Lewis Thornton Powell. LIEUTENANT Lewis Thornton Powell."

"Well, Lieutenant Powell, what do you think of our plan?"

"I think it sounds a little unfinished."

"What do you mean, 'unfinished'?"

"What if there's shooting from the President's bodyguard? What if the President should have a cavalry escort that day? What if he won't be chloroformed? What if this fellow Davy gives him too much chloroform and kills him? What are your alternate plans? How dependable are your men if things go wrong? That's what I mean by 'unfinished.'"

"Good questions, Lieutenant. And I confess I haven't all the answers. If the guard starts shooting we can overpower him. At least two of us, three if I judge you correctly, won't be put off by a little gun play. If there's a cavalry escort, we ride on by as if we weren't interested. As for alternative plans, I haven't any."

"Don't you think you should?"

"Yes, and I'm working on that. We've a man in the White House who may be helpful in that. What about the gunpowder Colonel Mosby's supposed to get to me?"

Powell was impassive. "I guess you'll have to develop an alternate plan for that. Colonel Mosby can't get it to you."

"Good Lord, I only wanted a keg. Just enough to create a small diversion."

"Well, the Colonel can't provide it. Not even a keg. You're probably unaware of it, but the South has a shortage of gunpowder."

Bishop stroked his smooth-shaven face. "Then we'll just have to get our gunpowder somewhere else, Lieutenant Powell. It looks like you've arrived just in time to be of some help."

Chapter 26

Wednesday, February 22

A thin line of gray was pushing its way up from the horizon to the east as Joshua Dancey slowly and laboriously slogged his way upstream. My God, but the Allmound Creek was a regular river. It had been difficult going since leaving the Osborne's Old Turnpike. The banks were overgrown and littered with debris from a dozen years' floods. The creek was knee deep at its lowest and over his head as often as not. And the mud! The sucking, slimy, all-pervasive mud! It was like a gritty lard, slippery and greasy. Josh had lost count of the number of times he had slipped and fallen. But four times, he knew, he had gone completely under.

Now, as he neared the Confederate works that made up the inner line of defense of the city of Richmond there was added to Josh's burdens the necessity of being quiet. He had planned to pass through here before daylight, but the going was too rough. The whole idea of following the creek bed was to go between the Rebel breastworks. But he couldn't go lumbering through like an ox dragging a sled, at least not in broad daylight. He had to be quiet.

The icy water and the February cold were taking their toll. His feet were getting numb. But on he went, doggedly dragging upstream. He had to get through. Miss Van Lew had told him it was very important to get his message through. The written message in the heel of his shoe was ruined, of course, from being in the water so long. But he remembered the message word for word. He had to.

-0-

The sentry on the breastwork was huddled around a small, smokeless fire, trying to fend off the bitter chill of the February morning when he heard the noise. At first he wasn't sure he had heard anything. The wind was stirring a bit with the coming of dawn and he thought perhaps it was roughing up the water or causing some of the debris from the banks to fall in.

Then he heard it again - a "plunk" followed by a "splash." He grabbed his musket and leaned over the muddy earthwork, peering into the gray dawn mist.

Nothing.

Then it came again - "plunk" . . . "splash." Someone was down there, in the creek between the two works. The sentry shouted: "Halt! Who goes there?"

There was no response. Not a sound. "You. Down there in the creek. I have my rifle on you." Still nothing.

He called to the emplacement across the creek. "Will! There's someone down in the creek! Can you see them?"

Will Dixon threw off the captured Yankee blanket he had been wrapped in, rushed to the parapet, and peered into the misty ravine between the two works. His eyes raced up and down the creek but he saw nothing but muddy water, tangled thicket and mist. He yelled back to the other emplacement. "Yes, Bud. I see him."

Dan Compton gritted his teeth. The word "Bud" told him the other sentry had not spotted whoever was down there. Well, he thought, at least he thinks we've seen him. Maybe that's enough to flush him. "You down there. Come out with your hands up. We've got you in our sights."

Josh held on to the root and jammed himself against the bank,forcing himself farther under the overhanging mud-caked root system. Only his head and right hand were above water and he would surely be nearly invisible in the shadow of the overhanging bank. Those sentries were no fools. They would have fired by now if they had spotted him. He clung fast to the root and stayed absolutely still.

-0-

After about an hour the sentries gave up. Will Dixon quit first, convinced this was just another of Dan Compton's ghosts. Finally Dan left the muddy parapet and went back to the fire. The hell with it. If there is someone down there we'll hear him if he moves again. No need to miss breakfast over it.

He grabbed a small metal pot and poured into it a mixture of parched rye and acorns that had been blanched in several turns of water to remove some of the bitterness. Then he added water and commenced stirring what the boys called "Rebel Coffee." The pathetic substitute was a long way from the real thing, but at least it heated up the stomach on a cold morning.

After he had stirred the mixture thoroughly Dan set it gingerly on two rocks nudged up against the small fire which he had carefully rejuvenated. Then he slipped back into the woods for his morning constitutional.

-0-

Josh's legs were no longer aching, they were nearly numb. There was no way he could walk the rest of the way upstream to Darby Road. Very slowly he slid out from beneath the overhanging root and began pulling his body upstream by grabbing tree roots and an occasional branch. Soon he developed a system to assure that his progress would be absolutely quiet. He held onto the last solid thing he had grabbed and reached ahead and tugged slightly at the next solid-looking object. If it gave at all he looked for something else. If it didn't give he pulled himself forward slowly.

Only once did a "firm" handhold give way and it, mercifully, slid into the mud without a sound. Slowly and painfully, with the numbness in his legs spreading, Josh crawled up Allmound Creek with only his head and hands showing above the muddy waters of the stream.

It took three hours to work his way out of sight of the earthworks. When he could no longer see the works beyond the bend of the stream Josh tried to stand up. It was no use. He had no idea where his legs were down there. He would have to drag himself to the Darby Road.

-0-

Corporal Tim Kennedy of the 8th Connecticut was nervous. Two days before a patrol had been ambushed along this same road. John Stone had been killed outright and Abner Prettyman had to have his leg amputated. The Rebels had concealed themselves in the high grass along the road and fired at the little patrol as they came up the road.

Today, Tim decided, there would be no ambush. The Rebel bushwhackers would get some of their own medicine if they tried to sucker this command into playing the role of a sitting duck in a shooting gallery.

As they came to a slight bend in the road Tim raised his hand and motioned the others to stay back. The little squad spread out along the sides of the road and squatted in the high grass at the edge of the pinewoods, eyes on their corporal.

Tim crouched down in the grass on the right side of the road and waddled forward on the wet pine needles that carpeted the ground until he could see down the road. It sloped away for several hundred yards through the tall pines to a creek and then slashed its way through the pines back up the hill on the far side of the stream and passed out of sight. The dark green evergreens absorbed all the spare light of the dismal day and only the road and its grassy edges were visible at any distance. But the pines were full of underbrush, "filth" the New England farmers called it, and a soldier hiding in there could see out only slightly better than he could be seen. If there were Rebels waiting in ambush they would be in the grass at the edge of the road.

For nearly a quarter of an hour Tim watched the road, paying particular attention to the tall grass along the edge of the road. He was about to go back and motion his squad forward when the tall grass near the creek began waving and thrashing about. Then Tim saw it. A man. Most likely a Rebel soldier. No one else would have any reason to crawl along on his belly like that. The dirty sons-of-bitches were setting up another ambush.

Very carefully Tim raised his Enfield musket. He peered through the little heart-shaped peep sight and cocked the hammer. The man was crawling toward the road.

Tim carefully set the site on man's head and slowly squeezed the trigger. The rifle crack was still ringing in his ears when the smoke cleared. Down the road the Rebel was lying still, his head a shiny mass of blood and brains. After a minute or two Private Jeff Lynch camp loping up and dived in next to Tim.

"What's up, Corporal?"

"Rebel ambush, down there. I caught one of them crawling through the grass. We'll sit tight and see if any more show themselves."

After a half hour Tim turned to Private Lynch. "Go back and bring the others up. Stay on the side of the road and keep low. We're going down the road."

When they had satisfied themselves there were no Rebel soldiers around, the little squad gathered about the dead man.

"Hell, Tim, you shot a poor old darkie. Probably a slave trying to get away. Look at him, he's caked with mud. Even his boots are ruined. What do we do with him?

Tim shook his head. "Well, I thought he was a Rebel soldier. Nobody can blame me for not being careful. If he'd only stood up so I could have seen him. Toss him back in the woods there. We can't do anything for him now."

Josh Dancey's body lay stiff and contorted, face down on the forest floor as the patrol from the 8th Connecticut continued on up the road toward Richmond.

Chapter 27

Thursday, February 23

Noah, Lieutenant Powell and a third man were waiting in the upstairs room at Mrs. Surratt's house when Bishop arrived.

Powell handled the introductions. "Captain Bishop, this is John Harrison Surratt, Jr., of our courier service." Powell looked toward Surratt. "I believe you've heard of Captain Bishop."

"Yes," Surratt replied softly. "You've quite a reputation in our service, Captain."

Bishop ignored the compliment and proceeded to business. He told the little group about his meeting with Poindexter and then pulled a sheaf of papers from his inside coat pocket.

"Here's a list of employees at the White House. Look it over and see if you recognize anyone there who can help us. The days and hours after their names are when they are at work. And here's a sketch of the second floor of the White House. Poindexter has marked where Lincoln sleeps most of the time, when he's not sleeping with his son. Tad. I also have," he pulled his hand from his pocket triumphantly, "a key to the White House, though, from what I hear, the place is hardly ever locked."

Noah coughed, then asked Bishop, "G.W., are you thinking of changing our plans and picking up Lincoln at the White House?"

"No, Noah, I'm just taking advantage of the opportunity Mr. Poindexter represents. Maybe we will decide to do something in the White

House, maybe not. It just seemed to me that the more we know about Lincoln the better off we'll be."

"Are you sure we can trust this fellow Poindexter?" Noah asked.

"I think so," Bishop said. "As a precaution I've had his son placed in jail in Richmond. He's going to be pressured into writing his father and explaining that he is being held pending his cooperation. The letter's being sent to me."

"There is one other thing," Bishop continued. "I had asked for Colonel Mosby to send us a small keg of gunpowder. Lieutenant Powell says Mosby can't help us there."

Noah looked puzzled. "Gunpowder? What in the world for? You've never mentioned this before, G. W."

"I thought we might try a little diversion. Set off a keg of powder at the Treasury about the time we were grabbing Lincoln. In all the commotion no one at the White House would miss the President for a few hours. They'd assume he was at the Treasury where the excitement was."

"Isn't that a bit risky for the fellows who have to set off the explosion?"

"Well, we have to live with some risk. And even if it doesn't go off there's bound to be excitement when they grab our boys. Excitement's all we need."

Surratt, who had not said a word since the introduction, spoke up. "I like the idea. But why not do some real damage while we're at it?"

"Well, I suppose it doesn't really matter now," Noah added. "We're not going to get the powder."

Bishop smiled. "Noah, you give up too easily. We're going to steal it ourselves."

"Where from?"

"The U. S. Magazine near the poorhouse. All we need is some Yankee kepis and overcoats, a horse and wagon, and the proper order from General Halleck."

"I can get a horse and wagon," Surratt said.

"Good. I'll take care of the rest. We'll meet here tomorrow evening at 8:30. Oh, yes," he looked at Noah, "the two of us will need horses."

Bishop walked to the door. "I suppose that takes care of everything."

Noah, who had started coughing, motioned for Bishop to wait. When he had finished and spit into the small can set at the foot of the bed, he looked directly at Bishop.

"I don't like this gunpowder escapade, G. W. Seems like we're taking an unneccessary risk for something that's not vital to our real mission. Could give us all away."

"If you're afraid to try . . . ." Bishop replied.

"'Afraid?' I deserve better than that from you, G.W., after all we've been through. I'm not afraid. I just think it's too risky, that's all."

"I don't. And I'm in charge of this operation," Bishop snapped. "Sorry to be so curt, old friend, but that's how I feel and I haven't time to waste discussing it."

"Anxious to get back to one of your lady friends, are you? Well, please don't let me hold you up with silly little matters like life and death."

"Don't drag my lady friends into this . . . ." Bishop frowned.

"Yes, we certainly would have a roomful, wouldn't we?" Noah was red-faced and angry.

"Noah, I don't know what's eating you but I haven't the time or the inclination to argue over something as trivial as this. Will you be here tomorrow night or not?"

"I'll be here, on horseback. But I still think it's foolhardy."

-0-

Bishop stood in the shadows, eyes intently on the door, as Belle delivered the message to Poindexter. He was to have several sheets of War Department stationery and a sample of General Halleck's signature.

Belle would meet him at a streetcar stop on Pennsylvania Avenue shortly after he left work tomorrow. Bishop smiled as he heard Belle deliver the warning, trying to sound so fierce as she did so: "If anything goes wrong, if anyone follows me or we have the slightest reason to suspect you've told the Yankees, your son Richard will pay. Do you understand?"

Poindexter nodded wearily and closed the door.

-0-

Bishop fidgeted nervously as he waited for Belle to emerge from the National Hotel. Booth must have been home or she wouldn't be taking so long. If anyone were watching the room they would assume she was just another of the actor's girls. So that was no problem. What did bother him, though he kept trying to suppress the thought, was the possibility that Belle and Booth might, well, they just might go to bed. Booth was a notorious womanizer and Belle loved a good romp in bed. He was handsome and she just might accept his offer to make love. Ah, there she was now . . . .

He waited until he was certain that no one was following her and then started after her, keeping to the opposite side of Pennsylvania Avenue. At 11th Street he crossed over and walked up beside her.

"What did he say?"

"He'll have them there at 9:15 sharp. He said for you not to worry, there'll be so much excitement that you'll be able to walk in and take what you want."

"I doubt it'll be that easy, but it's comforting to have him so certain. It probably didn't hurt anything to have the message delivered by a beautiful woman."

"I suppose I could have offered him a reward if he promised to help." Belle smiled at Bishop.

"I'll take all the rewards you offer, sweetheart." He put his arm around her and walked to the Van Ness House through the darkened city.

-0-

Everyone was on time and the weather was pleasant enough, cold but clear. They rode in silence up Massachusetts Avenue. At Delaware Avenue the wagon clattered across the B & O tracks. Surratt, who was driving, was jostled against Powell who rode on his right on the narrow spring seat. Noah and Bishop rode behind, on horseback, in absolute silence.

Bishop was glad for the heavy Union overcoats Colonel Lomax had provided, though their warmth and the luxurious feel of the wool served as a stark reminder of how much better supplied the Yankee army was. By now Lee's soldiers were in rags and their thin butternut overcoats offered little protection against the harsh February winds.

The fit of the overcoats and kepis was pretty good, too, considering the haste with which the outfits were assembled. Only Powell's was a poor fit and that was due more to his immense size than any error in requisition. Bishop was also pleased with the epaulets with major's oak leaves that graced his greatcoat. If any problems developed with the Yankees, he could always bull his way through by asserting his rank.

He made a mental note to thank the Colonel when he got back to the Van Ness house. The overcoats were only one more example of what a key role the old man played in Bishop's whole operation in Washington. The use of his mansion as a safe house, feeding the whole lot of them when they stayed there, lending his horses at will, and all because Bishop had befriended the Colonel's son when they served together in the 3rd Virginia Cavalry. All he asked in return for his assistance was that the Rebel couriers carry his letters to and from his son, a request that Bishop attended to diligently. Yes, he thought as he pulled the greatcoat about him, the Colonel was quite a man.

Seven blocks from the magazine, where Massachusetts Avenue crossed B Street, Surratt drew the wagon over the curb and stopped. Bishop rode up beside him. Surratt opened his greatcoat and made a shelter against the wind as Bishop struck a match and looked at his watch. It was 8:58.

"We'd better wait here for about six or seven minutes. It took me eleven minutes to ride from here to the magazine this afternoon. It will probably take us a little longer with the wagon. If we leave at five after nine we should get there a minute or so after the commotion starts.

No one spoke. The two horses pulling the wagons snorted and stamped their feet. And the minutes slowly ticked away.

It was 9:04 when Bishop checked the time again. "Let's go," he said softly, and the party rode off slowly.

Massachusetts Avenue ended at the huge fenced lot that held the jail, almshouse, workhouse and magazine. The party turned right on East 19th Street and rode toward the river and the magazine which sprawled across the lower part of the enclosure. As they neared the workhouse, a grubby three-story brick building situated at the corner of E and West 19th Streets, there was an explosion on the river off the point opposite the magazine. A man's voice screamed out across the water and flames licked up from a small boat. The party turned left by the workhouse and rode up to the iron gate where two sentries guarded the entrance to the magazine. Both men were out in the street, looking in the direction of the river.

Powell shouted at the soldiers. "Hello! Open the gates. We have a load of powder to pick up."

One of the sentries ran to the gate and swung it open. The party rode forward a few feet and stopped again. Powell handed the soldiers a paper and the man carried it to the guard hut and read it in the dim light of a lantern. Then he turned and spoke to Powell.

"What's 'Old Brains' want with twenty kegs of gunpowder?"

"I don't ask generals what they want when they give me an order," Powell replied. "General Halleck's aide gave me those orders and told us to transfer the gunpowder from here to the arsenal at Greenleaf's Point. That's what we intend to do. Now, may we please have the powder?" Behind him, Noah coughed violently and spit into the street.

The screams from the river were growing louder and the flames continued to leap up from the small boat. The soldiers looked toward the river. "I reckon everyone's busy watching that fire right now."

"Then get someone's attention and load the wagon," Powell snapped.

Bishop rode up beside Powell. "What's the matter here, sergeant?" he said.

Powell pointed toward the sentry. "Sir, this man says we can't have the powder because everyone is busy watching the river!"

"I didn't say you couldn't have your goddamned powder," the soldier replied. He turned to the other sentry. "Here, Jake, get two or three men and load twenty kegs of gunpowder on this here wagon. These men are in a hurry." Then the soldier stepped back and saluted as the party rolled into the Magazine grounds.

Fifteen minutes later they were on their way back up Massachusetts Avenue. The commotion on the river had died down shortly before they left the Magazine but everyone was interested in hearing the story from the men who had rowed out to rescue the man in the burning boat and no one paid the four bogus Yankees any heed.

The soldiers were convulsed with laughter at the description of the boatload of pitch that suddenly exploded when the occupant of the boat had decided to light a cigar. Fortunately there was another boat nearby, manned by a friend of the first boatman, and the occupant of the burning boat was able to leave his flaming skiff and get away to the safety of his friend's boat. There was little the soldiers could do except laugh and watch the barrel of pitch blaze away. No one seemed to question why a man would keep a barrel of pitch uncovered, why he would be so careless with matches around it or why his friend would be beside him in an otherwise empty boat.

Bishop could hardly conceal his elation at the success of their little mission. "Booth said he'd have a show on the river and he sure did. Herold and O'Laughlen were all right. They sure came through in a pinch, eh Noah?"

"Very lucky." He began coughing again and Bishop rode ahead. He drew up beside the wagon and spoke to Powell. "Well, what did you think, Lieutenant? Pretty nice little operation, wasn't it?"

"Yes," Powell replied matter-of-factly. "It came off the way it should have. But we still have to get the stuff hidden and get off the streets. I'll feel better then."

Disappointed that no one seemed to share his excitement, Bishop dropped back beside Noah, who was still coughing, and rode in silence. At West 18th Street the wagon turned left off Massachusetts Avenue and headed south toward B Street, the river and the old Van Ness mansion at the foot of 17th Street.

Colonel Lomax opened the huge iron gate and the wagon rumbled into the courtyard. Surratt maneuvered the wagon so it was hidden from the street by the brick wall that surrounded the mansion and the four of them, joined by Bishop's man William, began wrestling with the twenty kegs of gunpowder. William had brought a lantern with him and in the crazily flickering light of the two lanterns the men rolled the kegs, all clearly marked "gunpowder," into the carriage house and bolted the door securely, taking great care to keep the lanterns and their flames from the powder.

When they were finished Surratt and Powell drove the wagon to the ice house at the foot of Congress Street in Georgetown. Then they picked up their rented horses and rode back to the boarding house at 541 H Street.

By the time Surratt and Powell were back at their boarding house Bishop had been asleep nearly an hour in the second floor corner room of the Van Ness House. In the basement of the house William slept soundly too, wrapped in two thick blankets piled on a bed of straw.

Chapter 28

Saturday, February 25

It was the same dream he had had for the past three nights. He was at the office. David came in wearing a deadly serious expression. He walked over to Sam and stood there crying. Between sobs Sam could hear him saying, "You've been betrayed. Your family has betrayed you. Your stepmother has finally succeeded in turning your father against you. They've given all our secrets to the enemy."

Sam had jumped up screaming that it couldn't be so, yet he knew it was true. Anna Clarke Reid hated him. To her he was a constant reminder of her husband's first wife. Finally she had conceived a way to destroy him, she would betray him to the enemy.

David, who had turned into Colonel Baker, stopped crying. He was staring now, hard, quizzically. "You're going to hang, Lieutenant! You haven't captured Captain Bishop and now you've been our leak to the enemy. We're going to hang you!"

Desperately Sam sought to scream out. He worked his jaws and yelled with all his might. But nothing came out. He was paralyzed. Finally, with all his might, he broke his body free. His arms flailed about and he screamed out, "No! No! . . . ! No" His right hand slapped against the bedpost.

-0-

For a moment he was filled with relief that it was all a dream. He wasn't going to hang after all. Then he remembered David's diary entry. He WAS the leak. And he had not been able to figure out how, despite his going over every item on David's desk a hundred times. Sergeant Pollack too was stumped. The whole thing was very depressing.

He thought of his dream. Anna would never betray him to the enemy. He didn't even think she hated him. Resented him, yes, at least she had as long as he was living at home. But now, in a curious way, since she had her own child by Nathaniel Reid and Sam was no longer home, he sensed that Anna had warmed toward him. She had even added a brief note to his father's last letter, telling him how well the peach tree he had planted when he was nine was doing and how much little Clarke enjoyed "Sammy's peaches."

That had been a long time ago, at least eight months, for Nathaniel Reid wasn't much of a correspondent. Even so, she HAD added the note and it said volumes to Sam about the improvement in the often difficult personal relationship he had experienced with his family since his mother's death.

-0-

The dream still haunted him as he went over the papers on David's desk once again. He knew he had to find out what David had been talking about, for time was running out.

There was still only one paper that made any sense at all and Sam had concluded it must be the message David had referred to. It was the ad in the February 6 edition of the *Daily News*. "Andrew. Our man suspects nothing. Shall I send him to the well again? Robinson."

That HAD to be it. But what did it mean? Who were "Andrew" and "Robinson"? Why were they sending him "to the well" again? It was all very confusing and depressing.

He got up from his desk and walked across the hallway to John Burke's office. John was in Department V, Internal Security. He and Sam rarely talked business. Mostly they just consoled one another about the difficulties of being one of Baker's detectives. John was twenty-three, Sam's age, a relative newcomer to the headquarters and, like Sam, he was burdened with a constant sense of inadequacy.

John was very busy when Sam walked in, reading telegrams and scratching notes furiously. Sam walked over to the fireplace and backed up against it. "What's all the excitement about?"

"Twenty kegs of gunpowder were stolen from the Magazine last night. Colonel Baker's about to shit himself. Major Campbell put me on it. Like always, we're looking up a lot of dark alleys."

"Have you come up with anything yet?"

"No, not much. They were dressed in our uniforms and carried orders on War Department stationery signed by General Halleck. Just before they rode up a small boat exploded in the river and everyone was watching it. We don't know whether that was just a coincidence or if it was part of the plan."

Sam turned around and faced the fire. "I don't believe in coincidence any more. At least not until I've ruled out every other possibility." He smiled and looked around at John. "I guess this place is finally winning me over. I'm becoming hard and suspicious."

"Here, read these statements we took from the soldiers who dealt with these men last night. Maybe your hard and suspicious mind will spot something I missed." He handed Sam a sheaf of papers.

Sam read them carefully. It was a well-executed operation. One item caught his eye. A Corporal Bennett, one of the sentries, said in his statement: "One of the men on horseback, a tall thin man, coughed a lot, like he had the consumption."

Sam stared at the fire. The tall, thin man with the cough. First he invited Sam to Hooker's Division, then he gave "Davy" the instructions down by the Canal, and now he helps steal the gunpowder. One of the others must have been Bishop.

Sam carefully read the descriptions of all the men. Except for the man with the cough the descriptions were useless. They could have been anyone. Still, one of them must have been Bishop. The tall thin man with a cough was the key.

Sam handed the papers back to John. "Not much to go on, is there? But there never is. That's what makes this job so frustrating."

The messenger was standing in the doorway. "Sir, Sergeant Pollack said to give you this. It just came in."

Sam took the paper and walked back to his office. It was a message from "Dancer," a federal agent who worked in the Confederate Treasury office in Richmond. "$5,000 in gold has been sent to a Captain Bishop in Washington on orders of Pres. Davis. The President told the Secretary of the Treasury that the fate of the South rides on the Captain's mission."

Sergeant Pollack huffed into the room. "What do you make of Dancer's' message, Lieutenant?"

"Sounds to me like President Davis really considers Bishop's mission important. I mean, saying the fate of the South rides on it is one thing, but sending $5,000 in gold to further the mission is something else."

"I think you're right, Lieutenant. But, dammit sir, what IS that bastard Bishop up to?"

"I told you. I think he wants to kidnap President Lincoln. And, by the way, Bishop was the one who stole the gunpowder last night. I think I can prove that even to the Colonel's satisfaction."

"How?"

"Never mind, it's a long story. What do YOU think Bishop's up to?"

"Don't know. I'm still not convinced that Lincoln's the game they're after."

Sam stood silent for a moment. "Well, whatever Bishop's up to, it's big stuff. And I don't think we can afford to let the President go about unprotected without a warning."

Sergeant Pollack stood up. "Let me give you one piece of advice, sir. Don't you go warning the President unless Colonel Baker gives you the word. Otherwise you're a gone goose."

Sam sat quietly after the Sergeant left, staring into the dancing flames. He ran the known facts over and over in his mind. It all added up to a big mission, authorized by the Confederate high command, that involved stealing something out of Washington and getting across the lower Potomac in a hurry. The quarry was something big enough to involve Jefferson Davis personally, big enough to convince him it would win the war. Now they had twenty kegs of gunpowder to work with and $5,000 in gold to buy whatever they needed. This man Bishop was still out in front and Sam knew he HAD to get ahead of him if he were to stop whatever it was he was up to. Right now the chances of that didn't look very good.

Chapter 29

Saturday, February 25

Having decided that the stolen gunpowder was not safe at the Van Ness House, Bishop, Noah, Powell and Surratt loaded the kegs onto a wagon. They pulled a canvas cover over the load, leaving only the rear row of boxes visible, each box clearly marked "hardtack." Around six the wagon drove through the gate. It would take about twenty minutes for the load to reach the safety of the ice house at the foot of Congress Street in Georgetown.

Bishop had decided to move out of the Van Ness house to lessen the danger to Colonel and Mrs. Lomax. They were very important to the Confederate underground effort in Washington and would be much safer with the stolen powder and their Confederate underground guests no longer on their property.

After the wagon left Bishop spoke to Noah. "Are you going back to your boarding house now?"

"Yes. I agree that we need to clear out of here." He coughed, a deep throaty cough and spit onto the carriage house floor. "What are we going to do with twenty kegs of gunpowder anyway?"

"We'll create one thunder of a diversion when we capture Lincoln, or maybe even do some military damage. Haven't figured it all out yet."

"Well, I still think it's more risk than it's worth. Like your women friends."

"Noah, I'm not going to be drawn into an argument. I don't know why you are obsessed with what you view as my wild escapades with women. But I'm not going to argue with you." With that he left the carriage house and strode across the courtyard toward the house. Behind him he could hear Noah saying something about the "Seventh Commandment" and "the Judgement Seat of God".

Belle was waiting in their room on the second floor of the house.

"Are you packed, dear?" he asked her.

"Yes. I'm ready to go."

Bishop picked up the bags and they walked out North B Street behind the President's Park to F Street. After about twenty minutes a horse drawn trolley rumbled up and they got on. A half hour later they disembarked at their safehouse at 617 South L Street, a much humbler dwelling than the spacious Van Ness mansion. Bishop introduced himself to the lady of the house as Richard Milburn.

"I'm Mary Taylor," she said as she led them in.

Mary Taylor was a cheerful woman who at one time must have been quite a beauty. Ten years and twenty pounds had, however, taken their toll.

She lived alone, she said, since her husband's death. They could have the front room upstairs. It would be private there. She slept downstairs in the back. The colored man, William, who Bishop explained would be joining them later, could sleep in the pantry behind the kitchen. She'd fix a cot there. She smiled at Bishop. "Have you had supper yet?"

"No, we've not. We'd be much obliged if you could fix us a little something. But first, could you show me the house?"

Mrs. Taylor led him through a narrow kitchen and out a short hallway to a back door. She opened the door and pointed. "There's a privy and beyond that fence is the alley." The gate has a hinge broken and is hard to use, but it works." As she closed the door she brushed against Bishop. "It's going to be so nice to have a man around the house again," she said, looking directly into his eyes.

Bishop stared back. "We're certainly happy to be here," he replied smiling. "I hope there is some way I can repay your kindness."

Mrs. Taylor noticed the shift from "we" to "I". She answered quickly, "Perhaps some opportunity will arise. In wartime we must grasp the opportunities as they appear."

"Yes," Bishop replied. "Quite so. Now please show me the upstairs. I'm particularly interested in any way out of the rear of the house should that become necessary."

The upstairs had two large bedrooms, each with a roomy armoire. At the end of the hallway at the rear was a large window. Mrs. Taylor stood there and nodded toward the porch roof below. "You could open this window, step out onto the porch roof and jump to the ground. It's not much of a drop. You'd have to be careful of the ice on the roof, though."

Bishop surveyed the scene carefully. "Yes. Tomorrow I'll scrape a bit of the ice off the roof and spread some salt about. But it will be fine."

As they turned to go back downstairs Mrs. Taylor stopped abruptly. "Mr. Milburn, I want you to know again how happy I am to have you here." She pressed against him slightly.

Bishop smiled. "Perhaps tomorrow, when I send Belle out to shop, you will be even happier to have me here."

-0-

William arrived shortly after dark. Bishop motioned for him to sit at the table, ignoring Mrs. Taylor's look of shock and surprise at having a negro share her kitchen

Bishop stood up and started to leave. "You stay here with Belle. Mrs. Taylor will feed you supper." Bishop smiled at his incredulous hostess. "Won't you, Mrs. Taylor?"

"Yes . . . yes, of course." Mrs. Taylor stammered. She followed Bishop into the hallway. "May I have a word with you?"

"Of course," Bishop replied. "Is something wrong?"

"I don't like having a darkie sit at my kitchen table just like he's as good as a white man. It isn't proper."

"A lot of things aren't proper, Mrs. Taylor," Bishop said. He put his finger under her chin, tilting her head back slightly. "But that doesn't mean we don't do them. Now you feed William and show him where he's to sleep. He'll give you no trouble. And I promise you you'll not be sorry you've treated us so well."

Mrs. Taylor blushed and said nothing.

Chapter 30

Saturday, February 25

Colonel Baker burst into the room, eyes flashing and nostrils flared, like a runaway horse. "Where's that Goddamned letter?" he said, ignoring everyone present.

"Here it is, sir," Sam replied as he handed it to him.

The Colonel held the letter up at eye level and read it aloud:

> "Captan Bishop is staying at the home of Col. Lomax at the foot of 17th street, he shares a room on the secend flore with a Woman named Bell Gilbert. The twente kegs of gunpowder Stolen from the magazine is in the Carriage house packed in boxs marked hardtack.
>
> a Frend."

"Jesus H. Christ!" the Colonel exploded as he handed the letter back to Sam. "The foot of 17th Street! Right under our noses! The son-of-a-bitch has been staying right under our noses! And he hid the gunpowder there, too. You're sure this isn't a trap?"

Yessir, I'd bet on it," Sam replied.

"Then let's go. Everybody armed?" He looked at Sam. "You got your pistol, son?"

"Yessir." He held up the pistol he had retrieved the night he was attacked on the Island.

"All right. Now here's the plan. Major Wright, with twenty men, will cover the back of the property. I'll lead the rest of you in by the front gate. Shoot to kill! Any questions?"

There were none. Major Wright left immediately with his group of detectives. Three minutes later Colonel Baker led another twenty men out into the street. They walked two and three deep down 17th Street toward the Potomac. When they crossed North C Street one block from the river the Colonel stopped and faced the men behind him.

"I want the first six of you to cover the front of the house, facing the river. The rest of you follow me in through the gate. Two of you stay there and guard the exit. Lieutenant Reid, since you're in charge of catching Captain Bishop, you come with me. Now, let's go."

Everyone drew their pistols and followed the Colonel down the street. When they reached the house they stopped. The Colonel waved six men past him to cover the front of the house. When the last man motioned that his men were set, the Colonel spoke softly to Sam. "Let's go get the son-of-a-bitch, son."

They barged through the gate and into the dark courtyard. The Colonel motioned two men toward the carriage house on his right and then headed straight for the mansion. He motioned to two more men to stand guard at the door and then, without ceremony, opened the door and charged on in.

There were four people in the house, all in the parlor, seated before a blazing fire in a Franklin stove, Colonel Lomax, Mrs. Lomax, their niece Virginia, and a black maid. The house was searched thoroughly. The only sign that anyone other than these four had been there was found in a room in the cellar where, underneath a pile of straw in the corner of the room, the detectives found a small pocket New Testament. The room was quite damp but neither the straw nor the Testament were mildewed. Clearly, someone had slept there recently.

The men in the carriage house reported finding spilled gunpowder on the stone floor but the gunpowder kegs weren't there. Sam left the mansion and walked out to the carriage house with one of the detectives who had searched the place. He scooped up a bit of the black powder and placed his candle on it. It exploded in a cloud of acrid smoke that blew out the candle. It was gunpowder, no question about it. Then he searched the rest of the room carefully, moving in ever larger circles with his re-lit candle close to the floor. Near the door a shiny substance glistened in the flickering light of the candle.

Sam jabbed the blade of his knife into the substance. It was bloody sputum. The tall man with the cough had been here.

It was nearly eight when they finally got back to the headquarters. The Colonel had arrested everyone in the house and ordered them sent to the Old Capitol. On impulse, Sam took charge of the black maid as they waited for a wagon to arrive and carry them off to prison.

"Where did Captain Bishop say he was going?" he asked her.

"Massa, I don't know nothin', 'deed I don't." The girl was frightened, shaking like a leaf.

Sam decided to gamble. He took the girl aside, into a small room off the entrance hallway, and had her sit on a straight-backed chair.

"What's your name, honey?"

The girls eyes were looking down at the floor. "Sissie, that's what they call me."

"Sissie, are you cold? Would you like something hot to drink? We have some coffee."

The girl nodded. "Yessir, I'd like some coffee."

Sam shouted for an orderly. "Bring this young lady a cup of hot coffee. And add plenty of sugar and thick cream." He looked at Sissie. "Is that the way you like it?"

"Yessir."

Then Sam pulled a chair up to Sissie's chair, took her hands in his, and stared directly into the girl's eyes. "Sissie, I don't want to harm anyone, least of all Captain Bishop. But do you know what he's up to? Do you know what he's trying to do?"

The girl shook her head.

"Are you sure?"

"Honest, Massa, I don't know nothin'. I just cooks and cleans for Mrs. Lomax."

"Well, I'll tell you what he wants to do. He wants to kill President Lincoln, blow up the White House with that powder he brought home the other night, and stop freeing the slaves. That's what he wants to do."

The girl's eyes grew wide. "I never heard nothin' 'bout that. Onliest thing I heard him say was to tell Miss Belle the Yankees not gonna have no one to 'naugurate."

"Now think real hard. Did he say ANYTHING else that you remember? Be sure, because if he does what he wants to do, you might end up picking cotton in Mississippi."

"I heard him say one time at Breakfast - he were talkin' to Colonel Lomax, that Jeff Davis was countin' pretty heavy on him. He said he'd kill anything that got in his way. That's all I heard. Honest."

"Did you hear him say anything about where he was going to take the gunpowder?"

"Nawsir."

"Where were he and Belle going to stay when they left?"

"Don't know."

"What time did they leave?"

"Around six. Miss Belle had packed their suitcases and they walked out toward town. William left, too, but not with Captain Bishop and Belle."

"William?"

"Cap'n. Bishop's man. He's a fine lookin' darkie. Stayed to hisself in the cellar. Wouldn't talk to no one."

"Are you sure there's nothing else you remember about Captain Bishop or what he's up to. It's very important, especially to you negroes."

"Nawsir, honest. I don't remember nothin'."

The coffee had arrived and the girl took it greedily and drank in big, loud gulps. Sam rubbed his eyes and ran his hands through his hair. He was suddenly very tired. Captain Bishop was still way out in front and unless a miracle occurred it was very likely that the North would have no President to inaugurate on March 4. He decided to ask Sissie one more question.

"What did Captain Bishop look like? Did he have a beard?"

"Nawsir. And no mustache either. Shaved his mustache off after he came in one day. None of them had any hair on their faces."

"'None of them'? Who all do you mean?"

"Cap'n. Bishop, William, the man they called 'Mosby,' and Johnny. Oh, I forgot, Mr. Noah, he has a mustache, poor man."

"What do you mean 'poor man'?"

"He has the consumption. Coughs somethin' awful. And spits up blood. I seen him do that. He gonna die 'fore long. I know that. His cough sounds like the death rattle already."

Sam perked up. "Mr. Noah. Is that his last name?"

"No, his first name. Last name's Dyer. Ain't that a purty name, Noah Dyer. Sounds like he rode in on the Ark."

"Where does he live?"

"Don't know."

"That's a shame. We have some medicine, something new in from Europe, that cures consumption in just two weeks. We could probably help him if we just knew where to find him."

The girl got very serious. "I don't know where nobody lives. They never say. Maybe Colonel Lomax could tell you. I know he'd want to help Mr. Noah. Why don't you tell him about the medicine?"

Sam thanked Sissie for her help and went into the hallway looking for Sergeant Pollack. He found him seated in a stuffed chair, eating a ham sandwich. "Sergeant, does the name 'Noah Dyer' mean anything to you?"

The Sergeant thought for a moment. "Yessir. I think we got a file on a man by that name. I know we do. I'll bring it to you when we get back to the office."

Sam nodded. "Thank you. And, oh . . .have someone take care of the little darkie in the front room. Her name's Sissie, and she's scared."

-0-

Twenty minutes later, back in his office, a manila folder was lying on Sam's desk. Noah Lewis Dyer was a Virginian, from Lynchburg. He was Bishop's age and the two of them had roomed together at Franklin & Marshall college. He was known to spy for the South but the file contained nothing else, not even the name of his unit.

Sam closed the file and carried it back to Sergeant Pollack's office. "Sergeant, I'm going by to see Ellie now. Right now I just have to be somewhere where everything makes sense."

The Sergeant nodded.

What Sam didn't tell the Sergeant was that he was going to find a way to warn President Lincoln personally of the danger facing him, regardless of the possible trouble that could cause him with Colonel Baker.

Chapter 31

Saturday, February 25

Captain G. W. Bishop was deeply troubled by "Norton's" message that someone close to him was once more trying to get him captured. The letter announcing that he was in Washington had been bad enough but Bishop had dismissed it as something drafted by a bystander who knew he was in town and what he looked like.

But the more he thought about it the more it bothered him. Only a handful of people knew him and that he was here in town and they were all trusted friends: Belle, Noah, William, Colonel and Mrs. Lomax, Virginia Lomax, Sissie, Powell and Surratt. Of these nine, all but Powell and Surratt had known when he came to town and could have described his appearance.

William was out of the question because he couldn't read or write and the same was undoubtedly true of Sissie. All of the remaining seven, however, had to be considered potential suspects. But the possibility that hurt worst of all was Noah. Yet Bishop had to admit that he also seemed the most likely suspect.

Noah had become increasingly difficult to please. He harped on what he considered Bishop's "philandering" and his taking unnecessary risks. He had become a sour, dried-up man, the result, Bishop knew, of the ravages of the tuberculosis which was now killing him. A year ago he would have laughed at Bishop's dalliances and reveled in the adventures of the plot against Lincoln, but today he was curiously negative in his attitude toward his old friend and co-conspirator and his approach to the plot they were involved in. His disease was driving him insane and it was doing it at a moment when the South could least afford it.

It was a hard decision, but Bishop decided to freeze Noah out of any future plans. If that didn't work, painful as it was to consider it, the man would have to die. The fate of the South rode on this mission. President Davis himself had said so.

He laid his pistol out on the table and looked at it. A .36 caliber Leech and Rigdon percussion revolver, it was one of the best six-shooters manufactured in the Confederacy. He ran his hand along the gleaming octagonal barrel, sensing the power of the cold steel. He touched the rich walnut handgrip which was beginning to darken with age and handling. It was a marvelous little machine, a piece of beautiful craftsmanship as it lay benignly on the table. But, in the hands of one who knew how to use it, it was a cool, efficient instrument of death.

He hoped it wouldn't be necessary to use it on his old friend Noah.

-0-

Powell was not awake when Bishop called on him at the Surratt House. He splashed cold water on his face and dried it briskly with a towel in an effort to waken up.

"What's so damned important that I couldn't get another hour of sleep this morning, Captain?"

"I've worked out the final details of the operation and I want to go over them with you and get your advice. And then I want to prepare to strike.."

Bishop took a small paper from his shirt pocket, unfolded it and handed it to Powell, who walked over by the window to read it:

> "President Lincoln will attend a choral presentation at the Soldiers' Home at 2:30 p.m., Tuesday."

He handed the note back to Bishop."Who wrote this? How reliable is it? Could it be a trap?"

Bishop laughed harshly. "You're quite a 'doubting Thomas', aren't you? You question everything."

Powell stared back, unamused. "When you ride with Mosby and spend your days and nights behind enemy lines, you learn not to trust anyone or anything."

"Well," Bishop continued, "you can trust this message. It's from Lincoln's Chief Usher, William Poindexter. And it gives us just the sort of advantage we need - time to prepare for the capture with precise knowledge of when our man will be there. Now, here's my plan . . . ."

Bishop took a small hand-drawn map of Washington and its environs from his pocket and unfolded it. He laid it on top of Powell's unkempt bed and began talking.

"We'll meet Lincoln here, just after he turns off the 7th Street Road onto the lane that leads to the Soldiers' Home. There'll be you, me, Davy Herold, O'Laughlen, and Noah. Davy will chloroform the President and his driver while you and I hold them at gunpoint. The driver'll have the chloroform rag tied around his face and he'll be placed back in the pines, out of sight. He will never wake up.

We'll wrap the President in a heavy burlap sack and place him on the floor of the buggy. Noah will drive and we'll come back out to the 7th Street Road, go north about a mile to Shepherd's Road, then to Brentwood Road, about two miles all told." Bishop's finger moved rapidly along the map from left to right as he pointed out the route. "Then we'll turn south on Brentwood Road to Boundary Avenue and ultimately we cross the Anacostia River on Bennings Bridge, which O'Laughlin will blow up after we cross it. From there we'll head south through Maryland to Surrattsville. When we arrive we'll make our first switch to fresh horses, which are already there, and continue south."

Powell had not moved his eyes from the map, nor had he said a word. Bishop continued. "Now, this is the important part. We will intercept Lincoln around 2:15 p.m. At 3:00 John Surratt is going to drive up to the rear door of the Treasury building on a horse with two boxes marked 'Hardtack' strapped behind the saddle. Only the boxes won't contain hardtack, they'll be packed with some of the gunpowder we stole the other night. John will place the boxes in front of the door, set fire to the fuse, and ride away. There'll be plenty of smoke and noise and John will ride off toward the tavern at Surrattsville and meet us there."

Powell spoke for the first time. "What if the President's late and hasn't reached us when the Treasury gunpowder blows up and he turns back to see what the noise was?"

"Surratt will wait in Lafayette Park until he sees the President's buggy pull out onto New York Avenue. He won't set off the explosion until forty-five minutes after Lincoln leaves. That'll give us plenty of time to capture him."

"How's he going to get away with driving right up to the front door of the Treasury? It's been guarded every time I've been by there."

"I didn't say 'front door.' I said, very clearly, 'Rear Door.' The door will be unguarded. He'll be dressed in a Yankee uniform and, as I just said, the boxes of powder will be marked 'hardtack.' The only time he'll be the least bit suspicious is at the last minute or so when he unloads the boxes and lights the fuse. All right?"

"Yes, go on. There must be more."

"There is. When we head up the 7th Street Road toward Shepherd's Road after grabbing Lincoln, O'Laughlen will stop at the first bridge over Piney Branch and after five minutes he'll blow up the bridge with powder placed under there in advance. There are two more bridges where the road crosses Piney Branch. He'll blow them up, too, and continue on out the 7th Street Road. He'll set off charges all the way into Silver Spring, Maryland."

Bishop looked up at Powell. "This will lead the Federals to believe we've headed into Maryland with the President. And Booth will settle any doubts they might have. Around noon Tuesday a message will be delivered to his box at the National. He won't be there when it's delivered so the clerk will read and copy it for the man who follows Booth. He's been doing that all along. The message will tell Booth that 'the biggest haul of the war' will cross the Potomac just south of Lone Tree - that's the most logical route across the river from Silver Spring if you want to avoid the District. The message will mention Mosby by name."

"Between the Treasury explosion, the bridges blown up on the 7th Street Road and Booth's message, the Yankees won't think to look in the opposite direction - down lower Maryland where we'11 be going."

"On the contrary," Powell said coldly. "That's just where I'd look under these circumstances."

"Yes, assuming you had all this information at once, clearly outlined before you. But they won't. They won't even realize the President's missing for several hours. The people at the Soldiers' Home will assume he didn't show up because of the explosions they've heard. The folks at the White House will not miss him because they'll think he's at the Soldiers' Home and later they'll assume he went to check on the damage at the Treasury. I figure that by the time they realize Lincoln's missing, we'll have him across the Potomac. All the soldiers will have been prowling around the Treasury and at the bridge sites along the 7th Street Road."

Powell said nothing but studied the map for a long time. Then he looked up at Bishop. "It just might work, but what if it rains? How do you intend to set off the powder?"

"Fulminate of Mercury - a percussion cap. Here, I'll show you how."

Bishop sketched a firing mechanism from a Springfield rifle. "You place this down in a box of powder, wired tightly to the side of the box. Run a string from the trigger to someplace safe, go back and cock the mechanism, return to your safe place, yank the string and - BOOM - you've got your explosion.'"

"I think it's worth a try. Who else knows about this?"

"No one. I wanted your opinion first. After all, you've had far more military experience than anyone else in the group."

Powell nodded. "When do you propose to call the others together and tell them?"

"At the very last moment - Monday night." Bishop folded up his map and stuffed it back inside his shirt. "And for reasons I'd just as soon not discuss, I'd rather Noah didn't know about this until just before we take off. I'll be responsible for notifying him."

"Getting under your skin, is he? I've noticed how he keeps lecturing you about your women. Surely you have a better reason than that to keep him in the dark. He might be right about your women, you know."

Bishop looked closely at Powell to see if he could detect the slightest hint that he was making fun of him. But Powell was serious, deadly serious.

"I have my own reasons, Lieutenant, and that's all I need."

Powell sat down in the chair by his washstand and stretched his long legs. "Well, suit yourself."

Bishop walked to the door, stopped and looked back at Powell. "Be here Monday evening. I'll be calling the group together here that night."

Powell glared at Bishop. "I'll be here. You just worry about keeping that meeting and the next day's activities a secret from the Yankees. And - in case you want my opinion - I don't think Noah's your turncoat."

-0-

Powell's comment bothered Bishop. If it wasn't Noah, who could it be? Given their past association, Bishop was relieved to think it might not be his old friend, yet eliminating him meant the traitor could be any one of the others. They had to be given their specific instructions Monday night. How could the traitor be kept from warning the Yankees?

He tossed and turned in the old feather bed he shared with Belle. The clock in the hallway downstairs struck one, two, three . . . Just before four his answer came to him. He would pair them off: Booth and Herold; Surratt and Powell; Noah and O'Laughlen, with the pairs not to leave one another's sight until the capture was made. That would keep the traitor from running to the Yankees. With that settled at last, Bishop drifted off to sleep, two days before Abraham Lincoln would become his prisoner.

Chapter 32

Saturday, February 25

The lobby at Willard's was jammed with politicians, soldiers, statesmen and strangers, all jabbering away about the war, the government and society in general.

Sam slowly threaded his way through the huge room and into the dimly-lit bar that was located across the hallway from the lobby. As he paused in the doorway to let his eyes adjust to the dark interior of the bar he listened to the voices.

"Damned shame Lincoln dumped Hamlin for Andy Johnson. Johnson's a Southerner. May have been loyal but he's still a Southerner. Better to have a Vice President from Maine, like Hannibal Hamlin, than a Southerner from Tennessee . . . ."

"They can't last much longer . . . See here, we've cleared out the Shenandoah Valley . . . Sherman's split the South in two . . . Lee will fold before the end of the summer. Mark my words . . . ."

"Did you see Grant when he was in town the other week? Doesn't look like much but, God, what a fighter . . . ."

"Yes, I lost a boy at Gettysburg and another in the Wilderness . . . And I lost a brother at Antietam . . . ."

When his eyes had adjusted he spotted John Hay, standing at the end of the bar talking to a young Colonel whose gold-trimmed uniform announced that he was in the cavalry. Sam walked across the room and approached Hay, his stomach tightening nervously.

The Colonel was talking, telling about one of his wartime adventures. ". . . so there we were, all jumbled up, Yankees and Rebels shoulder to shoulder, sabers flashing, men and horses screaming . . . I mean, by God, it was bloody awful. Just then this Rebel trooper . . . ."

"Excuse me," Sam said politely. "Forgive the interruption but I must speak with you, Mr. Hay."

Hay turned around. He was a short, slight, dapper young man of twenty-five who exuded charm and the easy confidence that flows from success achieved early in life. "Ah yes, we've met before . . . the dining room here at Willard's."

"Yes, I'm Sam Reid, Lieutenant Sam Reid of the National Detective Police. I do apologize for interrupting you but I must speak with you, Mr. Hay, on a matter of extreme importance."

"Certainly. You'll excuse us, Colonel? Enjoyed chatting with you." Hay grabbed his drink and started to walk away from the bar. "Would you like a drink, Lieutenant?"

"No thank you, I don't drink." Sam looked at Hay's drink, felt the lingering chill of the late February wind outside and his own chill over what he was about to do, and said quickly, "On second thought, I believe I will. I'd like a bourbon."

Hay snapped his fingers to call a bartender. "Bring my friend here a bourbon. And put it on my tab." He turned back to Sam. "Where's your lady friend? I recall that when the crowded dining room forced us to share a table you were accompanied by an extraordinarily beautiful woman . . . dark hair, large -uh - eyes . . . quite charming." He smiled. "You can see I was quite taken with her. In fact it's remarkable that I can remember you at all."

Sam laughed. "You mean Ellie. She's at home now. I'll be going by to see her later. We're engaged to be married. I shall pass on your compliments to her and I know she'll be quite pleased. I must admit that she's the only truly beautiful woman I've ever known who is not carried away with her own beauty."

When the drink arrived Sam thanked Hay and the two of them walked over and sat down at an empty table against the wall. Sam sipped cautiously at his drink, but the bourbon was harsh and raw and he went into a choking cough, spilling some of the drink on his coat. When he had quit coughing he brushed off his coat and spoke softly. "As you can see, I'm not much of a drinker. I'm sorry to have interrupted your conversation with the Colonel."

"Oh, please don't be. He was just giving me his 'war hero' stories, hoping I'd be impressed and tell the Tycoon and get him a brevet to Brigadier General. But I've heard it all before."

"The 'Tycoon'?" Sam looked puzzled.

Hay laughed softly. "That's my nickname for the President. Call him that because no man ever had more personal power and used it less for his own personal gain. The president doesn't know I call him that. At least, I don't think he does."

Sam took a careful sip of his drink. Then he looked about the room to see if anyone was paying them any attention. At the table next to them two stout, prosperous-looking businessmen laughed over sturdy mugs of beer. One of the men spit lustily onto the floor and laughed loudly, shifting the huge wad of tobacco in his mouth from jaw to jaw. Sam looked at the floor which glistened like a spitoon from the capital's free use of tobacco. Only a week or two before the *Intelligencer* had declared angrily that the floors of most public places were so filthy with tobacco stains that if one were to drop a coin he would want to put on a glove before picking it up.

Sam had to admit that the *Intelligencer*, which was given to exaggeration in its editorials, was right this time.

He turned back to the table, leaned across toward John Hay, and spoke softly but, he hoped, with the voice of conviction. "Mr. Hay, I have reason to believe that the President is in great personal danger. I have been unable to convince Colonel Baker of the urgency of the situation and I know no other way to get a personal warning to him." Slowly and deliberately he outlined his concern for the President, beginning with the suspicions raised from intercepted Rebel messages and ending with the theft of the twenty kegs of gunpowder from the Magazine.

Hay listened intently without interrupting. When Sam was finished he spoke. "Well, I think we should go tell the Tycoon, not that it will do much good, mind you, he's not very concerned about his own safety. But I think there's a chance you just may be right. It certainly does make sense to me."

Sam took another drink. "I'm taking my life into my own hands by going over the Colonel's head to warn the President. I'll probably spend the rest of the war in the trenches before Petersburg, if I'm lucky enough to stay out of the Old Capitol."

"Baker! I never did like that old scoundrel. Wouldn't trust him the length of a musket barrel. He's no good, sir, no good." Hay's voice was suddenly harsh. "The only reason he hasn't been slapped into the Old Capitol himself is that he gets the job done the way Stanton wants it done." He peered at Sam through the bar's smokey haze. "A government is a hell of an organization to try to do anything with and there are only a handful of people who can make it work, push and jab the bureaucracy and make it do what they want. Unfortunately for those of us who care anything about the rights of innocent citizens, Baker is one of those people. Secretary Stanton doesn't care about the roughshod tactics and broken lives Baker leaves in his wake so long as he gets results. And results are Baker's business."

"It sounds like you're saying the end justifies the means, Mr. Hay."

"Well, of course it does - in politics and war. We say otherwise but when the survival of the Union is on the line any means to survival at all are quite acceptable. It's that kind of atmosphere, don't you see, that breeds and sustains a scalawag like Baker."

"Look at how he runs his operation, Lieutenant. I know a thing or two about it, never mind how I know. He has you divided up into five departments and stuck over in the War Department Annex on 17th Street. He never lets one department know what another one's up to. Even plays one off against the other at times. And he sits in his headquarters over the *Intelligencer* and watches over the whole picture. You're all just cattle to him, means to an end."

Suddenly John Hay stood up. "Well, enough about your boss. Let's go see the Tycoon."

They left Willard's and walked up Pennsylvania Avenue to 15th Street, crossed below the Treasury and entered the White House via the East Entrance. When they reached the Entrance hall on the main floor a genial little man with a thatch of white hair looked up from his chair and smiled at Hay. "He's still at work, so far as I know, Mr. Hay."

"Thank you, Edward," Hay replied as he led Sam up a set of stairs toward the second floor. When they reached the landing and turned onto the second course of steps Hay spoke to Sam. "That was Edward McManus, 'Old Edward' everyone calls him. He's been the doorkeeper at the North Entrance for many years. You can imagine what kind of protection that little Irishman would offer the President."

"Doesn't he have *any* protection?" Sam asked.

"No, but there has been talk of detailing a guard or two from the Metropolitan Police to cover the White House."

They were on the second floor now, in the wide corridor known as the Center Hall. The hallway was dimly lit by only a few small glowing gas jets breaking the gloom of night. On their right at the end of the hall they entered a small, old-fashioned office where a thin, balding man with a goatee sat at his desk writing. "Nico, is the Tycoon in? We need to see him about something important. Oh, this is Lieutenant Sam Reid of Baker's Detectives. Lieutenant Reid, John Nicolay, the President's Secretary."

Nicolay rose and the two shook hands. "Yes, he's in. General Halleck just left. I suspect the President is getting ready to leave, so you're just in time."

Sam looked around at the dark mahogany doors, the old-style mantel, the dark paneled wainscoting and the clutter of papers and books. Here, at the nerve center of the Union, the offices looked just as bad as his in the War Department Annex across the street. In a curiously negative way Sam found that comforting.

Hay rapped softly at the door to the next office. "Yes," a voice from within replied, and Sam was ushered into the President's office. It was a large square room, decorated in green and dominated by a massive walnut table that ran down the middle of the room. Ten straight-backed chairs were lined up along the sides and ends of the table and Sam realized that this was where the Cabinet met. Against the wall facing Sam were two chairs and a sofa, upholstered in rich green brocade. Three huge maps hung on the wall behind the furniture; a map of Virginia, a chart of the Charleston, South Carolina harbor, and a map of Kentucky.

The President's desk, a cluttered table with pigeon-holes stuffed full of papers, was against the wall to Sam's right. Like every other flat surface in the room, the desk was littered with maps, books and rolls of documents. On top of a pile of papers at an edge of the desk Sam noticed a delicate china saucer on which lay the remains of a piece of gingerbread. Beside the saucer sat a half-empty glass of milk balanced precariously.

The President stood. Sam had seen him at church perhaps a dozen times but he had never been this close to him. Now, though he had seen him before and though his height was almost a part of American folklore, Sam was surprised at how tall he was. His walk was loose-jointed, almost awkward, and there was an air of honest simplicity about him. He smiled, a tired smile that reflected his weariness as much as it did his pleasure in greeting his guests.

Hay came right to the point. "Mr. President, this is Lieutenant Sam Reid of Baker's Detectives. He believes you are in great personal danger. He expressed his concern to me and it seemed genuine enough that I thought you should hear about it first-hand."

The President took Sam's hand, smiled and led him toward his desk. He pointed to a straight-backed chair backed up against the wall. "Here, take this chair and tell me all about it." Sam noticed that he pronounced "chair" as though the word were "cheer."

Sam sat down and began outlining his discoveries of the past two weeks. The President plopped into his chair and crossed his legs and leaned forward, one elbow on his knee and his chin resting against his balled-up fist. It looked like an uncomfortable position but Lincoln never moved during all the time Sam was explaining why he feared for the President's safety.

When he had finished, Sam added: "I'm probably in trouble for having come here, Mr. President. Colonel Baker warned me against bringing you theories instead of facts."

"But you thought enough of your theories to act on them," Lincoln replied. "I like that. Shows initiative." The President leaned back and stretched his long legs out in front of him. "But I don't see how I can possibly do anything with what you've told me."

"When I came to Washington back in '61 I cooperated in extensive security measures which later caused me considerable political embarrassment." He looked over at his assistant secretary." You remember the trip in from Baltimore in the dead of night, don't you, John? I've always regretted that I let myself be used like that. The press had me sneaking into town dressed in a Scotch cap, cowering like a frightened puppy."

"But, Mr. President," Hay interrupted. "These are different times. We're at war."

"The times don't change that much, John. Remember how old Andy Jackson dealt with the lunatic who tried to shoot him back in 1835?" He pointed to a bad portrait of Jackson hanging above the mantel. "He was going to cane the man to death. Now, can you imagine what it would look like if I ordered a cavalry escort? They'd say I was acting like the Emperor Napoleon. No, I can't do it. Perhaps if Stanton were to become alarmed and order an escort it would be all right. But I can't order it and I can't hint that I want it. Wouldn't be proper. Just wouldn't be proper."

"As for kidnapping me, that reminds me of what old Jesse Dubois said to the preacher at Springfield when he was asked to lecture on the Second Coming of Christ. Jesse said that if Jesus had ever been to Springfield and was lucky enough to get away alive, he would be too smart to come back again."

"Well, I reckon if the Rebs knew how much trouble I would be they'd never bother coming after me. I'm sure that if they ever got me once they'd never come back a second time."

When he had finished laughing, the President stood up and walked to the door with Sam and John Hay. He put his hand on Sam's shoulder. "Lieutenant, I am much obliged to you for your concern about my well-being. And I am very sorry that I can do nothing about it. But I'm sure you understand."

Sam looked squarely at the President. "I'm not sure I do understand fully, Mr. President. But as a soldier I respect my commander's decision. Good night, sir, and thank you for hearing me out."

The President smiled. "Just remember what old Jesse Dubois said and don't worry so much."

When they had reached the Center Hall Sam said, "Well, Mr. Hay, I guess that's that. If he won't be protected we can't force it on him."

Hay looked surprised. "The deuce we can't. We're going to see Secretary Stanton. Your story is just the sort of thing to curl old Stanton's perfumed beard."

They left the White House and followed a narrow brick walkway, past the greenhouse that sprawled out from the western wall of the White House, to a gray-painted brick building that sat among the trees at the 17th Street side of the President's Park. The path was dark and difficult to follow and neither of them noticed the tall, muscular man, dressed in black, who watched them from the shadows of the trees at the edge of the greenhouse.

The Secretary's office was closed and Major Eckert, a big, burly man who ran the Military Telegraph Office on the first floor of the building, told them Mr. Stanton had gone home for supper about an hour before. No, Eckert said, the Secretary was not expected back that night.

Hay thanked the Major and led Sam out of the building and back along the path to the White House. The man in black watched them, motionless and undetected, as they hurried down the gravel driveway, through the iron gate and across Pennsylvania Avenue to 16th Street.

He could still see them as they walked up 16th Street, past the Sickles-Colfax House, where Congressman Dan Sickles had lived when he shot and killed the son of Francis Scott Key for committing adultery with Sickles' wife. Only when they turned right onto H Street and the shrubs and trees of Lafayette Park blocked them from his view, did the man in black take his eyes off Sam and John Hay.

Robert, the Stantons' butler, answered the door at the Secretary's home. He recognized John Hay and invited him and Sam into the parlor. A minute or so later Secretary Stanton appeared. His glasses were down on his nose and he was in his shirtsleeves.

He looked deceivingly meek and domesticated for a man who ran the northern war effort with a well-advertised iron hand. He spoke to Hay. "'Evening, John. What can I do for you?"

"Mr. Secretary, this is Lieutenant Sam Reid of Baker's Detectives."

Stanton held out his hand. "Yes, Lieutenant, how can I be of service?" He did not smile.

Sam decided to try to thaw out the Secretary's icy demeanor. "Mr. Secretary, I believe we've met before . . . in my father's store in Steubenville."

Stanton raised his eyebrows. "You're from Steubenville? What's the name again?"

"Reid. Sam Reid. I'm Nathaniel Reid's son."

"Nathaniel Reid? Of course. Know your father well. Used to trade with him when I lived there. Knew your mother, too, God rest her soul. How is your father? Haven't seen him in years."

"He's fine, thank you. I suspect I met you when you saw my father last. You were Attorney General in Mr. Buchanan's Cabinet and came back to Steubenville on a speaking engagement. You came by our store and my father introduced me to you."

"Yes, I remember. You were just a lad then, clerking for your father." Stanton was smiling now. "Let's see now, if Nathaniel is your father, then you were Aaron Reid's grandson. Thomas Reid, the one who owned the *Dorthea Lea* that ran between Pittsburgh and Louisville, was your uncle. I remember the night he was killed - the night the *Dorthea Lea* burned. She was a fine boat." Then he added hastily, "Your uncle Thomas, he was a fine man."

"Well, please take a seat." He pointed Sam toward a couch that sat beside an ornately carved walnut pump organ. "You didn't come here to reminisce with an old man. What can I do for you?"

Sam was amazed at the transformation in the usually gruff Secretary of War. Slowly, but very methodically, he began telling his story to Stanton.

The Secretary interrupted occasionally, asking for background, questioning Sam's theories, asking about the reliability of his facts. But from his manner and the tenor of his questions Sam knew he believed the theory being laid before him.

When Sam had finished talking Stanton stood up and began pacing the floor, hands behind his back. He had removed his glasses and he squinted when he looked at Sam.

"When do you think they'll strike?"

"Sometime before March 4. Sissie - the colored maid at the Lomax House - said she heard Bishop talking that the North would have no one to inaugurate."

"That's one week from today. Can you get any more precise than that?"

"No sir. And I haven't any idea how they intend to do it. I suspect the powder may be to blow up bridges and the like along their escape route - and to create a disturbance. But that's only a guess."

"Well, young man, that's quite a piece of detective work you've done. I congratulate you. And I'll tell you what," he jabbed his finger at Sam, "I intend to act on it. I'll surround the President with a squadron of cavalry - Ohio cavalry, by Jove. Ohio cavalry! What do you think of that?"

Sam grinned. "They're the best, sir."

"And I'll assign a bodyguard around the clock. By Jove, these Rebels will not carry *this* President off to Richmond.'"

Sam and John Hay stood up. "Mr. Secretary, Lieutenant Reid has been worried that he might get into trouble with Colonel Baker for going over his head, so to speak. I assume he can count on your consideration for having done his duty."

"Of course. I'll tell Baker it's all my idea, brought on by word we received from our people in Richmond. He's not the only one who has contacts in Richmond, you know."

They were standing in the doorway now, preparing to leave. Stanton smiled broadly at Sam. "Nathaniel Reid's boy, I'll declare. It's always good to see a hometown boy turn out so well. When this is all over I've a mind to write your father and tell him how proud he should be of you. Let's see, Nathaniel was an abolitionist, wasn't he? Always heard your home was a station on the Underground Railroad. Anything to that?"

"Yes sir," Sam replied evenly. "For over five years we helped runaways from across the river in Virginia. It was ..." Sam dropped his eyes, searching for words "... a powerful experience. Human slavery is a monstrous evil, Mr. Secretary. This war is the price we have to pay for letting the institution take root here."

Stanton was obviously moved by Sam's words. "Yes, I've no doubt you're right, Lieutenant Reid. And the cause of the Union is a holy cause."

"Holy cause." The words echoed in Sam's mind as he and John Hay left the Stanton home. It made the risk he was taking to protect the President even more worthwhile.

As the two prepared to part Sam stopped and placed his hand on John Hay's shoulder. "Mr. Hay, I can't thank you enough for giving me the chance to warn the President, and for the fact that Secretary Stanton is going to protect me from Colonel Baker. I truly believe the President is in danger and having the chance to get him protected means more to me than you can imagine"

John Hay smiled. "Lieutenant Reid, you represent the very best in this citizen army we have created to save the Union. You had the guts to risk your career to do what you believed was absolutely essential. I admire that more than you can even begin to imagine. I'm delighted to have had the opportunity to help you."

Sam was still smiling when he arrived back at his room.

Chapter 33

Monday, February 27

Bishop read the message from the Chief Usher of the White House very slowly and deliberately, giving John Surratt and Lieutenant Lewis Powell an opportunity to grasp the enormity of it all,

> "The new security arrangements are most extensive. They reflect Secretary Stanton's desire that President Lincoln be protected at all times and under all conditions. From eight until four each day two guards, detailed from the Metropolitan Police, guard the President's office or any other room he may be occupying. At night he is guarded by two separate policemen - one from four until midnight and the second from midnight until the day shift arrives at 8 a.m. The night shift is charged with escorting the President to and from the War Department and the theatre and patrolling the corridor outside his door while he sleeps. The policemen are armed with .38 caliber Colt revolvers. They are not in uniform."

He looked up at Surratt and Powell. Neither showed any emotion. He turned back to William Poindexter's letter.

> "When the President goes for his drives he is surrounded by a squadron of Ohio Cavalry, the Union Light Guard, riding

> with sabers drawn. An infantry guard has been stationed on the White House grounds, two companies of the 150th Pennsylvania Regiment, the Bucktail Brigade."

"Bucktail Brigade?" Powell interrupted.

"Yes. The men wear the tail of the white-tailed deer in their hats. They're a 'crack' regiment. Good soldiers." He returned to the letter.

> "The men are encamped on the South Lawn of the White House. Two sentinels pace their beats at the east and west entrances to the White House. Thus you can see, Mr. Milburn, it is quite impossible for anyone to approach the President and do him harm."

"Well, Gentlemen," Bishop folded the paper and placed it in his shirt pocket, "it looks like our plans have been radically altered. What do you suggest?"

Powell lay back on the bed, closed his eyes and spoke softly. "It looks like our naive little Lieutenant has outsmarted us again. I've just about given up on ever getting rid of him, and since we just heard the bad news, seems like we've had little time to come up with any plans. You, on the other hand, must have thought *something* about it. Why don't you tell us what you think? After all, you were supposed to get rid of Lieutenant Reid."

Bishop looked at Surratt. "I agree," Surratt said blandly.

Bishop walked to the window and stared out into the alley. "It looks like the original plan, to capture Lincoln on the way to the Soldiers' Home, is off. Assuming that Poindexter's not misleading us, and I don't think he is, we're not going to be able to grab Lincoln as easily as we thought and whisk him South. So, the question is, how else can we grab him?"

"What about kidnapping the Vice President or the Secretary of War or maybe the Secretary of State?" Surratt asked.

Bishop turned away from the window. "No. Nothing less than the President himself will do. And, despite what I just said, I think there is still a chance to capture Lincoln, and a chance that, even if we fail, will leave the North so touchy and insecure that Grant will have to move troops from Lee's front back to Washington."

Powell sat up, obviously interested. Surratt smiled. "Now we're getting somewhere."

Pleased with the interest he had generated, Bishop began talking. His tone was more the schoolmaster than the master spy.

"For some reason the Yankees seem to think that everything stands or falls on Lincoln being re-inaugurated. Poindexter told Belle that there is talk we've bragged there'll be no one to inaugurate on March 4."

"Anyway, they're going to be especially watchful between now and the inauguration. As March 4 grows closer I suspect they'll get more and more nervous and careful. But, once he's sworn in I expect they'll let up a bit. In fact, if we can encourage them to believe we're only interested in Lincoln before he's sworn in again, we can cause them to let up after the inauguration. Then, once he's sworn in, we can go after him."

"You think they'll cancel the guards and the cavalry escort once he's sworn in?" Surratt asked.

"No, not right away. But the state of alertness is bound to be relaxed."

Bishop reached into his pocket and withdrew a paper, unfolded it and lay it on the bed. It was a chart of the Capitol. "Now," he began, "Lincoln will be sworn in at noon on the 4th."

Surratt looked at the map of the Capitol and then at Bishop. "Wait a minute, Captain," he interrupted. "Are you suggesting that we try to grab Lincoln at the Capitol on Inauguration Day, with ten thousand people standing outside, the place crawling with soldiers and Lincoln surrounded by his bodyguards?"

"Hear me out, boys, hear me out," Bishop replied. "After the ceremony is over the President will come back through the Rotunda, turn right and walk toward the Senate wing. Very shortly he'll take a small set of stairs down to the ground level." Bishop pointed to a half-circle stairway on his map. "The plan is for the Presidential Party to go down those stairs and out to the East Front of the Capitol where his carriage will be waiting."

He smoothed out the map. "When Lincoln reaches here, at the stairwell, he'll be unprotected, except for his two guards. The others in the party will be his wife, his two sons, Marshal Ward Hill Lamon and possibly one or two other close friends. Only Marshal Lamon and the President's two guards will be armed. And," he looked up at the two men, "the guards will pose no problem because they will be OUR men."

"Our men?" Powell was puzzled.

Yes, our men. We're forging Mrs. Lincoln's signature to a letter requesting two of our agents from the Metropolitan Police be assigned to the White House guard detail."

"We have men on the Metropolitan Police?" Powell asked.

"Lieutenant, we have agents all over this city, including a couple of sympathizers in the House of Representatives and a member of the Senate whom we have compromised and who work for us on occasion." His voice turned harsh. "I know how you 'front line' soldiers feel about the soft life your spies lead. But we haven't exactly been sitting back and enjoying wartime Washington."

"I merely asked a question," Powell snapped. "I don't think it calls for a sermon."

"Forgive me, Lieutenant, but you're so quick to tell me when I've not met your high standards."

Powell glared at Bishop. "Don't push me too far, parson."

Before Bishop could answer, Surratt cut in. "All right, that's enough." He turned to Bishop. "Why are you using Mrs. Lincoln's signature instead of the President?"

"Major O'Bierne of the Metropolitan Police will probably be familiar with the President's handwriting. But he won't likely know Mrs. Lincoln's. Poindexter's given me two letters she has written. We can get our men assigned to the White House with no difficulty."

"Do you think they'll assign guards on Mrs. Lincoln's request?" Surratt asked.

"Mrs. Lincoln always gets what she wants, or hadn't you heard? Besides, who else would be more concerned over the President's safety?"

"What if O'Bierne gets curious and asks Mrs. Lincoln about the request?"

"Poindexter will intercept the letter, he handles all of the incoming mail for the family, and pass it on to me to answer. All right?"

Surratt nodded.

Bishop pointed to the map again. "Now, when the Presidential Party is here, at the stairwell, the three of us, my man William and Noah, will approach the party, draw our pistols and, with the help of the President's two bodyguards, take the President and his party back into the corridor linking the old and new Senate wings."

"By this time there will have occurred one of the most sensational explosions in this city's history. The twenty kegs of gunpowder which we stole from the Magazine will go off in the Rotunda, sending the Dome off into the air like one of Congreave's rockets, or at least causing it to collapse inward. For the next two or three hours no one will know or care where Lincoln is."

"Where will he be?" Surratt asked. "What are you going to do with him?"

"The moment the powder goes off in the Dome I'll shoot Marshal Lamon. He's the only one in the President's Party who can stop us and we have to get rid of him. Killing him will also let the others know we're serious. Then we'll lock the others in the crypt beneath the Rotunda where they had planned to inter Washington before the family refused to move his body from Mount Vernon. There's an iron gate on the crypt and we'll have our own lock. Davy will chloroform Lincoln and we'll put him on a stretcher, cover his face and haul him out of the Capitol to our waiting ambulance as a wounded victim of the explosion."

Powell spoke up. "When I came through here as a prisoner after Gettysburg, they were working on the dome. Someone said they had replaced an old one. Why?"

Bishop stopped, rubbed his forehead and stared into the distance. "The old dome was made of wood covered with copper and it was too short and squat after they enlarged both wings of the Capitol. They started tearing down that Dome before the war and kept on working on it even with the war going on. This new dome is cast iron. It was finished in December '63 with a big celebration. But all the powder we're going to set off will lift it off the Capitol even though it is cast iron."

Powell looked puzzled. "Well, when the dome goes up and then crashes back down, won't we be crushed under all that marble and cast iron?"

"Good question but, no," Bishop said, pointing at the chart of the Capitol. "When the dome goes up what comes back down will drop into the Great Rotunda. We will be here, away from the Great Rotunda on the steps leading down from the Senate Small Rotunda. We should be safe, especially since we will be halfway down to the ground floor, which means the floor of the main level of the building will give us more protection."

"Well, how do you propose to get the powder into the Dome?" Surratt asked.

"Leave that to me," Bishop snapped. "Just be ready for a bit of work tomorrow or the next day. And wear your Yankee uniform. I'll send word when you should get ready."

Bishop folded the map, placed it back in his pocket, and began putting on his overcoat. "Now, if these plans seem feasible to you gentlemen, I believe I'll leave. I have to take care of Lieutenant Reid once and for all." He glared at Powell, daring him to say anything about his failure to get rid of Reid before.

Powell glared back but said nothing.

Surratt spoke. "I think it's a risky business but we don't have much choice, we have to capture Lincoln. If you can get the powder in the Dome and set it off, this thing just might work. I'm for trying it. What do you think, Lewis?"

Powell looked at Surratt. "I came to Washington to capture Abe Lincoln. I'll try any halfway reasonable plan you come up with and I think this plan's just that, halfway reasonable. But that's enough for me." He turned to Bishop. "But what about the others, Noah, Booth, Herold, O'Laughlen, your man William? Will they go along?"

Bishop was at the door, ready to leave. "They'll give us no trouble."

-0-

Davy Herold was waiting for him at Harvey's Oyster Saloon, standing at the bar, one foot on the brass rail, nursing a beer and working his way through a plate of oysters.

He grinned broadly when he spotted Bishop in the gilt-framed mirror that hung behind the bar and motioned him to come over. "Evenin', sir. Here, try one of these here oysters."

Bishop shook his head. "No, Davy, I'm going to order a plate of my own. Oysters are just about my favorite food. But, Good Lord, are they expensive."

The fat Irishman behind the bar stroked his waxed mustache with one hand and scooped the oysters onto the heavy plate with the other. "Will you have a beer, sir?"

Bishop eyed Davy's beer with disgust. "No, I'd just like a tall glass of water."

The bartender shook his head. "Water'll kill you. Rusts your pipes. But all right, they're your pipes."

He filled a beer mug with water from a bucket that sat under the bar and slid it across the slick walnut surface to Bishop. The mug skidded to a sudden stop at the edge of the countertop and some of the water slopped out and ran down the front of the bar, adding to the elegant sheen of the wooden finish.

Bishop picked up the mug of water in one hand and, balancing the steaming plate of oysters on the other, led Davy across the sawdust-covered floor to a table in the corner of the busy saloon. Then he sat down and attacked his plate of oysters. When he was about halfway through he stopped eating and looked at the boy.

"I need some help, Davy, expert assistance from a man who knows chemicals."

"I reckon I'm your man. Guess I know as much about chemicals as anyone around," Davy bragged. He took a sip of beer and wiped the foam off his lips. "What you want to know?"

"I need a chemical that I can put in a coal scuttle along with the coal that will give off a poisonous vapor when the coal is burned. The chemical has to be something you wouldn't notice on the coal. What do you suggest?"

Davy stared into his beer. "Well . . . I don't know. That's a big order."

"Maybe we ought to get somebody who really knows chemicals," Bishop said. Then he scooted his chair back from the table as if to stand up.

"Hold on a minute," Davy protested. "I didn't say I couldn't help you. I'll just have to think about it."

"All right, Davy, you think about it. But I'll need an answer, and the chemical, by tomorrow night." Bishop stood up to leave.

Davy didn't budge but stared into his plate of oysters, his mind running past his knowledge of chemicals. "There's nothing that will give off enough gas to kill a man without most of the gas going up the chimney. You'll need to make an explosion. A small bomb, shaped like a lump of coal - that's what you need."

"A small bomb. Can you fix one by tomorrow? Will it really look like a lump of coal?"

"Yes, it will and I can do it. Where do you want it delivered?"

"Bring it to 617 South L Street. The lady who lives there is named Mrs. Taylor. If I'm not there give it to my black man, William, or to a woman named Belle Gilbert." He smiled at Davy. "It's good to have an expert in the group. You need some money to buy the materials for the bomb?"

Davy's grin evaporated. "Yessir, I will. I'll probably need five dollars or so."

Bishop handed the boy a gold coin. "Here's ten dollars. Buy all of the materials you need. I'll see you here tomorrow evening."

Chapter 34

Monday, February 27

Richard Maynard walked to the window and looked up toward the street. He could see the sky and part of the top of a big tree - an elm from the shape of it, though it was, of course, bare of leaves. The glass was filthy and the heavy iron bars over the windows added their obstruction. Still, it WAS a view of sorts, and after ten days in this damp, stinking basement cell anything was an improvement over what he saw inside.

He stood at the window for quite a while. An earthworm was slithering out from between the two boards that formed the window well and Richard watched the creature until it plopped to the bottom of the well. Then he turned and walked back to the straw tick and sat down on the filthy blanket that covered it.

What a mistake he had made going with the South. "Hurrah for Southern Rights, Hurrah!" He could still hear the crowd's excitement in the square in Leesburg that Saturday afternoon as the tiny minstrel strutted across the back of the wagon and sang out the "Bonnie Blue Flag" to the stomping and cheering of the crowd. John Landon had rushed forward to announce that he was enlisting in the Southern Army and the crowd had cheered him so and, before he knew what had happened, he and Fred Praeger had declared that they, too, were enlisting.

Mary Alice had been so proud of him that she had even let him walk her home. Dick Maynard - Dick the Bastard - walking Mary Alice Thomas home. It was as close as he had ever come to being accepted in Leesburg and it had lasted for such a brief time.

Then there was camp in Richmond where the measles killed Fred Praeger and Dick almost joined him, followed by the long slow recovery in Chimborazo Hospital in Richmond and, finally, the artillery corps and the batteries at Drewry's Bluff and Battery Brooke. That had been his war - measles, slow recovery, and nursemaid to a large siege gun overlooking the James.

But he had made Sergeant, on merit alone, no aristocratic family ties or big-time political connections were available to Dick Maynard. And his men liked and respected him. If it wasn't exactly military glory, neither was it anything to be ashamed of. And here, at least, he was no longer "Dick the Bastard." No, he was Sergeant Maynard, and a damned good sergeant at that.

Until last Friday. Now he sat rotting in a stinking cell, like a common prisoner. And all because his father worked for President Lincoln and the South wanted to put some pressure on him to learn something about Lincoln that apparently only his father could help them learn.

But William Poindexter would be too honest, too upright, to betray his President without some sort of skulduggery like this. Dick rubbed his hands together and blew on them. Now the people at the War Department wanted him to write his father and beg him to help the South, to tell him he was being held prisoner and that his life depended on his father's cooperation. The big, burly captain from the War Office had told him that if he didn't write this letter, and if his father didn't cooperate, they would send a man into Washington to kill him.

Dick thought of all the pleading he had done, calling up his honorable service in the Artillery Corps, his spotless record as a Southern soldier. But all the men from the War Office were interested in was putting pressure on his father. That Dick was a loyal Southerner mattered not at all.

His father! Poor man, he had lived a life of shame because of Dick's birth, yet he had bravely owned up to his paternity and claimed Dick as his own, had met his financial responsibilities over the years, indeed had been everything one could expect of an absentee father. And now, Dick knew, he would risk everything to protect his son, even if it meant betraying the President of the United States.

What a son he had been, Dick thought. The day of his birth had probably been the most unfortunate day in his father's life. And every day since then he had been a shameful reminder of a terrible transgression against the laws of God. Now he represented a cruel pressure device the South intended to use to force his father to cooperate in an act that was nothing short of treason. Somehow there had to be a way to spare his father this last agony.

-0-

The sun had dropped behind the hills but it was not yet dark when the guard turned the key in the heavy door. "Here's your grub, Sergeant Maynard. Food fit fer a king, grits 'n black-eyed peas. . . ."

The metal plate clattered to the floor and the guard went dashing out the corridor calling for the corporal of the guard. "Frank! Jesus Christ, come quick! Sergeant Maynard's done hung hisself!"

Chapter 35

Tuesday, February 28

Mrs. Taylor was alone when Bishop arrived back at the house. "Belle's gone shopping. She said she'd be back around six or so." She glanced at the clock over the mantle. "It's barely three now."

"So, my pretty. Would you like some more of the pleasure I gave you yesterday?"

"Yes," Mrs. Taylor replied immediately.

Bishop smiled, took her by the hand, and led her upstairs to the bedroom he shared with Belle.

It was nearly five when they came back downstairs. Mrs.Taylor was all smiles. "I declare, you are the best thing to ever happen to me. What did I ever do without you?"

"We humans are very adaptable, Mrs. Taylor. We do the best we can with what we have, or we do without." He grinned at her. "My guess is that you never did without. So after your husband died you managed to have a man around once in a while. Am I right?"

Mrs. Taylor came over to the parlor window where Bishop was standing, peering out into the street. She placed her arms around his neck and pulled him around toward her. "Actually, that's none of your business but, yes, I have managed to have a man now and then since Andy's death. But, honey, none of them have been half as good as you."

"Well, it's good to know a man's work is appreciated," Bishop replied coldly. "Now, if you'll excuse me, here comes Belle. I don't think she'd appreciate finding us this way."

Mrs. Taylor backed away, a hurt look on her face, as Belle walked up on the stoop and unlocked the door.

"Belle, sweetheart, how are you? Did you get the letter?"

"Yes, it's here." She looked at Mrs. Taylor who was swishing down the hallway toward the kitchen. "You two been having a little meeting in the parlor? Isn't it more your style to meet in the bedroom?"

Bishop ignored her questions. "Let me see the letter, please."

Belle handed him an envelope with the return address "Provost Marshal, District of Columbia" printed on the upper left corner. He opened the envelope and read:

Washington, D. C.
February 28, 1865

Wm. Poindexter, Esq.
Chief Usher
Executive Mansion

Dear Mr. Poindexter-

I shall be pleased to detail Messrs. Parker & Sheldon for guard duty at the Executive Mansion upon receipt of a formal request from Mrs. Lincoln or the President.

/s/James R. O'Bierne
Major & Provost Marshal

Bishop folded the letter and placed it in the envelope. "We'll have to move fast if we're to have our men assigned in time for duty on Inauguration Day. I'm going to draft a response to this letter, over Mrs. Lincoln's signature, and we'll have to get it to Poindexter right away."

"Oh God, G.W., do I have to go all the way to Georgetown tonight? I don't think I can manage. Why don't you send William?"

"I'd rather not. This is a white person's job. Besides, we don't have to go to Georgetown, only as far as the White House. Poindexter's on duty 'til seven, and there's always a little reward for you."

"All right, but I'm too tired for your 'little reward.'"

Bishop went upstairs, walked over to the bureau, and took a piece of paper out of the drawer with "Executive Mansion, Washington" printed across the top. He walked over to a small writing desk that sat in front of the double window overlooking the street and began to write:

> "This is to certify that John F. Parker and Joseph Sheldon, members of the Metropolitan Police, have been detailed for duty at the Executive Mansion, by order of,"

Then he dipped the steel pen into the bottle of ink and, keeping an eye on the sample of Mary Lincoln's handwriting on the table beside him, carefully signed the letter, "Mrs. Lincoln." When he had blotted the letter he folded it and placed it in an Executive Mansion envelope addressed to "Major James R. O'Bierne, Provost Marshal, Washington, D. C." Across the bottom of the envelope he wrote "Urgent - Immediate action required."

Then he placed this envelope inside a plain one and sealed it. On the outer envelope he wrote "William Poindexter, Chief Usher. *Personal and Confidential.*" When he was finished he glanced out of the window and saw a short, stocky, dark-haired man striding purposefully down the street carrying a small box. It was David Herold. Bishop rose from his desk and hurried downstairs to greet him. He opened the door just as the startled boy was reaching for the door knocker.

"How'd you know I was comin'? You watch the street all the time?"

"I do what I have to," Bishop replied. No need to spoil the spell he had over the boy. "Is that the bomb?"

"Yessir, just like you asked for. And it only come to two dollars. Here, I'll get your change."

"Keep the change for your trouble, Davy," Bishop told the boy as he took the box and opened it. "It looks like a plain lump of coal. You sure this is a bomb?"

"Yessir. Here, turn it over. See that there little black string? Right there? That's the fuse."

"What's it filled with, gunpowder?"

"Yessir, and it's got over two hundred match heads packed inside there, too. The cover's made out of lead so it'll splinter into a thousand pieces when the fuse lights the match heads."

"Why the match heads?"

"The odor will be more poisonous than gunsmoke."

"How'd you get the lead melted around the powder and matches without an explosion?"

Davy grinned. "Very carefully, Cap'n, very carefully."

Bishop laughed. "That's pretty good. You sure it'll work?"

"Yessir. I know what I'm doin'. This ain't the first bomb I ever made."

"Good. Say, Davy, are you busy now? Can you accompany me to the White House?"

"The White House? Why, yes. What you want to go to the White House for?"

"Got to deliver a message." He walked into the parlor where Belle sat, staring wearily out the window. "Sweetheart, Davy is going with me to the White House. No need for you to bother."

"Thank God," she replied as Bishop left the parlor.

-0-

Bishop sat down on the base of Andy Jackson's statue in Lafayette Park and watched as Davy walked across Pennsylvania Avenue and up to the iron gate where a pair of blue-clad sentries walked their beat. The sentries stopped when Davy reached the gate. One of them approached Davy with his rifle at "present arms."

"State your business, sir," he said in an officious tone.

"I have a personal message for the Chief Usher of the White House, Mr. Poindexter," Davy replied as he took the envelope from his coat pocket."

"You can leave it with me. I'll see that it's delivered."

"Hu, uh. No sir. I got orders to give this to Mr. Poindexter hisself."

"What is it that's so special that it can't be delivered to him by a sentry?"

"Don't know that it's any of your business, but it's a prescription for some medicine for Master Tad Lincoln. I'm from Ward's drugstore."

The soldier looked at the envelope for a long time, weighing his orders, to let *no one in* against his fear of Mrs. Lincoln's wrath if he prevented the delivery of a vital prescription for the Lincoln's youngest son. Finally he stood aside and jerked his head toward the White House. "All right. You can go see Mr. Poindexter, but you get right back here and check out through me. You understand?"

"Of course," Davy replied. "I'll be right back."

He started off up the driveway toward the White House, the hard gravel crunching beneath his feet. There were three soldiers standing under the North Portico, two of them guarding the doorway and the other one chatting idly with the guards.

Davy stopped at the ornately-carved door and repeated his story to the guard who motioned toward the gate. "Henry told you to come on up here?"

"If the guard's name is Henry, yes. You didn't see him shootin' at me, did you? He thought it was all right."

"Well, I don't know . . ." the guard said as he looked at the envelope addressed to Mr. Poindexter.

Davy feigned irritation. "All right. If you want Mrs. Lincoln crawling all over your back, that's your business. I sure don't."

The guard handed the envelope back to Davy and motioned him inside. "Go on in and ask Old Edward where to find Mr. Poindexter." Then he turned back to his two companions.

Davy walked into the huge white entrance foyer and closed the door behind him. On his right, asleep in a dilapidated old chair, was a little white-haired man with his head slumped forward on his chest. That would be Old Edward. Davy coughed softly.

Nothing happened.

He coughed again, louder. The old man looked up with a start. His face grew red. "Must have dozed off. It's a trifle hot in here. What can I do for you, sonny?"

"I have to see Mr. William Poindexter."

"Poindexter? His office is right here." He pointed to his left. "On the other side of the fireplace. Go on and knock, he's in there."

"Thank you," Davy said. He walked across the foyer to a dark, heavily-varnished door and knocked softly. A voice from within said, "Come in, it's unlocked."

Davy opened the door and walked into the room. It was about twelve feet square, with a high ceiling from which was hung a spindly gas chandelier. The chandelier was unlit but a bright gas jet burned on the wall above a tiny, immaculate desk. William Poindexter, his face pale and wrinkled in the harsh light, looked up at Davy. "Yes? What can I do for you?"

"Mr. Poindexter? William Poindexter?"

"Yes."

"Mr. Richard Milburn asked me to deliver this to you." He handed the envelope to Poindexter, who took it, stiffly, and opened it. He looked at the address on the inside envelope and looked up at Davy.

"Close the door, son."

When Davy had closed the door, Poindexter spoke again. "This involves the assignment of guards to the President?"

"Yessir," Davy replied. "And Mr. Milburn says this letter has to go out tonight."

"Tonight? The mail's already gone for tonight."

"Well, I reckon you'll have to send this out by special courier. I'm sure you wouldn't want anything to happen to your son."

Poindexter stared back. "You people never let up, do you?"

Davy said nothing.

"All right. I'll send it out right away by special courier."

"That's smart, real smart. Just see that it's done," Davy replied. With that he left the office, walked through the foyer and out the front door of the White House.

Bishop watched him come down the driveway and out the gate. He walked out of Lafayette Park and followed him up Pennsylvania Avenue, keeping to the opposite side in the gathering darkness. After a block and a half he crossed over the rutted cobblestone street and walked up to a streetcar stop where Davy had stopped.

"Everything went just like you said, Cap'n," Davy reported. He repeated his conversation with Poindexter, playing up his "threats" to the little man and described Poindexter's reaction.

"Good," Bishop replied. "Now, let's get this bomb to Norton and get Lieutenant Reid out of the way. Here comes a car now."

As the cream and white car of the Washington Horse Railroad Company rumbled up, Davy and Bishop walked out to the middle of the Avenue. Bishop signaled the conductor to stop and the pair stood motionless as the car came to a halt in front of them. They mounted the front platform, just beside a large sign that announced "Colored persons may ride in this car," paid their fare of five cents each, and sat down on the silk velvet seats that were the talk of all Washington. When the car commenced moving again the red glass lamp swayed gently back and forth to the rhythm of the horses' pace, casting shimmering crimson shadows on the polished woodwork and gleaming brass interior.

"I like ridin' the cars at night," Davy said. "Not so durned many crinolines takin' up all the room and you don't have to give up your seat to every woman that comes along."

Bishop nodded. "Yes, it is nice with no crowds. But in my business you get to liking crowds. They offer you some protection."

Davy looked around the car. There were only three other passengers, an old black man and two young men in their early twenties. The old man looked at Bishop, obviously thinking about his comment on crowds. But he said nothing.

At 15th Street and Pennsylvania Avenue, just across from the Treasury Building, they dismounted and walked into the shadows of the *Intelligencer* Building that occupied the corner. Bishop handed the box to Davy and gave him strict instructions on how to find the Rebel agent called "Norton."

In eight minutes Davy was back. "It's all set, Cap'n. Norton says he'll put the bomb in Lieutenant Reid's coal hod tonight his-self. When Reid puts coal on his fire and lights it, he'll set the bomb off. It's as simple as that."

"With Lieutenant Reid, nothing has been that simple," Bishop replied.

"Well, this is," Davy said, pounding his fist into his open hand.

"I made the bomb and I know my business."

Chapter 36

Wednesday, March 1

Ellie was radiant when Sam showed up at the door. She kissed him passionately, running her hands up the back of his neck and holding him close. "It seems like so long since I've seen you. I know, you were here yesterday, and the day before. But those visits were so short. I just can't seem to be with you enough. I love you so."

Sam kissed her again as they walked into the parlor and sat on the sofa. "Well, I've been busy. Working on some matters for the Colonel."

"Anything to do with catching that awful Captain Bishop?"

"In a way, but it's nothing you need to worry your pretty head about."

"Well, just so it doesn't interfere with our Sunday plans. Dr. Gurley has announced that a man from the Sandwich Islands will be at the Missionary Society Sunday afternoon. He's a converted Christian who was a pagan heathen just a few years ago. Dr. Gurley told us that he had been a most dreadful savage and now he just lives to be like Jesus. Isn't that wonderful?"

"Yes it is. But I think you're even more wonderful." He leaned forward and kissed her again.

"Oh, Sam, how can you think about that when we're talking about the church and our Savior?"

"I'll show you," Sam said. He pulled her down onto the couch, drew closer to her, and slipped his hand inside her dress top.

Suddenly Ellie's mother was at the doorway. "ELEANOR RICHARDS! Just what do you think you're doing? And you, Lieutenant Reid, watch where you put your hands!"

Eleanor! Something went off in his head, something awful and sickening and frightening. Ellie's formal name came searing into Sam's brain as he and Ellie sprang apart. He stood up instantly. He felt suddenly nauseous. He needed air, room to think, a chance to check out a frightening suspicion that had just been slapped across his face.

"I'm sorry. I guess I got carried away. I hope you'll forgive me, Mrs. Richards. It really wasn't Ellie's fault. I must be going now." He started for the door.

"Don't go, darlin'," Ellie cried. "It's all right, isn't it, Mama?"

Before Mrs. Richards could answer Sam had reached the door. "No, really, I must go. I'll call on you tomorrow, Ellie. Perhaps we can go to Willards for supper. I'll get back to you." He was beginning to sweat. He closed the door behind him and walked a few paces down the brick sidewalk and stopped. Wait a minute. What was he doing? When he left the house he always turned left, toward downtown, the direction from which he had approached the house. Why had he turned right tonight? And why was he charging out into the night in this direction? Clearly he was rattled, confused.

As he turned to go back in the other direction he glanced at the house. Ellie's mother was at the dining room window, moving the small fern that always sat at one side of the window to the center of the sill. He had often wondered about that fern as he had walked through the dining room, why it was always at the side of the window and never in the center. Now the dreadful suspicion came over him. The position of the fern in the window is a signal!

He unbuttoned his coat and removed his watch from the tiny watch pocket in the waistband of his trousers. Then he mounted the stoop to Ellie's house and rapped with the door knocker. Mrs. Richards answered the door. Sam tried to look embarrassed and awkward. It really wasn't too difficult.

"Ah . . . Mrs. Richards . . . I'm sorry to bother you, but I . . .uh ... I've lost my watch. It must have dropped out of my pocket while I was here. May I come in and look for it?" He started into the living room.

Mrs. Richards nodded toward the couch where he and Ellie had been sitting. "Yes, go right ahead and look. I have to check something on the stove." She left the parlor and walked through the dining room, on her way to the kitchen.

Sam walked over to the couch, reached down with his left hand and pretended to pick up his watch, which he already held in that hand. Then he walked briskly across the parlor to the dining room door to shout to Mrs. Richards in the kitchen.

The fern had been moved back to the side of the window sill.

"I found it on the couch, thank you, Mrs. Richards."

Mrs. Richards came to the kitchen door. "I'm surprised Ellie and I didn't notice it after you left."

"It was wedged down between the back and the seat. You had to be looking for it to see it," Sam lied.

"Well, I'm glad you found it."

"Thank you. I'll be going now."

On the sidewalk outside he turned right, walked a few paces to where he could see the dining room window and waited. After a few minutes Mrs. Richards moved the fern back to the center of the window.

There was no doubt. When he was in the house the fern was moved to the side of the window sill to announce his presence. When the fern was in the center of the sill, the signal was saying, "All Clear! You may enter."

The sense of nausea that had been growing since his suspicions were first aroused overwhelmed him and he vomited onto the sidewalk, and then staggered to a tree where he held on and retched several more times.

When he had recovered he began walking toward his office, anger and a sense of desperate conviction building within him.

He burst into his office and dashed over to David's desk, searching for the pile of *Personals* from the New York *Daily News*_and Washington *Star*. There it was, the one from the February 14, 1865 *Star*; "Eleanor. Your old teacher will call on you next week."

Sam shouted for the orderly and when the boy arrived he asked him if Sergeant Pollack was in.

"Nawsir, he out to supper now. But I 'spect he be back later. He usually drops by every evening."

"Well, leave a note on his desk that I want to see him when he gets in."

After the boy left, Sam wrote out a series of questions to ask the Sergeant. They were questions a good secret agent would have asked long ago. But Sam was under no illusions about being a good secret agent. He had let his love for Ellie interfere with his judgment. Now he would have to fight to keep his anger and hurt from blinding him further.

"Sergt. Pollack:

(1) Who were Bishop's students at the Georgetown Institute?

(2) Was Eleanor or Ellie Richards among them?

(3) Can you arrange around-the-clock surveillance of the Richards' house, immediately?

He lay the pen down and glanced toward the fireplace, suddenly conscious of the cold. He walked over to the fireplace and began building a fire. Someone had already arranged several lumps of coal in the grate and piled kindling wood and paper under it. As he poured some kerosene over the mound of coal and wood he thought of Ellie.

She had betrayed him, used him cruelly and brazenly. This woman he had loved, in whom he had confided his future, who had become his entire existence was a spy interested in him only because he was a source of information for her beloved South. She was his *enemy*. God, how that word hurt.

How many Southern men had she professed her love to, and meant it? The very idea made him angry. He would hurt her somehow, that's what he would do, make her feel something of the pain and anguish he was now experiencing.

He corked the jug of kerosene and took a match from a wooden box on the mantle and struck it on the hearth. The paper flared up in sheets of dark orange and brilliant blue. After a moment the wood chips caught and short blue flames began licking over the sides of the chips and flaring out onto the coal in the grate above.

It all fit together now. Ellie had always been interested in his work. Her innocent questions, he had assumed, grew out of her love for him and the natural interest in his work which would follow. But, no, they were the prying questions of an enemy agent. Her house, no doubt, was a way station or safe house for Rebel agents, why else would it be necessary to warn others of his presence with the clever window signal?

How many times, Sam wondered, had he sat in the parlor with Ellie while a Rebel agent, perhaps Bishop himself, lay hidden in one of the rooms upstairs?

The coal was catching now. It was good smokeless coal, Pennsylvania anthracite that cast out a strong, steady heat. Sam leaned forward and held his hands before the fire, palms out. Good God but his right arm hurt where the pistol shot had driven the splinter into the flesh. He stepped back from the fireplace and rubbed the arm, gently massaging the tender spot.

Suddenly there was a blinding explosion and jagged pieces of hot lead were hurtled into the room, ripping his uniform and tearing into his body. Sam fell backward and crashed to the floor, sending the coal scuttle sprawling.

A strong, acrid smoke poured into the room from the fireplace and Sam felt himself being whisked through a narrow, dark tunnel. He could hear his mother calling, "Sammie . . . Sammie . . ." But that couldn't be. Momma was dead. But still she called.

Sam lay still on the office floor, blood oozing through the ragged tears in his blue uniform.

Chapter 37

Thursday, March 2

The wagon was loaded with wooden boxes marked "Hardtack." John Surratt sat in the wagon seat dressed in the uniform of a Federal private driving the load right under the steps of the East Front of the Capitol. Bishop and Powell, who had been following on horseback, dismounted and tied their horses to a hitching post by the sandstone steps. The Yankee sentry, a blond soldier who looked to be in his late teens, saluted at the sight of Bishop's Major's epaulets and Bishop casually returned the salute.

"We've a load of hardtack here that's to be stored in the Rotunda," he said to the sentry. "I don't suppose our wagon will be in the way here for the next half hour or so?"

"Hardtack to be stored in the Rotunda?" the boy asked.

Bishop glared at him. "My God, man, where have you been? This whole building has been used by the army at sometime during the war. We've had soldiers billeted in the Rotunda and every other nook and cranny, and they've stored materiel all over the building. The vaults in the basement were converted to ovens to bake bread for the army. What's wrong with storing a little hardtack in the Rotunda? We'll stack it up on the balcony in the Dome where it will be out of the way. Won't even bother old Brumidi as he paints his murals on the ceiling. With any luck at all the war will be over before anyone has to eat this miserably hard substitute for bread."

The sentry blushed. "Sir, I didn't say there was anything wrong with storing it there. It just surprised me, that's all."

"Well, here's our orders, signed by Major Franklin of General Halleck's staff."

The boy glanced at the bogus orders. "Yessir. Go right ahead. And I'm sure your wagon won't be in the way here for the next couple of hours."

For the next two hours Surratt and Powell carried the heavy boxes into the Corncob Foyer, up the stairs to the main floor, across the North Small Rotunda and up the stairway between the two shells of the Dome. They stopped just beneath the Dome cap where a narrow walkway or gallery jutted out from the wall and circled the inside of the Dome, affording an excellent view of the Rotunda and a close-up of the inside of the Brumidi fresco under the Dome cap.

Brumidi wasn't painting today. He had suspended his work until the Inaugural festivities were over and his scaffold was bare. Bishop, who was dressed as an officer, did not carry any of the boxes into the Rotunda. But once he reached the gallery he began placing the boxes around the perimeter of the Dome.

Amid all the hustle and bustle of the inauguration preparations no one paid the three men any mind. After a half dozen or so boxes had been placed on the balcony, Bishop gently pried the top off the box marked with a small chalk "X". He checked the Philadelphia derringer that had been wired securely to the side of the box, cocking and snapping the hammer several times. It was a hair trigger, the result of shortening the spring. Satisfied, he tied a piece of thin copper wire around the trigger where he had filed a notch the night before. When it was tight he unwound a yard of wire and pulled it taut, cocked the hammer and pulled gently on the wire. As the pull increased the spring tripped and the hammer slammed down on the nipple with a sharp click. If there had been a percussion cap on the nipple, the spark from the hammer striking it would have ignited the powder in the box.

When all the powder had been delivered to the balcony Surratt walked over to Bishop, who was still fiddling with the derringer. "Here's your bucket, Captain." He handed him a wooden bucket with a hole in the side about three inches from the bottom. "I'm going to take off now, no need to leave the wagon around to raise suspicions."

"Fine," Bishop replied. "No one here will think anything about our two horses being tied down there. We'll leave when everything's arranged up here. Thank you for your work. Sorry I couldn't help carry the powder but I didn't think it would look right for a Yankee Major to work alongside his men. The army's funny that way."

Surratt grinned. "Next time I'll be a general and you can be a private."

Bishop smiled back. "If everything goes according to plan tomorrow we'll let Abe Lincoln be the private."

Powell, who was looking over the rail watching the tourists below, said nothing.

When Surratt had disappeared into the stairway Bishop turned his attention to the derringer once more. He placed the bucket beside the box marked with two chalked "X"s and wired it securely to the box. Then he ran the copper wire from the box containing the firing mechanism to the bucket and threaded it through a small hole near the top of the bucket.

From the box marked with the two "X"s he took a flat cobblestone, about an inch and a half thick and five inches in diameter that had been wired to a piece of inch-thick smooth pine measuring five by eight inches. He brushed the powder off it and placed the apparatus in the bucket and tied it to the copper wire leading to the box containing the derringer.

With a small pair of pliers he kept shortening the copper wire until it was taut when the rock and board apparatus was held about halfway down in the bucket. Then he spoke softly to Powell. "All right, cock the thing now."

Powell leaned over the box containing the derringer and brought the hammer back with two soft clicks as Bishop held the rock and board apparatus steady in the bucket. Slowly Bishop lowered the rock and board into the bucket. When it was around four inches from the bottom, still a good inch or so above the hole in the side of the bucket, the weight of the apparatus straining on the thin copper wire pulled the trigger and the hammer snapped home with a heavy "click".

Bishop nodded at Powell. "It works fine."

"Let's hope it does, Cap'n, let's hope it does," Powell replied.

Bishop sighed at Powell's lack of enthusiasm and placed the lid back on the box with the derringer. Then he reached into the box marked with two small "X"s and pulled out a cardboard sign that read, "Balcony closed until after Inauguration. Keep Out! By Order of Provost Marshal." On the back of the cardboard was another sign that read the same with the word "balcony" omitted. When he and Powell walked down the narrow stairway to the North Small Rotunda, Bishop stopped and removed a small length of heavy twine from his pocket. He threaded it through two holes in the sign and tied the twine to the two nails he had driven into the wooden door frame the day before.

There. Now, with any luck at all, no one would think of entering the Dome until the apparatus was ready to be set off. But "any luck at all" wasn't good enough and Bishop knew it. He looked toward the Great Rotunda where the sound of tourists was coming from. William was standing there, watching him carefully.

Bishop nodded and walked away, across the North Small Rotunda toward the spiral steps that led to the lower level.

As Bishop disappeared down the stairs William stepped over the sign and walked up the stairway toward the balcony. When he was out of sight he sat down and took up his vigil, keeping the explosive cache away from prying eyes.

-0-

A half hour later Bishop was back in the Great Rotunda, waiting for John Wilkes Booth. Outside, hammers pounded on the wooden platform that workmen were erecting before the East Portico.

Crowds of tourists, in town for the Inauguration, swirled about the Capitol. Bishop watched a family of four, parents and two girls all decked out in holiday finery, walk into the Rotunda and begin craning their necks backward as they took in the Rotunda. Back, back, back went their heads. The youngest girl's mouth flew open and she gasped at the incredible sight of one hundred eighty-three feet of vertical space enclosed under the domed copper ceiling. There was nothing else like it in all the land.

They were tourists, these people, raw country folks all gussied up for democracy's big show tomorrow. But, in a way, they typified something basic about the American character. They were proud of their Capitol, awed by the immensity of it all and just a little bit possessive. After all, it was *their* Capitol.

As Bishop watched he noticed that the man limped and he wore in his lapel a red, white and blue rosette, obviously some sort of veteran's symbol. No doubt, Bishop thought, the limp was a war wound. Bishop wondered if the man had ever faced the 3rd Virginia.

The little scene depressed Bishop. This prosperous family, the father a veteran, was representative of a strength and prosperity the South did not possess. Today they no doubt thought they were celebrating the President's Second Inauguration in the face of certain victory over the South. All the newspapers crowed that line. Well, he thought, we'll see about that.

A group of school children trooped into the Rotunda with John Wilkes Booth following, looking somewhat out-of-place. He smiled when he spotted Bishop and made his way over to him, weaving past the little knots of tourists.

"Good morning, sir. Thought I'd never get here. This whole damned building is packed with tourists and school children. You'd think they were here to celebrate the Second Coming."

Bishop smiled bitterly. "I believe some of them do think that. But we'll be changing their minds shortly. Now, if you'll just back over here against the wall with me, I'll tell you what I want you to do."

For the next ten minutes Bishop outlined in detail where the President would be and who would be in his party as they came through the Rotunda on their way to the Inaugural stand and on their way back through after the ceremonies were completed. It wasn't really necessary for Booth to have all this detail but Bishop gave it to him because it would increase the actor's sense of being in on the details of the planning, and also because Bishop could use another opportunity to run through the scene in his own mind.

"Now, after Lincoln has cleared the Inaugural stand with his party the lesser mortals will be permitted to leave. I want you to hustle into the Rotunda as soon as you can. The ticket we got for you puts your seat near the door to the East Portico, and after the President has had time to walk into the Senate Rotunda and start down the stairs, you start your demonstration."

"How long do you estimate that will take?"

"When we timed it Tuesday, it took four and a half minutes to walk from the entrance to the Rotunda, across the Rotunda, through the North Small Rotunda, and start down the stairs to the ground floor."

"All right. Four and a half minutes after Lincoln leaves the East Portico I will make a scene."

"Yes. Grab someone. Take offense at something someone says. Anything. Just cause a scene so that every policeman in the area will rush toward you."

"I suppose after the news gets out that the President has been kidnapped, I'll immediately be assumed to be a member of the gang that got him."

"Probably. But you should be on your way to Richmond by then. Your scene need last only a couple of minutes. Then you can apologize, identify yourself and get out of here."

Bishop did not mention the powder in the Dome or the explosion that was set to occur shortly after the President had passed through the Rotunda.

"The most important thing to remember, Mr. Booth, is to stay in the Rotunda when you make your scene. Whatever you do, don't leave the Rotunda."

Chapter 38

Saturday, March 4

Sam opened his eyes but he couldn't see, couldn't focus. There was someone, or some thing, there. But his eyes wouldn't focus. He was blind. No, he was dead. That was it, he was dead. And when you are dead you can't focus your eyes.

Whatever it was moved, and spoke to him, called him by name. Of course, it was an angel and she would know his name.

"We thought you were gone, Lieutenant Reid. For a while it looked like you wouldn't make it. But you're going to be all right now. You've lost a bit of blood, but you'll survive."

Suddenly Sam's eyes focused. He knew that voice and the form began to fill in before his eyes. It was Kate Huntt, the girl from Tee Bee and she was real and alive. At least that settled one question. He wasn't dead.

"Kate. Kate Huntt. So now you know I lied to you about not being in the army . . . ." His voice trailed off.

"Yes. I think I knew all along. It was just nicer to think maybe you were different from the others."

"I'm sorry," Sam said. He moved his head slightly but the pain shot through his cranium like a ricocheting rifle bullet. He winced and lay still.

"Don't move. It's not necessary." Kate wiped his brow with a damp cloth.

"What are you doing here? Where am I?"

"The army hospital in Georgetown, the old Union Hotel. They brought you here about an hour after someone tried to blow you up with a bomb planted in your fireplace. I was going off duty and just happened to see them bring you in. They said it was all right for me to sit with you. I think they expected you to die. Your friend Sergeant Pollack was beside himself. Kept fighting back tears and ranting about the 'rotten traitors' and 'bloodthirsty Rebels.' He must be very fond of you."

"Anyway, you were hit by several pieces of lead from a bomb but none of the wounds were very serious. You must have been turned away when the bomb exploded. You'll be in the hospital for a couple of weeks and your head will hurt from where a piece of lead tore into your scalp and where you hit when you fell to the floor. But you'll be all right in time."

"You still haven't told me what you're doing here," Sam said.

"My father died shortly after you stopped at our place. Just took sick one morning and was dead by nightfall. I closed the store and Smokey and I moved to Washington to stay with Pa's sister. Maybe after the war's over we'll go back and re-open the store. I don't know. But there was nothing to do at Aunt Cora's and I've always been used to working, so I volunteered to help at the hospital."

"Who's 'Smokey'?"

"My dog. You remember him, he was in the storeroom with us that night."

"Oh yes. Smokey. I remember." He was watching her eyes. There were flecks of gold amidst the emerald green, just like the first time he had met her. It was funny, Ellie's eyes had no gold."

Ellie! Suddenly it all came flooding back. "Did Sergeant Pollack say anything about a girl named Ellie? Ellie Richards?"

"He said you had been betrayed by a girl. Was that her name, Ellie?"

"Yes," Sam replied, and then he began to cry. It hurt his head and chest to cry. The sobs seemed to shake him apart. But he couldn't stop.

He had loved Ellie with every ounce of life he possessed and she had seen him as merely a convenient source of information for her Rebel friends. All her talk about love and marriage was just part of a bitter game. And he, 23-year-old naive Sam Reid, was the goat.

Kate tried to comfort him. She was leaning over him, holding him as best she could from an awkward position. "It's better to find out now, Lieutenant Reid. Better to know before you got married. There are always other women."

"No," Sam replied between sobs. "Ellie was special. I picked her out of all the girls in the world. She was special."

Kate wiped his face again. "No, we like to believe we choose our life's partners out of all those available in the world. It's more romantic to think that. But actually we choose from a very small group, usually only two or three at the most. We think we make a choice but really the choice is made for us."

Sam blinked away his tears and stared at the girl. "What do you mean?"

"I mean that when we reach the point where we begin to think seriously about someone of the opposite gender, we really know very few who we would consider and who are of the right age, religion, character and the like. So you really didn't pick Ellie out of 'all the girls in the world.' You probably picked her out of no more than three who seemed to fit what standards you had set." She smiled down at him. "And, as handsome as you are I'll bet she picked you, and made you think you had picked her. We women do that all the time, you know." She giggled. "I'm giving away one of our trade secrets."

"Maybe so, but I don't feel any better about being betrayed by Ellie."

Kate straightened up. "Well, it seems to me that, difficult as it may be, you had best begin preparing for what comes next, whatever that is."

"I'm not sure I understand . . . ."

"Well, Ellie betrayed you. What do you do next? You don't strike me as the type to sit around and cry about it for long."

Sam was quiet for a long time. The sounds of sleeping men wafted in from the next room, heavy breathing, snoring, a cough here and there and an occasional moan. Kate held his hand. Her skin was soft, reassuring, very . . . well, compassionate, if you could say that about skin. "What time is it? And what day?"

Kate looked at a watch pinned to her dark green dress. "It's 3:30. Saturday morning. Inauguration Day. Mr. Lincoln's going to be sworn in again today."

"Well, that settles that," Sam replied.

"What do you mean?"

"What I do next. I have to get out of here and to the Inauguration. Mr. Lincoln's in great danger. I know it sounds pompous, but I may be the only person who can save him."

"Lieutenant Reid, You can't leave the hospital that soon."

"Please, call me Sam. All right?"

Kate nodded.

Sam cleared his throat and began speaking rapidly. "Look, I know you say I can't leave the hospital so soon. But I have to." He looked at Kate. "Look, I lied to you before and you have no reason to believe me now. But I have to get out of here and get to the Capitol before noon."

"I can't imagine anything important enough to run the risk of losing your health."

Sam squeezed Kate's hand. "You sound like Ellie now."

"What's that supposed to mean?" Kate's voice had an edge.

"Like a little mother. 'You shouldn't do this' or 'you should do that.'"

"Well, you shouldn't leave the hospital that soon. I don't like being compared to your Ellie, but you shouldn't get out of bed that soon."

"I know. You're right. But I have to. And there's a very special reason why." He looked about him. The beds on either side of him were vacant. The men in the other beds appeared to be asleep. He motioned to Kate to lean forward and began to speak softly.

Slowly and deliberately he told her what he knew and suspected about the Rebel plot against Lincoln, how he had even visited the President to warn him. He left out no details, laying it all on the table for this girl from the Rebel-infested country who was barely more than a stranger to him. When he was finished he stared at her. "Well? What do you think?"

"I guess you do have to go to the Capitol. But you can't go alone. You'll need someone to lean on, physically. I'll go with you." She stood up. "I'm going home now, to Aunt Cora's. I'll be back around eight. We'll go to the Inauguration, don't you worry."

Sam smiled. "All right. I'll try to get a little rest but I'll be ready when you get here." Then he reached his hand out toward her. "It's 3:30 in the morning, midway through the night. Did you stay here all night with me? Why?"

"Yes. I was just leaving, around 8:00 o'clock, when they brought you in. I recognized you immediately. We were all afraid you were going to die. I just couldn't leave you. So I stayed." She smiled. "And I'm very glad I did. By the way, you'll need a disguise today, now that they obviously know who you are."

"Yes, it would help. But I don't know how I'd arrange one at this stage of the game."

"I'll send a courier for Sergeant Pollack. He'll be able to round up something. Now you get some sleep." She turned and was gone, all businesslike and proper. Just like a woman who had come of age running a country store and a post office, Sam thought.

He lay awake for what seemed like a long time, thinking about this girl who had walked back into his life when everything seemed ready to collapse about him. She was so direct, so straight forward. And she obviously cared.

From a bed in the far corner of the room came a long, low moan, followed by a racking sob and the cry, "Oh, mama, mama, mama! Please do something to stop this burning pain."

After a few minutes a woman came into the room and silently made her way past the coal hods, water buckets and teapots, to the groaning man's side. She perched on the edge of his cot, dipped a cloth in the bucket of water at the side of his bed, and began washing his brow. The man mumbled some more about "mother" and was quiet.

Sam looked about the little room, a hotel room in more peaceful times but now a hospital ward. The sickening smell of wounds, rotting flesh, bodies sweating from burning fever and the straw from the mattresses fought with the odor of the kitchen and the washrooms for possession of the air. The cots, there were eight of them, were set so close together that it was just barely possible to walk between them. The lantern hanging by the door streamed fitfully on the pathetic figures as they tossed and turned in their cots.

Outside, the cold moonlight fell on the silent figure of the sentinel, who stood guard to keep out idlers and gossips.

He had been lucky, and quite privileged, to have Kate sitting with him as a private nurse. He wondered if he had mumbled or cried out. And for whom? He hoped it hadn't been for Ellie. He wanted to forget her. He would think about Kate. She was obviously going to help him.

But, wait. Something wasn't right! Kate had left so suddenly after he had told her everything. And she was from Prince Georges County, Maryland. Rebel country through and through.

She had tricked him! She had got him to tell everything in his stupid, naive way and now she had gone to find someone who would come back and take care of him once and for all. It was no "accident" that she had been waiting here for him. He pulled the covers about him to fight the growing cold and determined to stay awake until help should arrive. If Kate Huntt's Rebel friends thought they could kill him they'd be in for a surprise. They might get him, but he'd take a few of them with him!

Within two minutes he was sound asleep.

-0-

It was after five when Sergeant Pollack showed up. He shook Sam gently until he woke up. "I'm sorry to disturb you, Lieutenant, but Miss Huntt sent a note that it was important I should see you right away. So I come right over. She mentioned a disguise. What's this all about? By the way," he was grinning broadly now, "it's good to see you lookin' so good. Thought you was a goner for a while there."

Sam smiled back. "I guess I'm a hard man to kill, Sergeant."

"Yessir, you are."

Sam thought for a moment and then looked at the sergeant. "I was worried about having told Kate about my concerns over the President and what we needed to do. Since she was from the lower neck of Maryland I began to wonder if she might be a Rebel spy, like Ellie. But, since she asked you to help me, I guess that means she's not a spy."

Sergeant Pollack laughed. "No, that girl's no spy and if I am any judge of women, she's mighty fond of you."

Sam smiled and remained silent for a while, thinking. Then he turned to the sergeant. "I'm going to the Inauguration, Sergeant. Since the Rebs know what I look like I thought I'd disguise myself somehow. Can you give me anything that would be helpful?"

"When I got Miss Huntt's message I throwed a few things into this here poke." He rummaged around in a small paper sack. "Here's a false beard and mustache. And I got glasses, with clear lenses, and powder to turn your hair gray."

"I don't want any whiskers. I haven't seen a pair of false whiskers yet that didn't look false. But the mustache and glasses sound good. And I'll use the powder."

"All right, sir. You go back to sleep now and Miss Huntt will be here around eight to help you get ready. I come over early so's I could get anything else if you needed it."

"There is one other thing I'll need. I want to spread the word that I've died. Let the headquarters believe it, including the Colonel if you think you can get away with it. And be sure to tell Ellie. That way whoever is working for the Rebs in our headquarters and whoever Ellie is sending messages to will be convinced I'm gone."

"Yessir. And, sir, I done a little lookin' into the questions you wrote out on the pad just before the bomb went off. Miss Ellie was one of Captain Bishop's students at the Georgetown Institute. She's listed as 'Eleanor Richards.'" The Sergeant was obviously embarrassed to have to tell Sam this. To cover his discomfiture he moved on quickly. "I've put a man to watchin' her house full time."

Sam lay silent. Conformation of his worst suspicions, though there had been little doubt about them, hurt deeply. But now, instead of wanting to cry, he felt angry.

"Well, you've settled the question about Ellie. She's a spy and she betrayed me, and, with God as my witness, Sergeant Pollack, she'll pay for that. By the way, does Colonel Baker know what I've been up to?"

Sergeant Pollack looked at the others gathered in the room. Then he leaned forward and began to speak very softly. "Don't like to have to tell you this, sir, but the Colonel knows everything you been up to. I tole him. It was my job."

"What do you mean?"

"Whenever you went anywhere or did anything I wrote a little report on it and sent it over to the Colonel's office by messenger. Like when you left for lower Maryland, I wrote him where you was plannin' to stop and all."

Sam laughed. "So . . . the Colonel knew all along what I was up to?"

"Yessir. I had to tell him."

"Well, where's the leak in our headquarters? Any ideas? Since it wasn't Private Selvern, I don't have any ideas."

"Sir, we realized that someone was readin' all the reports that came in. I'm not the only sergeant reporting on their officers. Everybody does it. We figured since all those reports came in from all over Baker's command, the leak was at the old man's headquarters. So we set a trap and caught a private, from all the way up north in Massachusetts if you can believe that. We think he was the only leak. Anyway, he's in the Old Capitol and probably is gonna hang."

Sam rubbed his sore arm. "By God, you're right. The colonel's office would be the logical place to keep track of everything. We all go our separate ways in our offices. But over there in Baker's office above the newspaper office, you can get the whole picture."

"I always figgered that's why the Colonel didn't have his office with the rest of us. He liked to be the only one to know the whole story."

"So, do you have to report to the Colonel that I'm alive?"

"No sir. Ever since I begin to suspect somethin' might be wrong over at the Colonel's office I been purty vague in my reports. And about you bein' alive and all, well, I didn't write nothin' about that in my report. I tole the Colonel personal, didn't write it down."

"Did you tell the Colonel about your suspicions about the leak?"

"No sir. The Colonel don't like to be told nothin', you know? He likes to figger it out for hisself. So I just hinted that maybe it was just as well I didn't have no time to write this report, tole him maybe the reports could get leaked out. You know, I got him to thinkin' about it. 'Fore long he'll stop the leak like it was his own idee."

"But you still didn't tell anyone but the Colonel I'm alive? There's no way anyone else could know?"

"Not lessen the Colonel tells, and you know that ain't gonna happen."

Sam smiled. "No, the old buzzard likes to keep a secret."

Sergeant Pollack said nothing for a long time. Finally he patted Sam on the arm and said, "I'm goin' now. You take care. Oh, here's your pistol. I brought it along in case you might be needin' it. I guess you will now."

Sam took the Army Colt and slid it under his pillow. "Thank you."

After the Sergeant left, Sam raced through his plans once more. He had been wrong about Kate, that much was certain. She had sent for Sergeant Pollack and she was obviously coming back to accompany him to the Inauguration. Kate . . . with those incredible green eyes, flecked with gold. What had he done to deserve her? And she had said he was handsome.

It was funny. He hadn't been able to stay awake when he had thought Kate was a spy and was going to have him killed. Now that he knew she was on his side, he couldn't go to sleep for thinking about her.

And then he thought about Ellie, how she had betrayed him and how much that hurt. He could see it all so clearly now, how cleverly he had been drawn into her web – the web of the Rebel secret service.

He had always considered it such a great stroke of luck that Ellie and her mother had approached his table at Willard's that night. He and David had just ordered their meals when Mrs. Richards approached, followed by Ellie. "Excuse me, gentlemen," she had said quietly. "I hate to interrupt you but, with the restaurant so crowded, I wonder if my daughter and I might share a table with the two of you."

Sam and David had been thrilled, of course, and the evening blossomed. Ellie paid David little notice but talked only to Sam, who was instantly smitten by the stunningly attractive young woman who was lavishing so much attention on him. As they were leaving she had even hinted that he should call on her some evening. And so the "romance" had begun.

Now he could see it all so clearly. She had been sent to him, to lure him into her web where she could question him ever so innocently about his work and then pass it all onto the Rebel underground. What a fool he had been.

-0-

Sam had planned to be awake and dressed when Kate got back that morning but he had drifted off to sleep again and was sleeping soundly when she arrived. Kate let him sleep until nearly nine and then shook him softly. He awoke with a jolt, flailing his arms and yelling.

Kate laughed. "Take it easy. It's all right. It's Kate, remember me?"

Sam calmed down. "Yes, I remember you. How could I forget?"

"I'll take that as a compliment and not ask what you meant. It's getting late so we'd better get you ready."

Sam blushed. "You'll have to leave while I dress. I don't have anything on but this shirt."

"I know," Kate said softly. "I was here when they brought you in. But I'll wait outside. Call me when you're ready. And, for heaven's sake, if you have any trouble standing or moving around, yell. There's no need to be modest."

After Kate left, Sam dressed quickly in the dark suit Sergeant Pollack had brought him. He was surprised at how steady he felt on his feet despite all the blood he had lost. "All right, I'm dressed."

Kate stopped when she entered the room. "You're taller than I remembered."

"I hope you don't mind."

"No. I like tall, handsome men."

There. She had done it again. She had called him handsome.

For the next ten minutes they worked with Sam's false mustache and his hair powder. Kate took a small mirror from her purse and handed it to

Sam. "Now look at this man whose hair is turning gray. Put these glasses on. Don't you look like a stranger to yourself?"

"Yes, that's a pretty good job. I think I might pass."

"There's one other part of your disguise that you haven't seen yet."

Sam looked at the girl, puzzled.

"I brought my niece and nephew along to accompany us. We'll go as a young family out for the festivities."

"Will the kids be any trouble?"

"No," Kate said with a giggle, "they'll listen to their mommy and daddy."

Sam smiled.

Chapter 39

Saturday, March 4

It was windy and rainy, a perfectly dreadful day to have to be out-of-doors. But the crowds were gathering in and about the Capitol for the spectacle of a Presidential Inauguration. The light drizzle of rain, which showed no signs of letting up, and the cold, gusty winds, drove more and more of them into the Capitol.

Major O'Bierne of the Metropolitan Police had ordered that the public be kept out of the hallways through which the Presidential party would pass as it walked from the Senate Chamber, where Vice President Johnson would be sworn in, to the Inaugural platform on the East Portico. But the crowds, too numerous for the police to control, went where they pleased.

Around mid-morning the President arrived at the Capitol, escorted by John F. Parker and Joseph Sheldon, members of the Metropolitan Police who had recently been detailed for duty at the White House at the request of Mrs. Lincoln. He went to the President's Room, an elaborately decorated room off the Senate Chamber that served as his office in the Capitol, and began reading and signing bills. He was there when Bishop arrived with Belle on his arm and walked casually up the staircase to the West Front.

The couple was disguised as a crippled, one-eyed Yankee chaplain and his wife. Bishop was on crutches and his left eye was covered by a patch. His hair was nearly white. Belle was dressed in a simple black dress, ornamented with no jewelry except a simple cheap cross which hung about her neck. The dress was cut low, after the fashion of the day, but not so low as to be unduly showy. Others might scurry about the Capitol in dresses baring their shoulders, but Belle Gilbert, wife of a chaplain in the United States Army, kept her shoulders discreetly covered. Her hair was demurely wrapped in a black bonnet, its inexpensive material not quite matching the color of her dress.

On her ring finger she sported a plain band which Bishop had picked up in a pawn shop on 9th Street. Belle had very carefully avoided any hint of showiness in her appearance, following the injunction of 1 Peter 3:3 against "outward adorning or plaiting the hair, and of wearing of gold, or putting on of apparel." She wore no makeup and had pulled her hair back severely from her face under her cheap bonnet. She was a preacher's wife and if she was not exactly a plain woman, that was God's doing, not the sinful vanity of a silly woman.

They entered the building through the West Portal, slowly climbed the West Stairway and made their way into the Rotunda as if they were visiting it for the first time. Only Bishop's swiftly moving eye, which took in the entire scene in seconds, betrayed their purpose as anything but tourism. He looked up toward the Dome, scanning the gallery carefully. There was no sign of the powder. After a few minutes they walked to the left around the edge of the Great Rotunda and into the corridor toward the Senate wing. A crowd of young girls, all in identical school uniforms, came giggling out of the North Small Rotunda, accompanied by a bevy of nuns. One of them bumped against Bishop's crutches and he almost fell. In the North Small Rotunda Bishop sidled up to the stairway entrance. He stooped down and wriggled under the "Do Not Enter" sign and disappeared up the stairway, leaving Belle standing there like a lost tourist. Halfway up the stairs he met William.

"Any problems? Anyone try to get in?" Bishop asked him.

William stood up and stretched. "No sir. Some schoolboys tried to sneak up here this morning but when they saw me they ran away. Nobody else has been near. I slept up on the gallery at the head of the stairs last night but the rest of the time I've been right here."

Bishop ignored his slave's effort at small talk. "I'm going up to check on the powder." He climbed the rest of the narrow stairs to the gallery, stopping to rest twice along the way. The guidebook had said there were 365 steps from the North Small Rotunda to the Dome, one for each day of the year. Bishop uttered silent thanks that the earth's years weren't any longer.

At the top of the stairs he laid his crutches aside and began carefully checking the boxes of powder. Everything was in order. Then he picked up a 2½ gallon bucket that sat by the top of the stairway and started down the stairs. On the way down the thought struck him that when he came back up the stairs into the Dome he would be the last person to climb into the unfinished Dome. If he weren't going to be famous for capturing Lincoln, that alone might be worth a line in the history books.

Bishop left the bucket with William, just out of sight of the entrance to the stairs. "Hold on, old friend," he said to William. "Your vigil will be over shortly."

At the foot of the stairs he slipped under the cord and joined Belle in the crowd.

-0-

It was nearly eleven when Sam and Kate, accompanied by their two "children", disembarked from the horse car at the foot of Capitol Hill. They passed through the iron gate and started up the mud-caked gravel walkway to the Capitol, walking slowly despite the steady drizzle. Sam held an umbrella over Kate who clung tightly to him. Annie and Will ran on ahead, calling back over their shoulders occasionally for Sam and Kate to hurry, unconcerned about the drizzling rain.

The zest and energy Sam had experienced when he got out of bed two hours before was gone and he felt utterly drained. Kate sensed his weakness. "Are you going to be all right?"

"I don't know," Sam replied. "I think so. I'll let you know if I have to stop." There was no need to posture with Kate, no need for artificial bravado. Sam was grateful for that, because he just didn't feel like "being brave."

Kate squeezed his arm and they continued on up the walk, dodging puddles of muddy rainwater.

Inside the West Portal Sam shook the water from the umbrella and stuffed it into a large stoneware jar already nearly full of umbrellas while Kate made a futile gesture at wiping the mud from her crinoline skirts. Then, with Annie holding onto Sam and Will clinging to Kate, they climbed the West Stairway to the main floor of the Capitol.

The papers had carried the schedule of festivities and Sam knew the President would be going to the Senate shortly before noon to see his new Vice President sworn in. So Sam and Annie began making their way through the crowds that lined the central corridor toward the Senate Chamber. Kate and Will followed close behind.

As they came through the North Small Rotunda Sam noticed the stairway to the Capitol Dome had been closed, "By Order of the Provost Marshal," the sign said.

He turned to Kate and nodded toward the sign that hung across the stairway entrance. "I'm glad to see that. At least no one will be trying anything funny from the Dome today." The crowds thinned out a bit before the entrance to the Supreme Court Chamber, perhaps because of the extra room afforded by the Foyer opposite the entrance to the Chamber. He pushed on, through the arcaded passageway, and into the South Corridor of the Senate Wing. There he stopped and waited for Kate and Will.

"Are we going up to the Visitors' Gallery?" Kate asked.

"No. We'd need special passes. We'll wait here."

Kate moved over beside him and took his arm. "If we're supposed to be disguised as a married couple we ought to act like we're married, don't you think?"

Her eyes were flecked with gold again.

-0-

Bishop saw Powell and Surratt as they walked along the corridor toward the Senate Chamber, dressed in uniforms of enlisted men in the Federal Medical Corps.

They saw him, too, but only the quick meeting of their eyes could have betrayed the fact that they were acquainted. Powell and Surratt walked on, keeping to the right of the corridor. Bishop, with Belle helping to steady him, followed at a leisurely pace. Occasionally, like a dutiful tour guide, he pointed out something of interest to Belle.

"The section we're in now, with the Old Senate Chamber and the North Rotunda, was the earliest part of the Capitol to be built. They built the House Wing next. The two wings were connected by a covered wooden walkway when the British burned the building in 1814."

"When they rebuilt after the fire they replaced the stairs here with a light well which is called the North Small Rotunda. Look at the top of the columns. See those carved tobacco leaves?"

Belle was fascinated. "Where'd you learn all this, love? I didn't know you were an historian."

Bishop leaned over and whispered. "I've prowled over every square inch of this place for the past week. And I've read everything I could find about it. It really is an interesting place. And after today, it'll be an even more interesting place. And we'll be in the guidebooks of the future."

They reached the South Corridor of the Senate Wing just as Mrs. Lincoln was arriving, accompanied by Marshal Ward Hill Lamon and thirteen ceremonial marshals, one representing each of the original thirteen states. The ceremonial marshals were dignified and correct, their eyes straight ahead and their chests thrown out proudly. But Marshal Lamon's eyes were on the crowd and his hand was inside his coat, where he kept his Army Colt revolver.

In the midst of this entourage with Mrs. Lincoln were her sons, Tad and Robert, a lady in a dark maroon dress who resembled Mrs. Lincoln very much and was probably her sister, and a pompous-looking gentleman who was obviously the husband of the lady in maroon.

Robert Lincoln wore the uniform of a captain of Grant's staff but he was unarmed and frail-looking. He would pose no problem. The thirteen ceremonial marshals would leave the party after the swearing-in. Only Marshal Lamon would give them any trouble, and he would be taken care of promptly when the action started.

The crowd was applauding now and Mrs. Lincoln nodded her head to the right and left, smiling proudly. "Where's Old Abe?" someone shouted, and a ripple of laughter passed through the crowd. Someone else shouted back from the crowd, "He's been here a'ready. I seen him come up a couple of hours ago. He's got a war to win!"

Bishop smiled grimly at this last comment. Yes, he thought, and a date with history that will eclipse his second swearing-in today.

As the marshals passed the crowd was pressed back and Bishop was thrust against an attractive lady whose gray-haired husband looked ashen-faced and exhausted. A veteran, Bishop thought, with war wounds and saddle sores. He ought to be home in bed. Bishop moved his crutches and apologized to the woman in a thick German accent and then spoke to Belle in his best schoolboy German. The couple could only believe he was German. It was a great disguise.

The official party was gone as quickly as it had appeared, passing directly into the Senate Chamber. When they had gone the crowd relaxed a bit and Bishop led Belle to the left up the corridor where Powell and Surratt stood, drinking in the scene. While he ostensibly admired the ornate clock which had been in operation since 1802 he whispered to Powell, "What do you think?"

Powell stared intently at the clock face. "No trouble at all unless those thirteen 'citizen marshals' are still around. Then the numbers are against us."

"They'll be gone." He pointed to the ornate hands, as if discussing them.

"Where are the others?" Powell asked.

"Davy's with the ambulance and horses at New Jersey Avenue and A Street, South, just across from the House Wing. He'll come into the Capitol right after the explosion. Mike is down by the crypt with a stretcher and blankets. He'll stay there. Noah's supposed to be waiting for me in the Rotunda now."

"Does he know what's up?"

"No," Bishop said softly. "I just told him to meet me there at noon. I'm late now."

"Well, that's your problem. We'll see you on the stairs when Lincoln's coming down." With that he sauntered away, and Surratt followed him. Bishop looked at the clock again. It was 12:18. A little over an hour and it would all be over. He'd best go meet Noah, he was late already. He turned to Belle and said in German: "Come dear, let's stroll back toward the Great Rotunda." Belle smiled. She understood "Come dear" and "Gross Rotunda" but the rest was beyond her meager German.

She placed her steadying arm on his elbow and they started back down the long corridor toward the Rotunda. At that moment, inside the Senate Chamber, President Lincoln took his place in the middle of the front row of spectators and the ceremonies began. Marshal Lamon relaxed for a moment. There would be plenty of time to worry about crowds when they left the Senate Chamber.

-0-

Sam was feeling weak and nauseous, the result of the heat generated by the large crowds packed into the Capitol and the debilitating effect of his wounds. Although the skies were still dark, the rain had stopped and people were beginning to find their way out into the plaza before the Inaugural Stand on the East Portico. Sam had begun to hope that, with smaller crowds, the corridor would cool off somewhat but, so far, he had noticed no difference. Kate sensed his discomfiture.

"Are you all right?" she asked.

"Barely," Sam replied softly. "I'd like some air, but I don't want to miss the President when he comes out."

Kate gripped his arm tighter. "I understand. Lean up against the wall and place your weight against there and on me. It shouldn't be too long."

Sam smiled weakly. "You've had some day. Mud and rain on the way up here, having your skirts crushed by that army chaplain's crutches and now having to hold me up. I'm sure you'll be glad when this is over."

"Actually, this day can go on for a long time. I rather like helping to hold you up."

Sam didn't reply. There was nothing to say. And, besides, he was just too weary to talk about it.

The clock on the wall showed 1:12 when the doors of the Senate burst open and the Presidential party started down the corridor toward the Rotunda, with the thirteen ceremonial marshals, identified by their gaudy blue sashes, pushing the crowd aside. Inside the little knot of people walked the President, his tall frame accented by the stovepipe hat perched atop his head. Beside the President, eyes sweeping the crowd and hand inside his coat at the ready, was Marshal Lamon.

Sam jerked away from the wall and started moving with the dignitaries, just behind the marshal representing Pennsylvania. Over his shoulder he told Kate: "Hold on to Will and Annie and follow me." Then he reached inside his coat and felt for his Army Colt. It was still there, as he had known it was all along.

On through the cheering, applauding mass of humanity the party went, through the arcaded passageway, past the North Small Rotunda and into the Great Rotunda, where members of the Metropolitan Police helped hold the crowds back. One of Lincoln's guards, John F. Parker, saw one of his old companions from the police force and waved boyishly. Finally the party passed out onto the Inaugural Platform and the great cast bronze doors slammed shut behind the dignitaries.

Sam stopped by the door and waited for Kate to catch up. Already the crowd was beginning to disperse, running for the other exits in order to view the Inauguration from the plaza outside.

Kate took his arm. "I guess the fact that nothing's happened yet is good news, isn't it?"

"Yes," Sam replied wearily, "it is. I hardly think anything is likely to happen now, but we may as well wait around and see."

Across the Rotunda the Army Chaplain and his pretty wife chatted with two enlisted men and a tall, thin civilian. Behind them a small boy wandered into the Rotunda and began looking up, up, up. Sam relaxed and took Kate's hand.

-0-

Noah was seething. "So this is it. This is our big move and you couldn't tell me about it. What's the matter, G.W., don't you trust me?"

"I told you to meet me here at noon with a pistol. That was all you needed to know. I told the others exactly what they had to know. I'm only taking basic precautions. We have a leak somewhere and I didn't want to feed it. Anyway, what's done is done. If I insulted you, I apologize. Are you with us or not?"

"I'm with you. My loyalty to my country is above question." He glared hard at Bishop who avoided his stare.

Finally Bishop spoke. "Powell, you and John go down to the bottom of the stairs at the Corncob Foyer. Wait there until you hear the Presidential party starting down the stairs. Noah, William and I will be right behind them. Stop the party when they're halfway down the stairs."

Powell and Surratt nodded. Bishop continued. "You'll hear a lot of applause when Lincoln finishes his Inaugural Address. Then he'll be sworn in and you'll hear loud cheering and a 21-gun salute. That will be near the end. The President will be on the stairs in about five minutes."

"Oh, I forgot to mention, wire the door from the Corncob Foyer to the carriage stop under the stairs shut and put a sign "Closed by Order of the Provost Marshal" across it. You can take the sign from the little stairway off the North Small Rotunda with you and use it. It's printed on both sides. Any questions?"

"How will you keep people out of the Dome if the sign's gone?" Surratt asked.

"William will still be in the stairway."

Both nodded again. Then they left the Rotunda and started out the corridor toward the North Small Rotunda and the stairs to the Corncob Foyer.

Bishop turned to Noah. "I want you to go to the stairwell to the Dome, walk up to where William will be sitting and get a 2½ gallon bucket which will be on the stairs behind him. Bring the bucket down and fill it with water from the pump just outside, the one beside the steps. Then take it back and leave it with William."

"Then what?"

"Wait there. I'll be by and tell you what happens next."

Noah turned on his heels and walked across the Rotunda.

Bishop turned back to Belle and began pointing to the huge painting of "The Baptism of Pocahontas." He pointed to an Indian sitting on the church floor behind the kneeling Pocahontas. "You'll notice he had six toes. No one is sure why Chapman painted him that way but it is one of the curiosities of the Capitol. The paintings were covered by canvas during the construction of the Dome and they've only recently been uncovered." Almost absently he added "I hope they're not too badly damaged by the explosion."

Suddenly loud applause sounded from outside. "He's finished his speech. Let's go." He spun around on his crutches and started toward the corridor to the North Small Rotunda. At the stairway to the Dome he stopped and held Belle's hand. "Darling, I want you to go back to Mrs. Taylor's and stay there. Don't leave the house for at least two weeks, someone might remember seeing us together. After two weeks leave for Baltimore on the evening train. From there go to Philadelphia, Harrisburg, and down to Cincinnati. Here's two hundred dollars in Greenbacks and an address in Cincinnati where you can get help in passing through the lines."

He pressed an envelope into her hands. "When we meet again in Richmond your 'Old Man' will be famous."

Belle squeezed his hand and whispered, "Good luck. Don't forget me when you become famous."

Bishop watched Belle for a moment as she walked down the corridor. Then he picked up the bucket Noah had filled and started toward the top of the stairs. "Wait here, Noah. I'll be right back."

When he reached the narrow gallery in the Dome he carried the bucket of water over to the other bucket with a hole in it. He reached into the bottom of the bucket and removed a small wooden plug and a piece of rag. He jammed the plug and rag into the hole near the bottom of the bucket and began filling the bucket with the water he had just carried into the Dome. As he filled the bucket the pine board with the rock wired to it floated to the top and the wire from the pine board to the box of powder nearby sagged toward the floor.

After he had satisfied himself that the plug was holding, Bishop walked over to the box of powder and lifted the lid. Very carefully he cocked the derringer that was wired to the side of the box. Then he slipped a fulminate of mercury cap over the nipple of the derringer and replaced the lid carefully. About seven minutes after the plug is removed, give or take a minute, the water will have run out of the hole causing the rock and board to sink to the bottom. When the rock is four inches from the bottom, the wire will have pulled taut, the trigger will snap, the hammer will fall on the cap and the powder will explode.

Bishop viewed the whole apparatus with a certain morbid pride. It was a simple device, so simple that it bordered on genius. Someday the design of a bucket with a hole in it would be almost an icon in the Confederate States. And he would be one of his country's saints.

The loud cheering and the steady boom of the cannon firing their Presidential salute signaled that the President had been sworn in. In a minute or so he would walk through the Rotunda on his way to the Corncob Foyer and his carriage to the White House. Bishop pulled out his watch and opened the cover. It was 1:43.

With his heart racing wildly he pulled the plug from the bucket and started toward the stairs. He walked softly, conscious of the fact that the firing mechanism was cocked. As he passed the boxes along the wall he hugged the gallery rail, as if his very nearness to the powder could somehow set off the lethal charge.

Finally he reached the door and started down the stairs. When he reached William and Noah he was flushed with excitement.

"Let's go. We're going to grab the President in a minute or so."

"Where?" Noah asked as he followed Bishop down the stairs.

"On the stairs to the Corncob Foyer from the North Small Rotunda."

Bishop stopped just out of sight of the foot of the stairs. He held out his hand to signal Noah and William to wait. "We'll wait here until we hear the Presidential party coming. Then we'll fall in behind them. They'll be here any minute."

Anxiously he removed his watch again and checked the time. It was 1:45. In five minutes the lid would blow off the Rotunda.

Chapter 40

Saturday, March 4

When the sound of applause reached the Rotunda Sam leaned away from the wall and pulled himself up to full height, stretching his aching limbs. "He's finished his speech. In a minute or so he'll take the oath. Then, only a few minutes after that, the Presidential party will pass through the Rotunda. We'd better get ready to follow them."

Kate grasped the hands of Will and Annie. "You children stay with me. Whatever you do, don't let go and don't disobey. This is very important." Her eyes told them she meant what she said. And their eyes replied that they intended to do as they were told.

Sam looked around the Rotunda. The chaplain and his wife had left at the sound of the cheering, as if it were a signal of sorts. It was curious, too, the way the chaplain had spoken with the tall civilian and the two enlisted men, like they were having a meeting.

No, Sam decided, he was making something sinister out of a series of coincidences. The cheering came again, this time accompanied by the boom of cannon. Only two or three minutes before the President would come through the massive bronze doors.

Sam stretched his neck and stared at the ceiling of the Dome featuring Brumidi's unfinished mural. Poor Washington! So long as the Capitol Dome stood he would be permanently fixed at the entrance to Heaven, legs wrapped in a lap robe, dressed in the buff and blue uniform of a

Continental Regular and holding a Roman short sword awkwardly in his left hand. It was immortality of sorts but, in a way, like the toga-draped statue of Washington that stood outside, it was sad. Americans don't just immortalize their heroes, they embarrass them so much they'd never dare to come back.

As he stared at the ceiling he noticed a small figure moving along the railing of the gallery that jutted out from the wall beneath the Dome. The sun had come out at last and sunlight flooded through the arched windows around the Dome. It was difficult to see but Sam could tell it was a man and that he was wearing what appeared to be a military uniform. He was working his way around the Dome, avoiding the wall of the structure and hugging the gallery rail, as if there were something along the wall that he was afraid of. At the doorway to the stairs he suddenly disappeared.

Sam was puzzled. What could the man be doing up there in that area that had been closed to the public by the Provost Marshal? He would have to see for himself. Something was wrong, very wrong. He touched Kate on the shoulder.

"I'm going to walk down the corridor to the North Small Rotunda and check the stairs to the Dome. Stay here and when the President's party comes through, follow it. I'll meet you in the small rotunda. But be careful, there may be trouble."

Kate nodded silently and Sam started down the corridor. That girl was no withering violet, Sam thought. She could take care of herself and her niece, nephew, and Sam, if it came to that.

At the Senate Rotunda Sam slipped into the tiny antechamber that led to the narrow stairway to the Dome. He stood for a moment at the doorway to the stair, listening. He could hear nothing. Then, just as he was preparing to start up the stairs, he heard a man cough, a deep, thick cough that shouted out "consumption!" In an instant it was all very clear to Sam. The short, stocky, "crippled" chaplain with the white hair and the attractive wife, the tall civilian with the consumptive cough, the gathering in the Great Rotunda that looked like a meeting. Bishop and Dyer and their gang were here ready to strike! At this very moment they stood just a few steps from Sam. He yanked out his watch and checked the time. It was 1:46. President Lincoln was due along here at any moment!

Sam turned as if he were speaking to his "wife" in the Small Rotunda. "I'm going up these stairs into the Dome, dear. They've taken the sign down so it must be all right." Then he removed his revolver and cocked it, covering the sound of the cocking mechanism with a small cough. He took a deep breath and started up the stairs, holding his pistol in his right hand, hanging loosely behind his right leg.

-0-

Bishop tensed at the sound of the man's voice. He quickly withdrew his pistol and motioned for Noah and William to do the same. As Sam reached the twelfth step, just out of sight of the door, he ran headlong into the Southerners. He acted startled.

"I beg your pardon, what's going on here?" He kept his pistol hidden behind his right leg, waiting for an opportunity to spring it on them.

Bishop leveled his pistol at Sam. "Stand right where you are, Mister, or you are a dead man. Noah, see if he's armed."

Noah put his pistol back inside his waistband and started to reach out for Sam. At that moment William spoke out plainly.

"Don't either of you move, or I will be forced to kill you."

Bishop spun around. William had his pistol leveled at Bishop's head. "You? You're the one? But I've always been so good to you. You've been one of the family. . . ." His voice trailed off in disbelief.

"Yes, Captain Bishop, you have been good to me. But I've always been your slave, nothing more. Your daddy sold my brother when he was just a baby, like to broke my mama's heart. We got feelin's too, you know, even though our skin is black. But you people never gave a damn about that, we're just property to you. Well the hell with you and your Confederacy! Me, a black man, I'm gonna keep you from capturin' Mr. Lincoln!"

Bishop caught the "Captain Bishop" instead of the familiar "Cap'n." "You talk mighty big for a slave, William."

William smiled. "I'm not a slave, Captain. I'm a Yankee now, a free man. As for my big words, I read a lot. That's somethin' else you didn't know about me." He looked at Sam. "You, sir, had best run upstairs and do whatever can be done to defuse the explosives that are rigged to go off any moment."

Sam moved toward the center of the stairs. As he started to pass between Bishop and Noah, Bishop shoved him roughly into William. Then he brought his pistol up in one quick movement and fired. The bullet grazed William's head and he collapsed, fell backward onto the stairs and began slithering slowly toward the doorway. His watch tumbled from his pocket and clattered onto the stairs. The time was 1:47.

Sam's pistol was still out, but he was off balance and could find no target. In an instant Bishop and Noah were gone, out into the antechamber, across the North Small Rotunda and down the stairs to the Corncob Foyer.

Bishop shouted to Powell and Surratt. "We've had a problem but I think we're still all right. We'll all wait here for the President. Whoever blundered into the stairway to the Dome may try to defuse the explosives, but we can still grab Lincoln."

In the Great Rotunda the bronze doors with their elegant bas-relief swung open and the Presidential party entered the Rotunda. The clock over the doors read 1:48.

-0-

Sam crawled back down the stairway, grabbed William's head and turned it. There was a deep bullet graze along the left side that was bleeding profusely. He lifted William's head and the black man's eyes slowly opened. "I 'spect Cap'n Bishop got away," he muttered softly.

"Yes, he and the other fellow are gone. But I have to get up these stairs and see about those explosives."

William shook his head slowly and stood up. "I'm comin' with you.".

Together they scrambled up the stairs where William had said something was set to explode. There was no time to waste. Kate and the children were down in the Rotunda. If the Dome exploded, they would die, along with the President.

Up the stairs they plodded. Sam was out of breath and his heart was pounding wildly when he reached the gallery. William was clearly having a difficult time but he crawled up beside Sam and pointed at the boxes marked "Hardtack" lined up along the wall of the Dome, spaced fairly evenly and completely encircling the Dome. "Gotta find the fuse. Follow me!"

Slowly and carefully they began walking clockwise around the Dome. When they were about a quarter of the way around the gallery William pointed to a puddle of water and, farther along, a bucket from which the water was leaking in a steady stream. "That's it," he said.

Sam stooped over the bucket and looked into it. A rock was wired to a pine board which was floating in the bucket. The rock was connected by wire to one of the hardtack boxes a few feet away and the wire was growing taut as the rock sank in the bucket.

Sam stooped down and placed his finger in the hole in the side of the bucket, stopping the leak. Then, with his free hand, he removed his handkerchief and carefully stuffed it into the hole in the bucket.

When the hole was plugged, he followed the wire to the hardtack box and removed the lid. The box was full of gunpowder, ready to explode when a derringer that was wired to the side of the box would be fired by the tightening of the wire attached to the trigger. Sam reached down, lifted the percussion cap from the nipple of the derringer and uncocked the gun.

Then he stood up and started on around the gallery, searching for other buckets and firing mechanisms.

Beneath him he could hear the sound of applause and scattered cheering. The Presidential party had entered the Rotunda.

"That's it, that's it," William said. He grabbed Sam and embraced him. "They ain't gonna be any 'splosion from this mess today. "Thank the Lord Almighty!"

-0-

Bishop was sweating profusely and his face was blood red. Noah had already lambasted him for the predicament they found themselves in. Now Powell added his bit.

"You don't look too well, Cap'n. You sure you can handle this?"

"Hell, yes," Bishop snapped. "I'm just a little upset. Can't you understand what has happened? I just shot one of my oldest friends up there, a man who was practically a brother to me. That'd unnerve anyone."

"You mean William? Your slave? He sure didn't act like much of a friend back there in the stairs, from what Noah just told us. 'Guess you've figured out by now that he's the one who wrote the letters to Baker's men that almost did you in." Powell smiled sardonically. "And you thought it was Old Noah here."

Bishop didn't answer. The truth was that Powell was right and Bishop knew it. His comment didn't call for any answer.

The little party stood in silence at the foot of the stairway waiting for the sound of the President's party. After a few minutes Surratt spoke. "The Dome should have gone up by now. Whoever it was that stumbled onto you in the stairs must have defused the powder."

"There's still plenty of time for it to go off," Bishop said quietly.

"That explosion was supposed to cover our operation," Powell said quickly. "Without that, I'm not sticking around much longer."

"You'll stay right here," Bishop replied. "The explosion wasn't to go off until after the President was in our hands. We still have a minute or so by my reckoning." He removed his pistol from his waistband and leveled it at Powell. "No one is backing out now. Booth will make a demonstration in the Rotunda that will cover us if the powder doesn't go off - we worked that out yesterday. Lincoln will be along any minute now and I intend to take him to Richmond. I've already shot one man today and I have no hesitation about shooting another one."

-0-

The President's party burst into the Rotunda to the polite applause of the handful of tourists waiting there. The President was walking beside Marshal Lamon; Mrs. Lincoln was on the arm of her son Robert, resplendent in his uniform. Behind Mrs. Lincoln walked Tad, the Lincoln's twelve-year-old son, and Richard Sheldon, one of the Presidential guards. The other bodyguard, John F. Parker, was to the side and slightly behind the President.

When they were nearly opposite Kate she suddenly rushed toward the party, dragging Will and Annie with her. "Mr. President, don't go down that corridor!"

Marshal Lamon was in front of Kate in a moment, pistol drawn in his right hand and brawny left hand ready for action. He grabbed the girl by the right arm, shaking Annie loose.

"What do you mean?" Lamon shouted "What are you trying to do?"

Lincoln laid his hand on Lamon's shoulder. "Just a minute, Ward. Let's hear what the little lady has to say."

Kate blurted out what had just happened, that she was there with Lt. Reid who was concerned about the President's safety. She told about the shot that had been fired in the stairway to the Dome, and the two men who had run across the small rotunda into the stairs to the lower level. She rattled on about Sam's suspicions of Rebel kidnapping activity and his own narrow calls with death.

The President patted Kate's hand and spoke softly. "Yes, your Lieutenant Reid visited me one evening and expressed his concerns for my safety. Where is he now?"

"I suspect he's lying dead in the stairway to the Dome, the two men who ran across the small rotunda right after the shot probably killed him." She let out a deep sigh. "I wanted to run to him but I knew he'd want me to warn you first."

Lincoln turned to Marshal Lamon. "Ward, I've met this little lady's Lieutenant Reid. If he says there's a danger and she believes him, I reckon we'd better change our plans. Send one of these other boys with her to check on the Lieutenant."

Lamon snapped to Richard Sheldon, who had heard none of the conversation with Kate, "You go with her. And you, Parker, get up here and keep your pistol ready. We're going to go down the stairs off the South Small Rotunda."

-0-

Bishop had put his pistol away. Surratt came back down the stairs and the others gathered around him

"They're all in a huddle up there in the Rotunda."

"What do you mean 'all'?" Bishop asked.

"The President, Marshal Lamon, some woman and a half dozen others."

Bishop spoke first. "Our game is up. We'd best scatter while we've still time." He yanked the wire off the door to the carriage entrance. "If we go now we can melt into the Inaugural crowd. I'll run an ad in the *Star* calling us together in two or three days. It'll be the same ad that we used to call the meeting at Booth's room."

"Where'll we meet?" Powell asked.

"The Wolf's Den in Hooker's Division. I'll arrange it."

"What about Mike and Davy?" Surratt asked.

"They'll go home when they realize nothing is going to happen. Don't worry about them."

Bishop flung the door open and walked briskly out of the Capitol. The others followed quickly. In less than a minute they were scattered into the Inaugural crowd.

-0-

When they reached the North Small Rotunda and turned into the anteroom Kate saw blood trickling down the stairs. She squeezed Will and Annie's hands and pulled them in front of her where she could look them in the eyes.

"I want you two to wait here. I'm going up this stairway to see if I can help Lieutenant Reid. Whatever you do, don't move. Mr. Sheldon here will stay with you."

She had barely started up the narrow stairs when she heard footsteps coming down. She stopped and waited. When they grew closer she spoke, her voice echoing up the narrow passageway. "Sam? Is that you?"

"Yes. Don't come up. There's quite a mess up here."

When Sam reached her she was sobbing. She flung herself at him and clung to him. After a few minutes they came down the stairs together. There was no need to say anything.

After he had directed Sheldon to stand guard over the stairs to keep visitors from stumbling over the powder cache, Sam left with Kate and the children. They stopped the first soldiers they came to and sent them for a ride, something for Sam. Finally, after what seemed like an eternity, the horse-car drew up before the West Gate to the Capitol. But the car was only going one way, to the Navy Yard. The westbound runs for the rest of the afternoon had been cancelled because of the Inaugural Parade.

Sam sagged down onto the stone base of the steel fence that enclosed the Capitol grounds. "I don't think I can walk very far, Kate. I'm spent."

"Wait here with Will and Annie. I'll get some transportation." Before he could answer, Kate was gone up the walk toward the House Wing of the Capitol.

In about twenty minutes she was back, riding in an army ambulance driven by a short, dark-haired boy in his early twenties. Sam stood up and walked to the curb with Will and Annie. "How'd you arrange this?" he asked Sarah.

"I told this young man his ambulance was being commandeered by order of Colonel Baker's detectives. He didn't want to come along but after he saw the President drive by and wave at me, he agreed to come with me."

Sam wearily mounted the ambulance and took a seat beside Kate. He extended his hand to the driver. "My name's Reid, Lieutenant Reid of Baker's Detectives. I appreciate the use of your ambulance. What were you doing parked up there by the House Wing anyway?"

"Sir," the driver replied, "I'm Corporal Will Evans. I drive for the V Corps and I was told to wait up there in case anyone got sick and had to be hauled off to the hospital during the Inauguration."

Sam nodded and rode on in silence. When the ambulance reached 17th Street Sam asked Evans to pull over to the curb. "Take Mrs. Huntt and the children on out to Georgetown. I have to go back to the office for a while." He looked at Kate. "I'll be there as soon as I can. But it may be a day or so. I have something very important to do."

Kate grabbed Sam's hand. "Be careful, honey." She stared deeply into Sam's eyes. "I like being called 'Mrs.'"

They rode on in silence until Sam dismounted a few feet from the door to his office.

Chapter 41

Saturday, March 4

Sergeant Pollack listened carefully to Sam's description of the scene at the Capitol. Two or three others crowded into the room to glimpse Sam, whom they had been told was dead.

"So the man who was trying to help us catch Bishop was his slave? Don't that beat all? I never would have guessed it, not in a million years." The Sergeant was sweating profusely and he wiped his brow with a dirty, stained handkerchief.

Sam nodded wearily. "Yes, and it came as quite a surprise to Bishop, too. I guess he just didn't understand that, no matter how well he treated him, William couldn't tolerate being owned by someone else."

"Still, Bishop got away from us again."

"Yes, but I think we just may be able to bring him to ground," Sam replied. "I have an idea, Sergeant. Write a report and send it to the Colonel that we are certain where Bishop is staying and plan to raid the house at 8:00 this evening. Say that our people know where he has been staying and will be certain to get him. Also write that we will be watching all known Rebel hangouts and public places in the city. Then get that traitor from Massachusetts who has been giving away our secrets to tell you where he reports to. Then make sure this message gets sent out, just like the traitor has been doing all along."

"Who am I gonna say is directin' all this?"

"Major Wright, who else? Then tell the Colonel in person that nothing big is up. Just tell him I'm testing his clerks. I'll take the heat if any is generated over this."

"What else do I do?"

"Nothing. Leave the matter to me. If this works we will flush Bishop from his safe house before eight tonight. I think I know where he'll go next.'"

"Where'd that be, Sir?"

"Sergeant, I'm not saying. Just let me have these men who were in here a few minutes ago. I'll have them back here by ten, and I'm willing to bet I'll have Bishop with me. Now, if you'll excuse me, I'm going to wash this gray powder out of my hair. I've been an old man long enough."

Sergeant Pollack stood up. "I'll have the men back here inside of ten minutes. I sure hope you know what you're doin'."

As the Sergeant walked through the door Sam called after him. "I want at least one of those men to be as mean as a snake, the kind of man who can slap women and children around and think nothing of it."

Sergeant Pollack called back over his shoulder. "I'll send Corporal Douglas, he'd beat up his own mother just for fun. He's a mean bastard."

"Good," Sam replied. "That's just the sort of man I need."

Chapter 42

Saturday, March 4

Bishop took the news calmly. After "Norton" had left he went up to the bedroom at the front of the second floor and began packing. Fifteen minutes later, as he walked along N Street toward the horsecar stop, he thought about Belle. She had been a fine companion, lovely in bed and a good cure for the boredom that was a natural part of the spy business. But her time was past. There was no need being sentimental about it, Belle was no longer of any use to him. In fact, she was a burden, a threat to his security. It was good that she was leaving. If she ever got to Richmond and if he ever did run across her, which was doubtful, he would just have to explain it all to her. But by then she would likely have figured it all out for herself. That was the thing about Belle, she was a realist. Those six months at Mrs. Wolf's place had taken care of that.

On the streetcar Bishop took a seat opposite the rear door. He laid his saddlebags on the seat beside him and watched out the window. The crowds had thinned out a bit now but those who were there were still celebrating. As the car crossed Virginia Avenue a soldier, with a painted prostitute on each arm, shouted at the car as it rumbled by: "Hooray for Long Abraham - four years longer!" The girls giggled and egged him on. "You tell 'em, honey. You set 'em straight!"

At F Street he disembarked onto the marble blocks that led to the dilapidated wooden sidewalk. The streets were full of carousing soldiers and Bishop gave them wide berth. Now was not the time to call attention to himself.

-0-

It took Sam about a half hour to position his men where they could watch the house and not be seen. Two of the men were stationed by the parlor windows of houses across the street, with the nervous acquiescence of the residents. Others were stuck beneath stairways, on top of roofs, and in filthy outbuildings. When he was satisfied with their placement, Sam walked up the street toward the house.

He stopped at the vacant lot and stared at the dining room window. The fern was in the center of the window. It would stay there tonight, by God. He took a deep breath, as if to fortify himself with the pure night air, mounted the steps to the front door, and raised the handle on the door knocker.

When Mrs. Richards saw Sam and the three others her face registered a mixture of shock, confusion and extreme discomfort. She stammered for a second and finally spoke. "Why, Lieutenant Reid. We'd heard you were dead. What a delightful surprise. Ellie, come here, dear, and look who just came in. Your prayers have been answered."

Sam's face told Mrs. Richards this was no usual social call. She tensed a bit and took a step toward the dining room.

Sam spoke. "Mrs. Richards, if you so much as try to leave this room I will have you bound and gagged and thrown into that corner. Is that clear?"

The woman stopped, turned and stared at him for a moment and then answered with a barely audible, "Yes."

"In case you're wondering, you and Ellie, and anyone else we find in or about this house - are under arrest."

"Why, what in the world for, Lieutenant?"

Before he could answer, Ellie burst into the room. "Sam, Sam darling. Oh, thank God you're all right." She rushed toward him with her arms outstretched.

Sam backed away. "Douglas, handcuff this woman's hands behind her back, gag her and throw her on that sofa, where she can't be seen from the doorway. If she moves or makes any noise whatsoever, let her feel pain."

Instantly Corporal Douglas grabbed Ellie's left arm, twisted sharply and brought her to her knees with a sharp cry. She dropped her eyes and submitted limply to the handcuffs and gagging.

Sam watched the whole process without blinking, though he found it not pleasurable, as he had expected, but intensely painful. Beautiful Ellie. It was hard to turn off love for someone even when they had betrayed you. Ellie caught him staring at her and looked back at him for a moment. Her eyes registered, Sam thought, understanding and perhaps even relief. But, then, it was hard to tell.

Ellie lay quietly on the sofa. She had shut her eyes and retreated into some private world. Sam turned to her mother.

"Mrs. Richards, we're expecting company before long. Whenever anyone comes to that door I want you to admit them without so much as a hint that anything is amiss. If anything goes wrong I will unleash Corporal Douglas on your daughter. The Corporal, in case you haven't sensed it, likes to inflict pain. Any questions?"

Mrs. Richards shook her head slowly.

"Good. Now you stand there in the middle of the parlor and wait for your company."

"May I sit down?"

"No, you may as well get used to a bit of discomfort. The Old Capitol prison isn't exactly Willards."

The clock over the mantel boomed out seven o'clock and its loud ticking filled the room with sound rushing upon sound. Mrs. Richards shifted nervously from foot to foot. Twice in the past twenty minutes she had asked to go to the privy and twice Sam had refused her, saying there would be a privy in the Old Capitol.

7:30 came and went and then 8:00. At 8:10 Sam motioned to Privates Boles and Ransom. "Search the house again, every square inch. Poke and jab into every possible spot where a man could be hiding, use your bayonet. If you find anyone, cuff them and bring them down here. If you don't find anyone and no one shows up by 9:30, we'll leave and set fire to the place just to be sure."

Mrs. Richards looked up at Sam with a jolt. "Burn our house down? Surely you wouldn't do that?"

"Mrs. Richards, you cannot begin to imagine the physical and mental abuse I would heap upon this household without so much as a moment's hesitation. So don't waste your breath. I'll burn your house down to make sure that no agents are hiding here undetected, though, quite frankly, your discomfiture at seeing your home burn would be reward enough."

The minutes ticked by slowly. After about twenty minutes Boles and Ransom were back, reporting that they had found nothing. Then as they were settling into two hard-backed, velvet-bottomed chairs, the door knocker sounded. Sam motioned everyone out of sight and whispered to Mrs. Richards: "You're on stage now. Unless you want Ellie broken in two and a soft lead bullet lodged in the back of your brain, this had better be good."

Mrs. Richards walked slowly to the door and opened it. Sam stood behind the door, pistol jabbed harshly into Mrs. Richards' ribs.

"Why, good evening, Captain Bishop. Please come in."

"I'm sorry to inconvenience you, but I have reason to believe the Yankees are after me . . . . ."

Sam brought his pistol down sharply across Bishop's head and the spy buckled and fell to the floor. Mrs. Richards screamed and covered her mouth with her hand.

"Shut up," Sam yelled at Mrs. Richards. "Boles! Ransom! Handcuff this man and disarm him!"

It was all over in an instant. Boles and Ransom helped Bishop to his feet and the spy stood there, shaking his head, his hands securely behind his back. A small trickle of blood was running down from his left temple where Sam's Army Colt had struck home.

After a moment he looked at Sam. "So, Lieutenant Reid, we meet at last."

Sam looked at the man standing there before him in the dimly-lit parlor. He looked so ordinary, so very unlike a man who would try to bring a government down about his shoulders. There was nothing about him of the ruthless killer, no hint of the successful ladies' man, no suggestion of dash and glamour and color. He was an ordinary little man, broken and helpless.

"Captain Bishop, forgive me, but I must relish this moment. Knowing that President Lincoln is safe at last gives me a great deal of satisfaction."

Bishop did not reply.

Epilogue

Kate was watching the street as Sam came up to the house. Before he could rap the door knocker she had torn open the door and thrown herself at him.

They said nothing but simply held tightly to one another, oblivious to the fact that they were standing on a fashionable Georgetown stoop in broad daylight. Then they kissed passionately. At last Sam backed away and looked at the girl. She had been crying but she was smiling now.

And her eyes were flecked with gold again.

CHARACTERS

Name	Role
Colonel Lafayette C. Baker	Ruthless head of the National Detective Police, the U.S. counterintelligence agency where Sam Reid works
George Washington (G.W.) Bishop	Very successful spy for the Confederacy
William "Bishop"	Slave body servant of G.W. Bishop
John Wilkes Booth	Prominent actor and underground agent for the Confederacy
Noah Dyer	Rebel spy with consumption who assists G.W. Bishop
Thomas Harbin	Confederate agent in lower Maryland
John M. Hay	Secretary to President Abraham Lincoln
Davy Herold	Co-conspirator with Bishop & Booth
Kate Huntt	Daughter of shopkeeper in Tee Bee, Maryland
J. B. Jones	Clerk in office of Confederate Secretary of War
Richard Maynard	Sergeant in Confederate Army, son of William Poindexter
Captain Archibald Miller	U.S. Quartermaster Corps officer responsible for sending supplies to isolated U.S. army posts in Northern Virginia & West Virginia
Michael O'Laughlen	Co-conspirator with Bishop & Booth
Lt. David Petersen	U.S. Army counterintelligence agent who shares an office with Sam Reid
William Poindexter	Chief Usher at U.S. White House

Sergeant Angus Pollock	Enlisted assistant of Sam Reid
Lewis Powell (aka Mosby)	Co-conspirator with Bishop & Booth
Lt. Samuel Alexander Reid	U.S. Army counterintelligence agent
Ellie Richards	Sam Reid's girlfriend
John Surratt	Confederate courier and co-conspirator with Bishop & Booth
Major Tom Swanson	U.S. Army counterintelligence agent who is Sam's immediate superior
Elizabeth "Crazy Bette" Van Lew	Resident of Richmond who provides valuable military intelligence information to the U.S.
Major Thomas Wright	U. S. Army counterintelligence agent who is above Sam in the command structure of the National Detective Police

Any references to historical events,
real people, or real places are used fictiously.

If you liked this book you should also look at Forest Bowman's other novels:

The Secret of the 48th Foot: When a chest of gold and silver coins is up for grabs, all hell can break loose. And usually does. Academicians Ben & Julia discover this in a coded message from a student who has turned up missing. After they break the code they find themselves in a life-and-death struggle with a band of cutthroat militiamen who are after the same treasure the missing student's message put Ben & Julia after. Things heat up from there. To keep ahead of their murderous pursuers the pair must rely on their wits, a former student and even the town fool. Blind luck doesn't hurt either. Using faked documents, a series of desperate and unexpected aggressive moves, clever disguises and gutsy maneuvers, they careen across West Virginia and western Maryland, pursued by armed killers. Finally, they zero in on the buried chest. But they never expected it to be their potential burial site . . . .

All Our Yesterdays: Living well is not always the best revenge. Sometimes getting even in grand style is better. Undersized 14-year-old orphan Adam is sent to live on a hardscrabble farm where he is treated miserably by two brutal brothers who live there. He escapes back to his hometown and, through hard work and an occasional bit of chicanery, becomes the owner of a furniture mill and a prominent citizen in the community. But the brothers continue to torment him, including setting fire to his mill. When they finally commit what to Adam is an inexcusable act and he is criticized for his reaction against them, he contrives a blood-curdling revenge that the brothers can't believe is happening. And the citizens of the community never realize that Adam has extracted his revenge.

The Secret of the 48th Foot and ***All Our Yesterdays*** are available on Amazon.com in both eBook and paperback format.

Made in the USA
Columbia, SC
24 June 2025